Frogs & Toads

Stacy Lynn Carroll

Pink Frog Press

ISBN: 978-0615904863

To my two beautiful princesses and my handsome little prince. May you forever believe in "happily ever afters"

Other books by author Stacy Lynn Carroll:

The Princess Sisters

Chapter One

Cinderella glided gracefully around the dance floor, her beautiful blue gown swishing around her feet. She looked up into Scott's dark eyes and he smiled. The way he smiled made Cinderella feel slightly faint, but his strong arm around her back kept her from falling over. A country song began blaring out from the speakers in front, and Scott quickly pulled her into his arms as he had done once before. Cinderella felt warm in his embrace as they Cowboy Cha-Chaed their way across the dance floor. Then things started to get a little blurry. The people twirling around them turned into a fuzzy haze and Cinderella felt her eyes opening.

She awoke in her room. Cinderella sighed and, glancing over at the pillow next to her, felt the warmth of Scott's gaze once again. She picked up his picture and kissed it lightly. Then she gathered the remainder of her dance pictures, which were strewn about the bed, and placed them in a neat stack back on her nightstand. *I must have fallen asleep looking at them again.*

Disappointed that her dancing had only been a dream, Cinderella stared hard at the digital clock on her nightstand. Her brain didn't want to come back to reality quite yet. She could see the bright red numbers, but it took a moment to register what they were reading. 8:13 AM. Cinderella grabbed her phone off the nightstand and punched in a familiar number.

As the phone rang, she picked up the top picture again, the one of Scott looking directly at the camera. She had snapped it before he could protest and it remained her favorite. The picture captured the intensity of his dark eyes.

"Good morning, Princess!"

"Hey Scott, you excited for Lagoon today?"

"Of course! We're stoked! But isn't this a bit early for you?"

"Not if we want to be the first ones in the park!" Cinderella said.

"Too true. So where are we meeting you?"

"Let's just meet right inside the front gates, before you get to the first ride."

"Sounds good!"

"See you soon," she said and she snapped her phone shut again. With a little flutter in her stomach, Cinderella finally got out of bed and began getting ready for the day. It had been several months since she'd last seen Scott and she couldn't wait! It sucked that he went to school so far away. They texted or talked occasionally, but it wasn't the same as actually getting to hang out with him. She missed his playful smile, his teasing hands, and the way he always scooped her up in a hug and twirled her around when they hadn't seen each other in a while.

Cinderella rushed into the bathroom and ran a brush through her long, brown hair. She couldn't make up her mind if she should pull it back into a ponytail for convenience, or leave it down to look nicer for Scott. As she started applying makeup to carefully outline her sunflower eyes, her mind couldn't help but go back to the dream. It wasn't even a dream so much as a memory from Homecoming last year. Scott and his college friends had swooped in and taken her and her lowly sophomore cousins to the dance in order to prove a bully wrong. The rescue made him a valiant prince in the girls' eyes. Cinderella started to feel restless and she reached for her phone again. It only rang once.

"Are you ready to go?" she asked, without saying hi.

"Someone is a bit anxious," Snow White laughed.

"Maybe just a little," Cinderella said, smiling.

"Give me five more minutes."

Cinderella sighed before conceding. "Alright, but I'm timing you!" Even though she couldn't see her face, Cinderella could almost feel Snow White's eyes rolling.

After hanging up, Cinderella immediately had the next number punched in and the phone started ringing again.

"How's it coming?" she asked.

"We're almost ready," Ariel said.

"Who is that?" Cinderella could hear Aurora's voice in the background.

"Guess," Ariel said.

Cinderella could hear Aurora laughing. "Tell her we'll meet her outside in ten minutes."

"Aurora says you're a freak."

"She did not, I could hear her."

"Fine, then, I think you're a freak."

"Yeah, yeah, I know. So see you in ten?"

"Yup. You're driving, right?"

"Yeah, see you soon."

Cinderella hung up and dialed one last number.

"Hey Belle, you ready to go?"

"Actually Craig is picking me up; we're taking our own car. Where should we meet you?"

"Just inside the gates."

"Okay, we'll see you there." Cinderella heard a honk outside. "That's him, I gotta go."

Cinderella placed the phone in her pocket and walked over to the large window, pushing the curtains aside. She watched as Belle climbed into Craig's car below and the two of them drove off. She then looked at herself in the mirror one last time before hurrying out the door. Cinderella stood by the front of her mom's Outlander, twirling the car keys around her index finger. They clanked together each time the keys made a full circle. Cinderella tried to be patient as she glanced back and forth between Snow White's and the twins' front doors.

She couldn't help feeling even more anxious, now that she knew Belle and Craig were going to beat them there. This had been her idea in the first place! After missing the trip to Lagoon last year, she and Snow White suggested they make a yearly tradition of going right before school started. Plus it had given her an excuse to invite Scott and his friends to hang out with them again.

Snow White's front door opened and she came bounding down the steps.

"Am I first?" she asked.

"Yeah, we're just waiting on the twins. Belle already left with Craig."

"Oh, I didn't realize they weren't driving with us. Not really surprising though."

"Not really. They like their alone time."

Snow White gagged, then the two girls shared a smile.

Cinderella opened the doors and climbed in, adjusting the seat back a little further. Over the last year, she had finally succeeded in growing taller than her mom, a fact she liked to point out to Dana whenever possible.

Cinderella looked up just as Aurora and Ariel emerged from their house. They climbed in the back seat and the four of them set off toward the amusement park.

Cinderella tapped her fingers on the steering wheel and kept glancing at the clock on the dashboard. *Was time moving in slow motion?!*

"Are you nervous?" Snow White asked gently.

"What? Why?"

"Because you've looked at the clock at least ten times and we're not even on the freeway yet." Ariel nudged the back of Cinderella's chair playfully with her foot.

"You wanna kiss him again, don't you?"

The car swerved sharply and a horn honked.

The twins laughed. "Geez! You trying to get us killed?"

"Oh come on, Ari, you know as well as I do that Cinderella thinks of nothing else but Scott Prince. I say you get him on the first dark ride you can. Alone. Then make your move."

"She can't do that, Rora, she's jailbait to the guy."

Aurora brushed her sister's comment away. "Go for it."

Cinderella's face turned scarlet as the girls continued to talk.

"Come on guys," Snow White spoke from the front seat. "She's excited to meet up with a cute guy. It's not like you've never had crushes before."

Cinderella gave her a grateful smile.

After what seemed like an eternity in the car, they finally pulled into the large parking lot. When purchasing their tickets, the girls began scanning over the waves of people who were making their way into the newly opened park.

"So much for being here first," Cinderella muttered.

"Over there!" Ariel shouted.

Cinderella's heart skipped a beat until she followed Ariel's gaze and caught sight of Belle. They pushed their way through the crowd over to where Belle and Craig were standing against a brick wall. They all said their greetings to Craig, who had his arm draped over Belle's shoulder. Her hand wrapped around his thin waist in return. This was not an uncommon sight. Belle and Craig started going out shortly after the Homecoming dance the previous year. Between dating and being in student government together, the two had quickly become inseparable.

"Any sign of Scott yet?" Cinderella asked.

"No," Belle said. "But I have to admit, I was only really watching out for you guys."

Cinderella's phone began buzzing in her pocket. She pulled it out and glanced at the new text message. Her heart fell. "They're going to be late," she said. "Scott says to start riding without them and they'll call us when they get here."

"Shall we?" Craig asked, pointing up the cement steps toward the first ride. The cousins all nodded and followed Craig's lead. Cinderella walked a little more slowly than the others. She kept turning her head back towards the front gate, hoping to catch sight of them. She felt an arm land on her shoulder and she looked forward again.

"He's still coming," Snow White said. "It's okay to have a little fun before he gets here."

"I know. You're right," Cinderella said. The two of them quickened their pace to catch up to the others.

The small group stayed near the front of the park and only went on rides with shorter lines so they could easily meet up with Scott and his friends once they arrived. They made it on three rides and were standing in line for the Tilt-A-Whirl when Cinderella's pocket started buzzing again.

"Hello?" she had to practically yell into the phone.

"Where are you guys?" Just the sound of his voice made a rush of warmth fill Cinderella's body.

"By the Tilt-A-Whirl. We'll start heading towards the front gate."

"No need. I can see you from here."

The warmth turned to heat and Cinderella knew her face had to be bright red. She turned around and pushed her way out of the line, the others following close behind. She looked around briefly before catching sight of him. Scott grinned as he moved toward her, but Cinderella froze. Walking next to Scott was his friend Jenny. Cinderella had met her once when she went up to Utah State University with Scott's little brother, Dave. She had been really sweet and had even let Cinderella stay at her apartment overnight. But now Jenny stood next to Scott. Too close to Scott. And the two of them were holding hands.

Chapter Two

Cinderella remained frozen in her tracks. She desperately wanted to move forward and give Scott a hug or even a high five, something to show she wasn't completely weirded out by the sight in front of her! But her inability to move or speak gave her away.

"Hey Princess!" Scott said. The typical greeting he always gave her sounded forced this time. He seemed to be nervous. He didn't move towards her and scoop her up in a big bear hug like he usually did. Instead, he held his hand out in front of what Cinderella expected was probably his girlfriend. "You remember Jenny, right?"

"Yeah!" Cinderella said, trying to muster up some enthusiasm. "How are you?"

"Great!" Jenny responded. She rushed forward and gave Cinderella a quick hug. "It's been awhile, hasn't it?" she asked casually. Cinderella nodded in return. "These must be your famous cousins!" she exclaimed, looking around their tight group.

After one look at Cinderella's face, Belle suddenly stepped forward and began making introductions. Grateful for the attention shift, Cinderella stared down at her shoes while she tried to process. The knot that had formed in the pit of her stomach now felt like it was moving up to her throat. Cinderella looked up at Scott with questioning eyes. Their gaze locked for a brief moment. Scott looked back at her guiltily, before quickly looking away again. Jenny continued shaking hands with all the cousins and seemed completely oblivious to any weirdness between Scott and Cinderella.

"What do you guys want to ride first?" Belle asked the newcomers.

"We're still waiting for a couple people," Scott responded, glancing back.

"Oh yeah, who?" Aurora asked.

"No!" Belle shouted, when their "couple people" came into view. "What is HE doing here?!"

Dave Prince strutted towards them with two of Scott's friends from school.

"He wanted to come," Scott said. "I know you guys have a history," he added, putting his hands up in defense, "but I was kinda hoping we could put some of that behind us today."

If looks could kill, Scott would have burned on the spot from the glare Belle gave him.

"It'll be okay," Craig said, tightening his arm around her. "I'll protect you," he grinned. He was trying to lighten the mood, but Belle found no humor in the situation.

"Fine, let's go then," she said. Belle took off toward one end of the park before Dave had even made it to the group. The others turned to follow and Dave and his companions had to jog to catch up with them.

"So she still hates me, huh?" Dave asked, catching up to Snow White.

"Yeah, pretty much," Snow White responded.

"Well don't sugarcoat it or anything for me," Dave teased.

"You know Belle," Snow White said, nodding her head toward the front of the group where Belle charged forward. "She doesn't let things go easily."

"I guess not," Dave said. "What about the rest of you?"

Snow White remained silent for a minute as she pondered the question. It had been a whole year since Dave had kissed each of the girls and torn them apart. But a lot had happened in that year and the girls were closer because of it. Even though she'd barely spoken to him in the last twelve months, she realized the sight of him didn't make her want to run away screaming anymore. She was over it, and she hadn't even realized it. "No," she answered honestly. "Not all of us still hate you."

"Really?" Dave asked, sounding hopeful.

"I mean, I don't want to go out and buy matching friendship bracelets or anything, but I can honestly say I don't hate you...anymore."

"Do people still wear those?" Dave asked facetiously. Snow White just glared at him. "Too soon for jokes. Got it."

Snow White gave him one of her famous eye rolls and continued, "Just give it some more time. They'll all come around eventually."

While they were talking, the rest of the group got in line for a free-fall ride. The huge, red, circular tower held seating for twelve people at a time. Each person sat with their back to the ride, facing out with their feet dangling below. The massive landmark ferris wheel was the only ride in the park that stood taller.

"We better hurry," Snow White pointed ahead of them.

They pushed their way past the crowds of people, making it to the end of the line just in time, before another large group. As they stood in line for The Rocket, Dave weaseled his way past Scott and his friends, ending up at the front, right next to Craig.

Belle pretended to ignore him, but she found it took all the energy in her possession to focus solely on her boyfriend. Her eyes had a mind of their own and wanted to glance at Dave, to see what he was up to. But every time they began to stray, she would quickly pull them back to Craig's mouth. He really did have a great mouth! Not a bad kisser either. He didn't quite curl her toes the way Dave had when they first kissed, but maybe that was just a first kiss thing. *Stop thinking about Dave!* she screamed at herself. Belle moved her eyes back to her focal point. Craig's lips were perfectly formed, like a tiny pink, soft heart. She had spent many hours studying these lips with her own. Why was it so hard now to even look at them?

"So how is the basketball team looking this year?" Dave asked.

Craig finally noticed that Dave had sidled up behind him. He turned his head, giving Belle the excuse she needed to finally glance at him as well. She studied the lips that had spoken, different from Craig's in almost every way. *Just like their personalities.* Belle snapped her eyes back to Craig, who was looking at her for reassurance. She gave a small nod and he turned to Dave again.

"Really well, actually," Craig said. "Tommy and Jet have really been working on their free throws and Coach has some awesome new plays we've been trying out."

Their conversation allowed Belle to resume her study of Dave. His lips were more red than pink, and larger than Craig's small heart shaped ones. Dave's lips also were longer, more drawn out in comparison, firm where Craig's were soft. Belle noticed his lips start to curl up in a grin and realized she had been staring. And Dave had noticed. Her own lips tightened in anger, anger that she had been caught. But Dave didn't say anything; instead he smiled and resumed his conversation with Craig.

"It's just too bad you have to wait until football season is over. We're gonna kill it this year! After we win the championship, people will be so focused on us, they'll forget all about those tall, skinny nerds out on the court."

Dave's words made Belle angry and she opened her mouth to rebut when she noticed Craig was smiling.

"What is it you guys do out on the field again? Oh, that's right," he said, without waiting for an answer. "Run ten feet, break ten minutes, run ten feet, break ten minutes. Strenuous!"

The boys both laughed. They were making fun of each other, yet they were both smiling. Belle so did not understand boys! Dave started to say something back, but right then the gate opened and Belle grabbed Craig's hand, pulling him onto the ride. "What was that?" she whispered, once they were securely fastened in their seats.

"What?" Craig asked innocently. "Oh, well, the basketball team and the football team have always fought over who is better."

"That's not what I meant," Belle said crossly.

"You nodded. I thought that meant it was okay to talk to him."

"Talk to him, yes. But you didn't have to be nice to him."

Craig just laughed and gave her hand a squeeze as the ride started and they blasted straight into the air.

Chapter Three

"Keep your head up, Kid." Ariel grabbed Cinderella's shoulders from behind, and guided her forward. She broke into song, hoping the upbeat tune would help distract her cousin for a little while.

Cinderella smiled and soon found herself singing along with the catchy melody. The pair grew louder as they neared the end of the song, but Cinderella couldn't finish the rest of the line when she realized several people around them had stopped to watch their impromptu performance. She and Ariel both burst out laughing and picked up the pace to catch back up with the rest of their group.

"Thank you," Cinderella said. She put an arm around Ariel and gave her a quick hug.

"You looked like you needed it," she said, shrugging.

"This day is not going at all how I thought it would," Cinderella sighed. "I thought we'd be here till closing, but now I don't know how much longer I'm going to last."

"I know," Ariel said. "But it could be worse. You could be Craig," she said, pointing in his direction.

Cinderella glanced at Craig and they both started laughing again. He was trying desperately to be the nice guy and make Dave feel included while at the same time trying to cheer Belle up, who'd been irritated from the moment Dave arrived.

"Poor Craig," Cinderella said. "He looks exhausted!"

"I know I wouldn't want to be alone with her in the car tonight! Reee reee reee!" Ariel added, making stabbing motions in the air.

Cinderella gave an appreciative smile, but it quickly turned into a frown when she looked in Scott's direction. He and Jenny had sat down at a table to share some dinner. Her head rested comfortably on his shoulder. Cinderella felt a sharp pain in her stomach as she watched Jenny tilt her head up to meet Scott for a tender kiss. She quickly turned her head away, fighting the tears that threatened to escape.

Ariel and Aurora quickly jumped into rescue mode and pulled Cinderella away, shouting an excuse over their shoulders as they disappeared into the evening crowd. Once they were safely out of earshot, Cinderella couldn't hold on any longer. Tears poured down her cheeks and she found herself in the middle of a twin sandwich. She wiped her eyes quickly, shaking her head.

"This is stupid! It's not like he was my boyfriend or anything."

"But you liked him," Aurora said.

"A lot!" Ariel added. "I think he's being kind of a jerk, flaunting it with Jenny in front of you like that! He knows you like him!"

"What kind of a name is Jenny anyway?" Aurora said, sounding disgusted. "Jen-ny. So boring! So plain!"

"Do you want me to hate her for you?" Ariel offered.

"I already do," Aurora stated.

Cinderella smiled at her cousins' attempt to make her feel better. "Thanks guys. I wish I could hate her! It would make life so much easier! But truth is, she's really nice. I actually like her a lot." Cinderella glanced around at all the happy couples passing by and shook her head. "I need to do something," she said.

"Like break into song?" Ariel asked. "'Cause we kinda started that and then I lost my backup singer." She nudged Cinderella playfully.

Cinderella smiled. "No, I want to *do* something. Something active to get my mind off of him...*them*..."

"I know exactly what you mean," Aurora nodded. "I didn't end up like this from nothing," she said, patting her bright red hair. "When everything happened with Dave last year," she paused to make a gagging gesture. "I went for a long walk to ease my frustrations and found myself in front of a hair salon. In that moment I needed to do something drastic, so I went from blonde to red. Now, I don't see any hair salons around, so a dye job is out. What were you thinking instead?"

Ariel glanced around, looking for inspiration. Then she grinned. "Got it." She took off in the opposite direction of the park.

"Where is she going?" Cinderella asked.

"No idea," Aurora responded. "I just hope it has something to do with a kissing booth, I'm feeling antsy." The two of them turned to follow and had to run to catch up with her.

***

"You're going to fly," Ariel said, proudly holding her hands up in the air to display her idea.

Cinderella and Aurora both looked up at the huge metal arch towering above them. Three tiny specks hung from ropes at the top, in the center of the archway. Suddenly a loud, high-pitched scream fell down on them from above as the specks plummeted toward Earth. At the last second their ropes tightened and they went from freefalling to swinging overhead. As they got closer, the specks turned into two guys and a girl, all strapped together, flying over them in their harnesses.

"No freakin' way!" Aurora said, shaking her head.

Cinderella watched the three people laughing as the workers brought them in and began undoing their harnesses. Her stomach twisted into knots and looking up at the top of the tower made her head spin. This is exactly what she needed.

"Let's do it," she said, walking forward.

Ariel squealed and gave Cinderella's hand a squeeze. Then she turned around and pulled the frozen Aurora forward, toward the booth to sign up for a ride.

***

Half an hour later, the three girls were shaking as they climbed onto the stand, harnesses tightly in place around their bellies. With a tight jerk from the ropes, they felt their feet lift off the ground, followed by a steady ascent up, up, up. They waved to their friends below, who had all gathered to watch the girls free-fall to sudden death, according to Aurora. She had almost backed out, until one of Scott's friends told her how impressed he was. Then she became all smiles and giggles, like freefalling 143 feet was the easiest thing in the world. She tossed her hair and winked at the boy as she climbed onto the platform, keeping a smile plastered on her face until they were high enough to be out of sight.

Now Aurora's pale face demonstrated her true feelings. Her eyes squeezed tight as she muttered, "We're gonna die, we're gonna die."

"Not exactly helpful," Cinderella said through gritted teeth.

Ariel, on the other hand, enjoyed every minute of it and couldn't stop giggling. "Wow, look how small everyone is!" she exclaimed.

Aurora peeked her eyes open and shrieked. "Aren't we there yet?!"

With a sudden jerk that made Aurora scream again, they stopped. Cinderella felt terrified, but she opened her eyes anyway and looked at the world below her. The sky swirled in pink and orange as the sun began dipping below the lush green mountains. She could see all the city lights coming on as they twinkled in the last of the sunlight. Everything looked so small from up here; it felt very surreal.

"Are you ready?" Ariel shouted.

"No! I want down!" Aurora screamed.

Ariel laughed and looked to Cinderella, who simply nodded. Ariel reached up and pulled the cord that kept them suspended. With a huge gust of wind they were falling, head first, toward the ground below. All three of them screamed and then laughed as the ropes caught and they went from falling to swinging over the crowd. Cinderella closed her eyes, relishing the moment. In those few seconds of falling, she felt like she really had been flying, free from any cares or worries.

When she opened her eyes again, she saw Scott watching her with a grin on his face. He wasn't watching Aurora or Ariel; his eyes were glued to her. Even when Jenny whispered something in his ear, Scott didn't bat an eye. He continued to stare at Cinderella and his smile widened when she got down and began high-fiving everyone around. Her heart skipped a beat when she realized Scott had broken free of Jenny and was making a beeline straight for her, eyes intense. He scooped her into a huge bear hug, lifting her toes off the ground.

"Way to go, Princess!" he exclaimed, laughing as he set her back on her feet again.

Then Scott returned to Jenny as quickly as he had appeared, leaving Cinderella speechless.

"What was that?" Ariel whispered, nudging Cinderella in the ribs.

"I really don't know," she said, a smile creeping over her face. She wasn't going to give up hope on Scott just yet.

Chapter Four

"Wait! Shhhhhh! It's starting!"

Aurora and Ariel stopped talking mid-conversation and turned their focus to the TV. Belle picked up the remote and turned up the volume as the theme song began playing a dramatic tune. Without moving her eyes away from the screen, Cinderella passed a bag of peanut butter M&M's to Snow White, who sat beside her on the couch. Their eyes were completely glued to the screen during the opening scene of their new favorite show.

School had only started a few weeks ago, but this new teen drama filled every conversation in the halls between classes. No one talked about anything else. The cousins had turned it on the first night out of curiosity, and were instantly hooked. Now, every Thursday night, a similar scene could be found in Belle's basement as the girls gathered to laugh, gasp, and ogle at the super-hot teacher on the screen. Then as soon as the first commercial started, the girls began talking again as if there had been no delay.

"Oh, this show is so good! Why do they have to ruin everything with dumb commercials?"

"To make us anticipate what's coming even more."

"We could always set the DVR to record *Locker Partners*, and just watch it later. That way we could fast forward the commercials," Snow White suggested.

Ariel looked at her like she had gone crazy.

"And just stare at the clock for an hour while we wait for it to record? Are you insane?!"

"I dunno you guys, I think I can make it through some lousy commercials to get to see Lucas Ferreira for an hour," Aurora stated.

Her cousins all nodded with enthusiastic agreement. Then the show came back on and the room went silent once again. The scene opened with Mr. Ferreira himself, leaning over a beautiful blonde student as he helped with her writing assignment. The girls simultaneously sighed, not one of them noticing the others, as they all wished for a *Freaky Friday* moment to transport them into that girl's shoes. Everything from his tan skin to his dark hair and eyes reflected his Latino roots. But his flawless American accent indicated he was second generation.

His character grinned down at the student when she found success, revealing his perfect white teeth, embellished by a dimple on the right side. His dark, long lashes winked right into the camera during a close-up shot and Snow White actually giggled. She quickly covered her mouth in embarrassment, looking around, but her cousins were too lost in his charming voice to notice.

When the show went to another commercial break, the girls were quickly broken free of their trance and resumed conversation.

"So have you heard from Prince Charming since Lagoon?" Belle asked. This is what they had taken to calling Scott since his sudden show of affection at the park.

"No," Cinderella said, looking down. "It's all kinda awkward with the whole Jenny thing..." she trailed off.

"So no phone call, text, nothing since that day?" Aurora asked, reaching for another handful of candy.

"Nothing. He did apologize that night though." Cinderella had her cousins' full attention now.

"Apologized?" Ariel asked.

"As we were leaving the park late that night, he hung back a little bit and just said he was sorry for not telling me about Jenny."

"Why didn't you tell me about that?" Snow White asked, indignant.

"It was weird, and a little awkward. I'm not sure why he felt a need to apologize."

"He led you on last year, and then you guys have been talking a lot. Don't tell me he couldn't find a moment in one of your conversations to mention he had started dating someone! He owes you way more than an apology!" Ariel shouted.

"I still think you can win him back," Aurora stated. "I say you just grab his face and kiss the crap out of him!"

Relief washed over Cinderella when the show came back on at that moment, pulling the attention off of her once again. She didn't want to reiterate how she had tried that technique once already, only to be shot down.

At the next commercial break, Cinderella fired off a question before the conversation even had a chance to return to her and Scott.

"What do you think it would be like having a teacher like that?"

"Oh, I would definitely pay better attention in school if all my teachers looked like Lucas Ferreira!" Aurora said emphatically.

"I dunno," Belle paused. "I think I would be daydreaming so much, I'd probably fail all my classes!"

"Only one way to find out," Ariel piped in. When the others looked at her quizzically she continued. "You're friends with a lot of the student body officers, just get them to put in a request to hire Lucas Ferreira as the new English teacher, Belle."

Cinderella and Aurora both launched pillows in Ariel's direction, who laughed in return.

"If only I had that power!" Belle replied.

Then the show returned with its final climatic minutes, filled with cliff hangers to keep the viewers wanting more, and insuring their return next week.

Mary came walking down the stairs after getting off work and paused at the bottom step. "Hey Belle, I need you to—"

"Shhhhh!" all five girls shouted.

"Well, this must be some show!" Mary said more quietly.

"Hold on Mom, you haven't seen the best part yet," Belle said. "There!" she pointed to the screen as the gorgeous actor appeared. "Isn't he great?"

Mary stood frozen to the spot. Usually she was the first to agree with the girls when it came to cute guys, and her sudden silence caused them all to turn in their seats.

"Mary?" Cinderella asked. "Is something wrong?"

"He…" Mary started, but couldn't finish. Her brain wouldn't form the right words. She reached out for the handrail and sat slowly on the bottom step, never taking her eyes off the screen.

"He plays one of the high school teachers," Ariel said, looking at Mary quizzically. "His name is—"

"Luke Ferreira," Mary finished, breathlessly. She could feel the room spinning around her and was glad she had chosen to sit.

Belle looked at her mother curiously. "Yeah, how did you know?"

"Because," Mary answered, pointing at the TV, "that is your father."

Chapter Five

No one moved. No one spoke. When the next scene showed one of the girls kissing their favorite boy on the show, a moment they had all been anticipating, the cousins still remained motionless. Even Mary just continued to stare at the screen, long after Lucas Ferreira moved off camera.

Belle felt slightly sick to her stomach. She had spent many nights, weeks even, lusting after her own father. Mary always told her that her father had been an actor, someone back from her own acting days, but somehow this is not what she had pictured. A slightly balding, old guy acting in off-Broadway shows flashed through her mind. She never could have pictured an ultra-hunk who every girl in school talked about each Friday. He was a smile shared between the younger teachers, a picture in every third locker, and the sole subject of several stalker-looking notebooks. *My dad?*

No, that word felt far too intimate for the man who wanted her dead. For wasn't that what he wanted? He had told Mary he would pay for the abortion, pleaded with her, even. He wanted her to stay in Hollywood and go after their dreams together. From the looks of it, Lucas Ferreira had gotten exactly what he wanted. Suddenly, Belle wanted to explode as her body filled with a fiery fury. She jumped up and shut the TV off with as much force as pushing a button could do. Then she ran up the stairs, past Mary, and out the front door before anyone knew what was happening.

It took Craig almost an hour to get any words out of Belle. She had arrived on his front porch crying and completely out of breath. Belle had never considered herself a runner before, but the three miles to Craig's house had only seemed like a jog to the end of the street as the battle raged in her head...and heart. Once she had collapsed into Craig's arms, all feeling returned to her numb body. Her lungs burned as she tried to gulp down air between sobs. He supported Belle's weight as she stumbled inside and fell onto the nearest couch. Her bare feet, now black from the pavement, stung under Craig's touch while he tried to rub out the blisters.

"My father," she finally squeaked out.

"What?" Craig asked, softly. Her big, dark eyes looked up into his. Craig nodded his encouragement and Belle continued.

"My mom was always straight with me about him, which I appreciate. Some of my cousins know almost nothing about their dads. But I never asked for details. I guess knowing he didn't want me, made me not want to care about him in return. If I had asked to see a picture or something, I'm sure my mom would have shown me. Wouldn't she?"

This is what Belle loved the most about Craig. She knew she wasn't making any sense to him at all. She was only half telling him what happened, the other half was thinking aloud as she tried to process. But rather than press her for more information, he held back. He simply sat quietly and held her tight, patiently waiting for what she wanted him to do next.

Belle's breathing had finally returned to normal. She could no longer feel her heart racing against her chest. And with the loss of adrenaline, she suddenly felt completely exhausted. She turned her head, resting it on Craig's firm chest and closed her eyes. She knew he had been patient long enough, but Belle didn't even know where to start.

"I met my father tonight, so to speak," she began slowly.

"Really?" Craig knew instinctually it was okay to respond now.

"You know that show all the girls at school love?"

"*Locker Partners?*"

"Yeah, that's the one. Have you ever seen it?"

"I watched it at your house a couple weeks ago, remember? Aurora almost took my head off for asking questions."

"That's right." Belle smiled at the memory. And as she recalled, he had made fun of it a little too, thus ensuring he wouldn't be invited back for future viewings. "Do you remember the English teacher, Mr. Rodriguez? He's played by an actor named Lucas Ferreira."

"Only because your cousins all squealed whenever he came on screen," Craig replied. He distinctly remembered Belle had started to join them too, then tried to brush it off as a sneeze or something. Because of the seriousness of their night thus far, he didn't bring it up.

"That's him." As Belle said this, she released a huge breath of air, admitting it out loud for the first time.

"That's who?" Craig asked. She looked at him meaningfully and he understood. "That's *him?*" he repeated.

Belle only nodded at first, the pair of them sitting in silence for several seconds. "What do you think?"

"Wha...how?" Craig didn't even know where to start.

"My mom used to live in Hollywood to be an actress. It's been a long time since we talked about it so I don't remember all the details. But they were on a show together and started dating. Then when she found out she was pregnant, she quit the show. He wanted her to get an abortion and she wouldn't. So she left Hollywood and moved back home with her sisters.

"When we were watching the show tonight, my mom came downstairs right as he came on screen and she freaked a little. Told me that was him. Then I just took off. I don't really know why, I just couldn't sit there any longer, with all my cousins staring at me."

Craig wasn't sure if she wanted him to respond, but he didn't really know how to. Finally he asked, "So how are you now?"

"Better, I guess. It's just weird, ya know. I mean, I haven't even thought about the man in years and suddenly BOOM! There he is, shoved right in front of my face. Right in front of everyone's faces, really, for the whole world to see."

The doorbell rang, causing Belle to jump, and Craig felt for the first time he understood the saying "saved by the bell." He carefully lifted Belle off his lap as he stood, and set her gently back on the couch. "Be right back," he whispered, kissing the top of her head.

Craig opened the front door to find Mary standing on his porch. At least he thought it was Mary. He had never seen her looking anything but perfect before, so seeing her now, with red, swollen eyes and looking disheveled, he froze.

"Hey Craig," her voice broke his trance. "Is Belle here?"

"Yeah, she's in here," he said, stepping back so Mary could enter. Then he closed the door behind her and led the way to his den.

Belle lay curled up on the couch, almost in fetal position. Looking at her, Mary briefly felt as though her daughter was six years old again, the first time she asked the question: "Mommy, do I have a daddy?"

Belle could sense eyes watching her, so she quickly jumped up and turned toward her mother. "You found me."

"It wasn't hard," Mary replied.

Belle looked at her mom, then really looked at her, and saw the obvious signs that she had been crying. Her super strong, super tough, always joking mother had been crying. Mary held out her arms and Belle moved into them. The two women held each other for a long time, new waves of emotion attacking them in unison. Craig, the smart boy that he was, quietly crept from the room, leaving them alone.

"Can we go somewhere and talk?" Mary asked, breaking their embrace at last. "Why don't we get some ice cream?"

"Ice cream, Mom? Really?" Belle questioned, her snarkiness returning. "What am I, four?"

"Oh gosh, I hope not!" she said, with equal sass. "The sticky hands, the constant whining, no thank-you!"

Belle smiled. "Okay, but only if I can get gummy bears on mine," she said in a childish voice.

Mary gave Belle a shove with her shoulder. "Let's go find that boyfriend of yours and tell him we're leaving. Poor boy! He's probably afraid we're both PMSing or something."

"If that's the case, I don't think we'll find him," Belle replied. "He's probably halfway to China by now!"

Chapter Six

"The first time I saw him, we were in a waiting room together. It was a tiny room, with two rows of chairs facing each other. It's like they wanted us to sit face-to-face with the competition and weed ourselves out. But sitting across from the other girls only made my confidence grow. I knew I had a better chance than all of them, I was certainly prettier."

"So you were super humble then?" Belle asked, grinning. She and Mary sat across from each other in a dark booth at the very back of the restaurant. They each had a delicious looking chocolate ice cream and cookie creation in front of them, but neither had touched theirs yet. The occasion didn't really generate hunger.

"You couldn't afford to be humble in those days," Mary continued. "I'm sure it hasn't changed much now. You had to absolutely exude confidence in every step of the audition process."

"And you never got nervous?"

"Oh I certainly got nervous plenty of times, but I would bury the nerves deep inside and not let on that they were there."

"So you were in a waiting room?"

"Yes," Mary sighed as she remembered that first day. "He was sitting across from me, on the opposite end of the row of chairs. He kept glancing in my direction, and smiling whenever he caught my eye, but I pretended to be focused on something else and looked away. He emanated confidence; you could just feel it radiating off of him from across the room. He obviously knew he was attractive, and charming, and I'm sure he knew he was a dang good actor too. But I didn't want him to know I had noticed. He was playing *my* game, and I think that's what bugged me most of all. I was the one who was supposed to be confident and scare away any potential threat. But the truth is I had never seen anyone like him before. I literally could not keep my eyes off him, no matter how hard I tried! His gorgeous smile made my heart beat faster. I was really glad when they called him in, I needed to be rid of the distraction, but I also paid close attention to his name.

"When my turn finally came, I nailed the audition. It was definitely the best one I had ever been to!"

"What was the part?" Belle interrupted.

Mary's eyes glistened at the memory. It had been her dream role. "It was for a sassy nurse. She was no-nonsense, didn't take crap from anyone, especially the doctors she worked with."

Belle broke into laughter from this. "A sassy, no-nonsense nurse, huh? How on earth did you act that part?"

Mary looked down at the scrubs she still wore from work and gave an appreciative laugh. "I guess it was meant to be my role, whether on the screen or in real life."

Belle shook her head, still chuckling at the irony, and finally took a bite of her gooey, melting dessert. The intensity that surrounded their discussion finally started lifting.

"I was really excited when I made callbacks and then asked to return the following day. When I got there, they had us doing readings in pairs, to test our chemistry. And you'll never guess who they paired me up with."

Belle's smile faded as she remembered the topic of their discussion, but she continued to listen intently. "I was ecstatic to see him again, but felt twice as nervous to be playing across from him. I was supposed to be completely in control, but it turned out my feelings worked perfectly with the scene we were reading. "The nurse, me, starts falling for one of the new doctors, which really pisses her off. She is used to being in control, but gets really flustered by his charms and good looks. "I played the part perfectly! And the more I acted with Luke, the more comfortable we were together. We had some awesome chemistry, on and off the screen." Mary mumbled the last part, but Belle still heard.

"What do you mean by that?" Belle asked with faux innocence.

"Just that...uh...even when we rehearsed our scenes together, away from an audience, we still had chemistry." Mary shrugged and looked at her daughter, waiting to see if she bought it.

"Really?" Belle asked doubtfully.

"Yes," Mary said with a single nod. "And when you're twenty-one I'll tell you the real answer. ANYWAY," she said loudly, over Belle's snickers, "the producers were just eating it up! They loved the two of us together. Then when the auditions ended, I started walking out of the building and he caught up to me. He asked if he could buy me a cup of coffee and we ended up having coffee for three hours! We talked and talked until we each received a phone call saying we were wanted back at the studio the next day. We were both so excited we went out and had a celebratory dinner together. We honestly had an amazing connection! I couldn't imagine one of us getting the part without the other. We just fit together so well."

Belle swallowed the lump that had formed in her throat. It felt weird to hear her mom talking about her dad—er, father with such a happy look on her face. She hadn't asked questions in a really long time. She didn't remember how in love with him her mom had been. Belle scooped up her last bite of ice cream as her mom continued.

"After two more rounds of auditions and screen tests, we were both cast as the leads for the pilot episode. By that time, we were already seeing each other almost every night."

Belle coughed a little as the realization of what her mom said sunk in. "Wait a minute...you were a lead? On a TV show?!"

"Yeah I thought you knew..." Mary trailed off at the stunned look on her daughter's face.

Belle slowly shook her head, looking down. "I knew you gave up an acting job, I just didn't realize it had been so huge. I thought it was maybe...well...I don't know what I thought it was. I just never pictured you on a big time TV show or anything."

Belle's words sank in and Mary immediately grabbed her hands, forcing Belle to look her in the face. "I have never, for a single minute, regretted my decision to leave acting and have you. Do you understand me?"

Belle saw the earnestness in her mother's eyes and knew her words were true. It didn't completely rid her of guilt, but it did help a little. "Okay," Belle said. Then her guilt quickly flashed to anger. "But *he* didn't want me. And he didn't want you to have me either."

"We were so young, Belle. I'm not saying that as an excuse, but you can't completely blame your father."

Belle couldn't believe what she was hearing.

"He didn't want to lose me, but he wasn't willing to give up everything to keep me either. I told him I was moving home and having the baby. He didn't want me to leave the show; he said actors have babies all the time. But I knew in my heart I couldn't continue acting and be the mother I wanted to be. My mom wasn't around most of the time growing up. Dana practically raised us, you know that. I didn't want to do the same thing to my own daughter. I wanted to be there for you, be a mom, not pay someone else to do it for me. That was my decision. Your dad only wanted me to...to..."

"Have an abortion." Belle stated matter-of-factly.

"He saw it as his only option. He was just scared, you need to understand that. He wanted kids someday, he really did. We had even talked about it. But he wanted to pursue acting too. I wouldn't stay in Hollywood to raise you, and he wouldn't quit acting and move home with me. We were both too stubborn to budge. So I just left. I left my mother's phone number, so he could change his mind if he wanted to, but he never called. I never saw or heard from him again. Until tonight. Seeing him on that TV show was like seeing a ghost!"

"A super handsome ghost that all the girls at school drool over," Belle said dryly. She shivered and gagged a little over the memory, then dropped her head onto her folded arms. "I can't believe I called my own dad hot," she said miserably.

Mary laughed and patted her daughter on the arm for comfort. "That is pretty gross," she joked.

Belle glared at her, then stuck out her tongue.

"But in all fairness," Mary continued, putting her hands up in supplication, "I never showed you a picture. So you had no idea what he looked like."

Belle slammed her head back onto her arms, shaking it slightly as she willed the past to be undone.

"It is still a little icky though," Mary whispered.

She then received a hard punch in the arm for her joke.

Chapter Seven

Belle walked into school the next morning cautiously. She felt as though the entire student body was looking at her as she walked quickly to her locker, head bent low. But no one was watching her. She felt like they should be; if anyone else knew about this new discovery, she'd be the talk of the school! Thankfully the only people who did know about her father would never spread it around. So even though her entire world changed last night, everyone else's had remained normal. All the girls, and a few guys, were talking about the latest episode of *Locker Partners*. Many went off about her dreamy father, but most were talking about the kiss. The kiss. Belle had almost completely forgotten about the epic kiss. Funny how something that would normally have been so monumental to her seemed completely trivial now.

As Belle reached into her locker to remove the large history book, she felt a pair of arms wrap around her waist.

"How are you doing today?" Craig whispered in her ear.

Belle turned around and smiled at him, encircling her arms around his neck in return. "Much better now that you're here." She kissed him lightly on the lips. "Thank you for last night."

Craig stepped back in surprise. First of all, Belle was not a big fan of the public displays of affection at school, other than hand holding. And on top of that, she seemed really somber this morning. Belle was acting completely out of character, but given the circumstances last night, he decided to brush it off. "Can I walk you to your next class?"

Belle pushed her locker shut, swung her bag over a shoulder, and grabbed Craig's hand. "That would be great."

Belle really didn't want to be at school. Even though no one knew, with the exception of her cousins and her boyfriend, she really didn't feel like talking to anyone. And no matter how hard she tried to seem normal, she almost walked into open locker doors twice. Her mind was obviously focused elsewhere. She really didn't want to deal with the "what's wrong?" question, asked with puppy dog eyes and a head tilt. It was so annoying! Yet every girl she knew could pull that one off. Thankfully all four cousins were in her first period history class. So she could avoid the obnoxious fake concern for at least one class period.

Belle kissed Craig again when they stopped at the entrance to Mrs. Payne's classroom. His eyebrows shot up in surprise but, like a good boy, he didn't complain. He just kissed her back before waving good bye. Even though Belle didn't normally like PDA, she wanted Craig to understand just how grateful she was for his presence today.

Belle walked to the back row and slid behind the table, alongside Cinderella and Aurora. Ariel, Snow White, and some other girl sat at the table right next to theirs. Poor girl. She was like an outcast among the cousins; none of them even knew her name.

This history class was the first time since Kindergarten that all five cousins were in the same class together. The girls were so excited to be together again, but poor, crazy Mrs. Payne could never keep them all straight. They didn't even look alike, but the same last name really seemed to throw their teacher for a loop.

They each offered Belle a supportive smile, but knew better than to ask how she was doing. Instead, Cinderella tried to keep the mood light.

"What do you think we're doing today?"

"I just hope we watch more TV," Belle replied, grumpily. "I could use a good nap."

"Who wants to take bets on who today will be?" Ariel asked, leaning over Snow White so the others could hear. Ariel and Belle both guessed older actors, while Aurora wished for a young, hot one.

"Just so we can look at him for the next hour," she said.

Snow White piped in with her guess, smiling mischievously as she did.

Mrs. Payne stood up to start the class. The girls watched as she pushed the large TV to the front of the room, and looked at Cinderella expectantly.

"Ummmm...I dunno!" Cinderella whispered.

"Today," Mrs. Payne announced, holding up a tape, "We are going to watch another actor discover his history."

She said the name and all four eyes shot to Snow White, who sat up in her chair, bouncing her shoulders excitedly. She grinned back at them and then mouthed, "I saw the name on the tape before class." The others sunk back down in their seats and rolled their eyes in return, while Snow White continued to grin impishly.

For the last several weeks, Mrs. Payne had been showing her class episodes from a documentary-type show that followed actors and actresses as they researched their genealogy. She said in order to understand history, you have to know where a person comes from. The girls thought it seemed more likely that their teacher enjoyed the nap she got during each episode, but they weren't about to complain. It was even kinda fun watching stars discover their ancestry. History became far more exciting when the students were able to make connections with real people, who were alive today, rather than learn about unknown historical people who lived hundreds of years ago.

"This is going to be our last time watching this show," Mrs. Payne paused while her class all moaned. "But," she said, putting her hand up to stop the complaints, "I have a really fun and exciting project in mind. I'll hand out the assignment after the episode. So," she held up the VHS tape and waved it in the air before placing it in the VCR. "Without further ado." She pushed play and then turned off the lights.

"Who uses VHS anymore?" Ariel whispered.

"A dinosaur maybe?" Snow White grinned.

"I didn't even know they still existed!" the girl sitting on the other side of Ariel exclaimed. The cousins all turned and stared. They weren't intentionally trying to exile her, but this was the first time any of them had heard her talk. They all looked at her now, stunned by the sudden decision to speak up. The pitiable girl's smile faded, her shoulders returning to their hunched position, as she returned her gaze to the screen. She peeked at the Princess sisters one more time and when she found them still staring in disbelief, she tried to cover her face with her brown, mousy hair.

"I'm sorry," Ariel shook her head, breaking them all of the awkward moment. "You just surprised us. None of us have ever heard you speak before."

"Which was probably our fault," Cinderella added quickly, trying to prevent the pitiful creature from crying.

She smiled meekly at them. "Well," she squeaked out, "it is extremely intimidating to be in the presence of the famous Princess sisters."

Aurora smiled, like she didn't quite get the joke. "Famous?"

"Of course!" the girl's confidence grew a little more each time she opened her mouth. "Everyone knows about you guys! The way you showed up Cynthia and her crew at the dance last year, that was classic!" Her eyes brightened at the memory, as though they had defeated some great beast. Although they kind of had, according to some. The way the cousins had all shown up to the dance, dressed in their fairy tale princess gowns, proved they weren't ashamed of their names. The way they'd stood up to the bullying was still talked about in reverent tones throughout the school.

"What's your name?" Belle asked quietly.

"Mona," she whispered back, in awe that such a marvelous being would even care.

"Well, Mona," Belle said. "Welcome to the group."

"Ahem!" They all jumped at the sound of Mrs. Payne clearing her throat behind them. But in typical Mrs. Payne fashion, she didn't scold or even say another word. Her message had been received. The girls all quieted and focused on the show instead. Within a few moments their teacher began snoring loudly behind her desk.

"*Now* she falls asleep," Mona commented.

Ariel nudged her arm playfully, giving her an appreciative smile. Mona's grin in return split her face ear to ear.

***

As the closing credits ran up the screen, the final music blared and Mrs. Payne jerked awake. She quickly jumped to her feet and returned light to the room. The students all squinted for a moment, trying to readjust their eyes.

"Wasn't that great?" she asked excitedly. "Now for the best part." She proceeded to make a drumroll noise with her mouth. "Over the next few weeks, you will all get to do your own ancestry exploration!" Mrs. Payne held up her arms, like the next words out of her mouth should be "Ta da!"

She briefly waited for a reaction, but most of the students didn't understand yet. "I want you all to speak to your moms, your dads, your grandparents, aunts, uncles, second cousins three times removed even! Dig up some dirt, or some good stories from your family's history. We're all going to be filling out these family trees." She held up a piece of paper with a blank diagram on it. "Then we will report our findings in three weeks to the entire class! Some of you can even videotape your search, if you'd like. Make your own sort of TV episode about your own families."

Most of the class began buzzing with excitement. History usually carried the stigma of boring, standard assignments. The project their teacher proposed actually required creativity and fun. Mrs. Payne reveled in the enthusiasm from her students; this was the reaction she had been hoping for. Everyone could feel the excitement bubbling through the room with the exception of the Princess sisters, who all looked like they were going to throw up.

Chapter Eight

Cinderella sat back in her chair, completely stunned. She licked her lips, which were growing drier by the second. She started to raise her hand, in preparation to ask a question, but she didn't know what to ask. She didn't know where to even begin.

The few brief moments in her life when she tried bringing up her father resulted in Dana usually being angry and bitter. Then she typically followed it with guilt. "Why would you even bring him up? Haven't I been a good enough parent to you?" Blah blah blah. Cinderella had even tried to Google him once, but without the knowledge of his last name, she knew she wouldn't get anywhere. All she knew about him was that his name was Steven...or Stephen. Since she wasn't sure how it was spelled, she tried both. "Stephen" brought up 94, 600, 000 results. "Steven" brought up 528, 000, 000. The only thing the search had taught Cinderella was Steven with a V was clearly a more popular spelling.

She wanted to ask a question about the assignment, but didn't know where to start. She quickly gave up and dropped her head into her hands. Cinderella was *not* looking forward to talking to her mom tonight.

Aurora and Ariel exchanged worried looks. Their father was in jail, that's all they knew. After hearing from their aunts how abusive he was to their mother, they didn't really care to know any more. What kind of man could hurt such a tender, sweet woman like Rachel? They made a pact when they were young not to bring him up, or even think about him. They had each other, their mom, their cousins and aunts. They didn't need to know about a man who still gave their mother nightmares. The few times he was brought up when they were little resulted in Rachel freezing in terror, shaking violently, or having a full-on panic attack. She couldn't talk about him, she couldn't even look at wedding pictures without losing it completely. The girls had a vague idea of what he looked like, from glancing at the pictures a few times. But the pictures were destroyed one night after Rachel had gone to bed, when Dana and Mary came into their house and burned them all. When the twins had questioned them, their aunts simply said it was for Rachel's own good and then left quietly as soon as the deed was done.

Several years ago Rachel received word that he had been transferred from the California state prison to the one in Draper, Utah. He had gotten in a fight with another prisoner or something. The girls didn't really know the details surrounding his transfer, nor did they care. But they had never seen Rachel so scared in all their lives. Even though Draper was a good 40 minutes south of Layton, Rachel was seriously contemplating whether she should pack up the twins and move. Thankfully her sisters had been able to talk her down.

"Do we have to explore both our mom and our dad's sides of the family?" Ariel asked without raising her hand.

"In order to complete the family tree, yes," their teacher replied. "You can choose which side to explore further, but you need to at least know the basics of both of your family lines."

Ariel blew out a huge breath, shooting her blonde bangs into the air. She hadn't even realized she'd been holding it in. Now she wished she could take that breath back. *Maybe if I forgot to breathe and passed out, I could play the sick card and get out of this assignment.* She heard a similar exhalation from her sister and looked over at her. Call it twin intuition or whatever you want, but from the look Aurora gave her, she knew they were thinking the exact same thing.

Snow White sat in her desk, wringing her hands silently on her lap. She felt completely dumbfounded. She didn't even know her dad's name! The few times he was brought up, her aunts simply referred to him as "the sperm donor". When she questioned her mom, Elizabeth would just treat her like a little kid and say the stork had dropped her off. No matter how much pushing or questioning she had done, Snow White always came up empty. Maybe she didn't really have a father at all. Maybe her aunts weren't kidding when they said he was a sperm donor. It's not like her mom ever dated, or even appeared to like men for that matter. Snow White looked around at her cousins and knew this was going to be the most difficult assignment they would have.

Belle sat frozen to her chair. She was already trying, no, trying wasn't the right word, more like being forced into the idea of her father existing outside her imagination. Now she had to somehow get in touch with him and have a father/daughter chat over cocoa about his parents and where he came from? Absolutely not! She would simply refuse and take an F on the assignment. She didn't even care anymore.

"And if some of you are thinking of skipping out on the assignment, perhaps it seems like too much work, well..." Mrs. Payne paused for effect. "It will be twenty percent of your grade, so I don't recommend it."

The witch can read minds! The fire that began boiling down inside of Belle suddenly built up so intensely, it shot her hand straight into the air. She didn't wait to be called on before diving in. "What if our fathers aren't a part of our lives?" she asked, eyes narrowed. Belle did not want her classmates knowing this information about her, but she had to let Mrs. Payne know how unreasonable she was being.

"Well, even if you have step-fathers, or no real contact with your dad at all, there's always someone you can talk to. Your mom, a grandma or aunt maybe, you just need the basic information for the tree itself."

Without even thinking, Belle found herself running away for the second time in less than twenty-four hours.

Chapter Nine

Belle ran down the halls and out the front door of the school. She knew she was over-reacting. She knew she was being immature. But after the physical and emotional draining from the night before, as well as barely sleeping, she didn't really care what anyone thought right now. She just wanted to run and run, and hope that when she eventually returned all her problems would have vanished. BAM! Belle was so lost in her own world, she ran straight into someone's very muscular shoulder.

"Are you okay?"

Belle looked up into those all-too-familiar blue eyes of Dave Prince and her knees finely gave out. She buckled and collapsed on the grassy ground. Dave immediately sunk down beside her. "Belle? What's going on?"

Belle hated Dave! She hated that he made her fall for him, she hated that he used her, but most of all, she hated him for being here at this very moment because she was just too shattered to put up a fight. Instead, she laid her head on his shoulder and cried. Dave put his arm around her and gently rubbed her arm with his thumb. He didn't ask questions or even speak. He just savored the moment she was back in his arms because he knew, as soon as Belle became herself again, she would be back to hating him.

***

"How does this sound? Dear murderous jerk-face, I think you're scum but I have to do this stupid assignment for school..."

"Well, it's honest," Cinderella said, trying not to smile. "But I somehow don't think he'll be interested in reading far enough to find out what you need, with an opening like that."

Belle gave a dramatic sigh and crumpled the paper she had been writing on.

"So where did you go after class?" Aurora asked.

Belle thought back to her moment with Dave and her cheeks grew warm. He held her for almost half an hour without a word spoken between them. Then, after composing herself, she whispered a thank you and immediately called home sick. Dave had seemed genuinely nice, like he actually cared for her. *No,* Belle told herself, shaking her head. *Dave is a user and a player. He probably has some ulterior motive. As soon as he gets what he wants, I'll be thrown to the curb again.*

"I just needed some fresh air," Belle answered. At least it wasn't a lie. "Then I went to the office and called my mom. I didn't really sleep last night. I'm feeling better now."

Aurora knew she wasn't getting the full truth, but she also knew she probably wouldn't, so she let it go.

"What did Mrs. Payne think about my little exit?" Belle asked.

"She was pretty shocked, to say the least," Cinderella answered.

Belle couldn't help smiling. She loved the idea of Mrs. Payne standing at the front of the classroom, her mouth gaping open, as she helplessly watched Belle run away. *Serves her right.*

"I know exactly what you're thinking," Cinderella said. "And whatever triumph you may have had today, you still have to do the assignment."

Belle narrowed her chocolate eyes at Cinderella, who glared back. Neither of them backed down, until they both lost control and burst out laughing.

"You're right," Belle said, blowing out a huge gust of air. "I guess I better write this stupid thing. If I'm lucky, he will ignore it and then I have a good excuse for the old bat. 'I couldn't do the assignment, Mrs. Payne, honest I tried, but my Daddy wouldn't write me back.'" Belle crinkled her nose at the unfamiliar taste of that word in her mouth.

Then she went back to scratching ideas down in her notebook. "You know, you all have to do the assignment too," Belle added, without looking up. "What's the plan?"

"My only hope is if it's for school, my mom will loosen up enough to give me a last name. Then maybe I can find him on Facebook or e-mail him or something," Cinderella shrugged. "I need to time this thing just right. Wait for a moment when she's in a really good mood, possibly distracted, then be really subtle with my questions."

From downstairs they could hear the front door open and close. "Cinderella, I'm home!"

"We're up here, Mom!" Suddenly, Cinderella's stomach was feeling very tight.

Belle grinned, "Here's your chance," she said, waving to the door.

Cinderella slowly got to her feet and walked to the top of the stairs. Looking down, she could hear her mom fidgeting around in the kitchen. She promptly turned back and sat next to Snow White on the carpet. "I don't think now is the right time," she said. "Let's finish your letter first."

Belle smirked and then began reading aloud:

Dear Mr. Ferreira,

My name is Belle Princess, I believe you knew my mother, Mary. I know you probably never expected to hear from me, your daughter, but I find myself having no choice. I have an upcoming school project where I need to make a family tree. I just need to know your family line; names of parents, grandparents, whatever you can provide me with would be greatly appreciated. Here is my e-mail address, if you could just send the information to me there, I promise never to bother you again.

Sincerely,
Belle

"Very formal sounding," Ariel commented.

"It's simple and direct, I like it," Aurora added.

"I like that you still managed to zing him just a little, but in a very casual way," Cinderella said. 'I know you never expected to hear from me, your daughter.' Like he forgot he even had one."

"Exactly what I was going for," Belle grinned, scanning her own words again.

"How are you going to get it to him?" Snow White asked. "I'm sure he gets hundreds of letters from fans every day."

"Oh, I'm counting on it," Belle said, shoving the letter into an envelope. "If it just gets passed over, then I really don't ever have to deal with the guy and I can tell Mrs. Payne that I did everything I could."

After finishing with the letter, the Princess sisters each headed home for dinner. Belle was the last to leave.

"Good luck with your mom," she said with a wicked grin.

Cinderella closed the door behind them and turned around. Suddenly she understood Belle's smile as she was leaving. Belle seemed thrilled that her cousins suddenly had to deal with the truth about their own fathers as well.

Dana was standing in front of Cinderella, her eyebrows raised. "Good luck with what?" she asked.

Chapter Ten

Cinderella took a deep breath and, without responding, led Dana over to the sofa.

"I need to ask you about my dad," she said. With a scowl on her face, Dana immediately got to her feet and began to protest. Cinderella gently grabbed her hand and pulled her back down to sitting. "Before you get upset with me, please give me a chance to explain."

Dana gave the smallest of nods to indicate her consent. Cinderella was going to take what she could get at this point, and she proceeded. "For my class at school, I need to make a family tree. The teacher has made it very clear that we have to include both sides of the family."

"What kind of class is this?" Dana was skeptical.

"History."

Dana raised her brows in question, but Cinderella quickly put her hand up to stop further argument.

"But before you say anything," she added, "You have to understand, Mrs. Payne is very…eccentric."

"It sounds like I just need to go have a talk with your teacher."

"Mom, please!" Cinderella started feeling very frustrated, and a little ticked off at Belle. "I know you hated your father. He cheated on Grandma, and left you and your sisters, and you've never been able to forgive him for that. And I know you feel jilted by my dad because he did the same thing to you. But he's still my dad. You at least knew yours and chose to shut him out. Don't I at least deserve a chance to make that same choice?" Cinderella's face grew hot and her eyes burned as she let the anger flow. She hadn't realized how frustrated she had become over not knowing, until she suddenly burst like a pipe, leaving all her frustrations running down her face.

Dana put her arms around Cinderella and began stroking her hair. Cinderella wanted nothing more than to pull away, but she knew that wouldn't help her case. She was playing the pity card now and, so far, it seemed to be working.

"Alright," Dana finally whispered. She said it so quietly, Cinderella wasn't sure if the words had actually come out, or if she had imagined them. Dana slowly got to her feet and went upstairs. "I'll be right back."

Cinderella sat in silence for several minutes, wiping futilely at the mascara that was now smeared all over her face. Dana came back downstairs a little while later carrying a small shoebox. She placed the box gently on Cinderella's lap and sat down beside her. Cinderella looked at her mom, but Dana waved her on without an explanation. She slowly opened the lid and the first thing she saw was a wedding picture. Tears again streamed down her face as she picked up the yellowing photo. She was looking at a much younger version of her mother, who looked genuinely happy. But what she really focused on was the man with his arm around her. Cinderella could not tear her eyes away from that face.

He was tall, much taller than Cinderella ever imagined. He had straight brown hair and sunflower eyes; *her* sunflower eyes. They were brown with yellowish edging and they were the only thing Dana had ever mentioned about him. He had a warm smile and he looked, well, normal. Cinderella didn't know what she had expected, but Dana had made him out to be such a bad guy, she had almost envisioned greasy black hair and a dirty mustache. Steven looked like an ordinary dad.

"Why have I never seen this before?" she asked. Cinderella tried to hide the anger in her voice, but the question came out more biting than she had intended and Dana flinched.

"I kept it to show you one day. I knew you would want to see what he looked like, and our wedding day, but then I never had the courage to bring it out. I wanted so badly to protect you from getting hurt by your father the way I was hurt by mine, that I never realized how much I was hurting you myself by keeping him from you."

Cinderella didn't know how to respond, so she didn't. Instead, she set the picture aside and picked up the next paper. It was a marriage certificate for a Dana Princess and a Steven Phillip Barnes. If she had a normal family and her parents were still together, Cinderella's last name would be Barnes. *Weird.* The box contained a few more wedding photos, along with Dana and Steven's divorce papers, and Cinderella's birth certificate. It was a perfectly concise containment for everything that pertained to Steven's existence. Here he was, living in a box her whole life, somewhere hidden in her mother's room.

Cinderella noticed a tattered looking envelope at the bottom of the box, and she carefully pulled it out. It looked like a letter addressed to her mom. But before she could examine it closer, Dana snatched the envelope from her hands. "Sorry," she said. "Forgot that was in there." Then Dana quickly escaped up the stairs.

Cinderella continued to look through the handful of pictures from their wedding day. She studied her father's face, his smile, the way his eyes lit up while gazing at his new, beautiful bride. It was hard to believe the same happy couple in this picture would be angry and divorced only a short time later. *What happened?* she wondered.

Looking at the pictures started making Cinderella feel more sad and lost, so she set them aside. She pulled out the divorce papers instead and examined them closely. She looked at her father's signature carefully, she did a little curly at the top of her N's just like he did. Steven was starting to become a real person to her now! Cinderella went back to the beginning and read each word carefully. Maybe somewhere in these papers, she could understand what went wrong. Then she saw it: *No children were born to or adopted by the parties during their marriage and the Petitioner is not now pregnant.*

Chapter Eleven

Later that night, Aurora and Ariel walked into Rachel's room as she was getting ready for bed. This was not a moment they were looking forward to. Ariel grabbed her sister by the hand, for added strength.

"Mom?"

"Hmm?" she responded without turning around.

"Mom, we have a project we need to do for school," Ariel began.

"Yeah, or we would never ask this!" Aurora added.

Rachel finally turned around and, upon seeing her daughters' clasped hands, knew this was a serious matter. "What do you need?"

Aurora and Ariel exchanged a nervous glance, each bidding the other to speak. Finally Ariel stepped up. "Did our dad have any relatives? People who might still be around somewhere for us to talk to?"

Rachel's face went pale as she sat on the edge of her bed. Seeing her reaction, both girls moved forward.

"We have to make a family tree for this stupid history class project. So all we need to know is information about our dad's family. Just enough to fill it out," Aurora spoke quickly, hoping her explanation would give her mom some comfort.

Rachel nodded slowly, trying to process what she was being told. Then she shook her head, "No, your father didn't have any family. You'll have to talk to him yourselves."

It was the girls' turn to go pale now. Ariel sat beside Rachel on the bed, and put an arm around her. Aurora sat in the armchair beside the bed. They sat in silence. Ariel looked down and began picking at a loose string on the bedspread. Aurora looked at her sister and motioned for her to say something. Ariel shook her head vigorously and mouthed, "You do it." Aurora shook her head in return and then suddenly became very interested in the picture hanging on the wall beside her chair. Rachel, who had been staring down at her white hands and wringing them finally sighed.

"I guess it's time, isn't it?" Rachel spoke so quietly, her voice was barely a whisper. "It's about time you two met your father." She looked from Ariel to Aurora, trying to gauge their feelings. "Do you want to?"

Ariel thought for a moment. All the horror stories she had heard about the abusive man never gave her a desire to meet him. And yet, there was a curiosity somewhere deep inside her, pulling her towards a decision she never thought she'd make. Slowly, very slowly, she nodded her head. Aurora glanced at her sister with wide eyes. It was one of those "twin" moments where she knew Ariel's thoughts. It would be scary, but they could go through with it if they went together.

Rachel simply nodded in return, somehow knowing what their answer would be. "I never wanted to take you to that horrible place, but now that you're old enough to decide for yourselves, well, I can't blame you. I'll call and set things up tomorrow. I can drive you down there, but I can't...I can't..." Rachel started to tremble.

Ariel wrapped her arm tighter around her mom's shoulder, and Aurora got up and did the same thing on her other side. "We can go in on our own," Aurora said, looking to Ariel for confirmation. Ariel nodded vigorously. "We would never expect you to come in with us, Mom, don't worry. We can even drive ourselves, if we need to."

They were both glad when Rachel shook her head in response. "No, I will drive you. I will be right out in the car if you need anything."

***

Aurora and Ariel held hands tightly as the guard opened the large door for them to enter the visiting room. Everything felt like a dream, drifting at them in waves. It was only a few days ago that they told Rachel they wanted to come here and talk to their father. Then the hour drive to the Utah State Prison felt like a few seconds. Then going through security, getting searched, and having their ID's checked were all a blur too. Now here they were, after seventeen years, with only a doorway between them and their father. They briefly squeezed hands, took a deep breath, and walked in.

The guard led them over to a small table and there he sat, hunched over with his head on his hands. He was a smaller man, maybe 5' 10" at most, with a slender build. This was him? This was the man who made their mother tremble at the mention of his name? They couldn't believe this man, barely bigger than they were, could have inflicted so much pain. When the girls approached he looked up, surprised. "What do we have here?" he sneered. "Did I win some sort of prize?"

"Are you Daniel McCaw?" Aurora's voice was barely above a whisper.

Daniel slowly looked the girls up and down, licking his lips. His dark eyes were cold as stone, as he continued to look them over without responding.

Ariel could feel her skin crawl as his gaze seemed to linger on her curves. *This was a bad idea!* But there was no going back now. She plopped down into one of the chairs across from him, pulling Aurora with her. If they were sitting, maybe he would stop looking at them like that.

But then Daniel smiled, relishing in the fact that he had made them uncomfortable. Smiling makes most people appear more attractive, but not in the case of Daniel McCaw. When he grinned, both girls visibly flinched. He just looked evil. There was no other way to describe it. Daniel leaned back in his chair, folding his arms across his chest. "Yeah, I'm Dan. Who wants to know?"

"I...I'm Ariel and this is my sister, Aurora. We're Rachel Princess' daughters."

They waited for the information to sink in and watched as it did. Daniel's eyes turned from grey to black. His large, brown eyebrows turned down and he scowled, muttering obscenities under his breath.

Ariel and Aurora sat frozen. Under normal circumstances, they would have gotten upset with someone calling their mother by such awful names, but they were too terrified to be upset.

"What does she want now?!" he half-yelled, throwing his arms up. Then after a warning from the nearest guard, Daniel brought his voice back down. "Money? Now that you two have appeared, I gotta start child support or somethin'? 'Cause if you haven't noticed, I ain't got nothin'!" He waved his hand around the room, indicating where they were.

"No, she doesn't want or need anything from *you*," Ariel countered, finding some courage now.

"Wanted to come find some connection with your long, lost Daddy, is that it? 'Cause I got news for you girls, I never wanted you! I never wanted kids and your mom knew that, but she went ahead and got herself knocked up anyway!" Daniel was raising his voice again. "In fact, the night I found out you existed, I tried pounding you right out of her stomach!" Daniel got to his feet, his face red with rage. He banged his fist on the table, as several guards ran over to intervene. "But I guess I didn't finish the job, did I!"

Ariel and Aurora jumped to their feet and ran from the room as fast as they could escape, while three guards contained Daniel and dragged him back to his cell. Now they understood where the fear came from.

Chapter Twelve

Snow White was the last to arrive at the twins' house after their first visit with their father. She walked into their room, only to find Ariel sobbing into Cinderella's shoulder. Aurora sat frozen, staring at her bed, while Belle tried to get her to talk.

"What happened?" Snow White asked.

Cinderella and Belle both shrugged. Snow White plopped down on the bed beside Ariel, and began rubbing her back. Ariel started talking through her sniffles as she tried to regain control of her emotions.

"It...was...just...awful," she managed to get out. "I'm ss...sorry...guys," she added, looking around the room. "We...dd...didn't...want...our...mm..mom..to..see." Ariel took a deep breath.

Finally Aurora spoke up. "We...we didn't want our mom to see us break down. She'd probably blame herself. We both held it in until we got home." A few silent tears began slipping down Aurora's cheeks, which she brushed away quickly.

Belle rubbed her arm and asked, "So what happened exactly? Was he just mean to you?"

Aurora's silent tears turned into labored breathing as the terrifying moments from her afternoon kept replaying over and over in her mind. Her heart began to race and she suddenly couldn't sit any longer. Aurora paced around the room, as her chest tightened and her breath came out in gasps. Every time she tried to close her eyes, Daniel's dark, cold gaze was staring at her, licking his lips. Her mind rang with his nasty voice and the awful things he'd yelled at them.

"Aurora?" Her cousins were starting to get worried.

When she didn't respond, just continued to stumble around the room aimlessly, wheezing as she walked, Cinderella jumped to her feet.

"I'm going to go get Rachel."

"No! My mom can't see us like this," Ariel was broken from her trance. "She's having a panic attack. I've seen my mom have them before. Just go get a paper sack."

Cinderella ran from the room and returned moments later with a small, brown lunch sack. With the help of Bell, they slowly coaxed Aurora back onto the bed. Then they handed her the bag and reassured her that all would be alright while stroking her back. Aurora breathed into the bag, making it puff in and out, until her breathing returned to normal and she was finally able to speak.

Aurora didn't even know where to begin, as she tried to explain the terror that now consumed her. After starting and stopping several times, while the frightened tears continued to come, she was finally able to gain composure. Aurora took a deep breath and tried again. "He basically told us he never wanted kids, and tried to kill us by beating our mom. He got so upset, the guards had to drag him out," Aurora said, wiping the sorrow from her cheeks.

No one knew what to say. They had all dreamed about meeting their dads since they were little. Now two of them finally had, and it was the worst experience of their lives!

"So I'm guessing that means you didn't get any information out of him for class?" Belle asked.

Ariel scoffed.

"What are you going to do?" Snow White asked.

"Well I'm not going back there!" Aurora exclaimed.

"Not unless we have bodyguards with us," Ariel added. "Do you think Prince Charming is available?" For the first time in hours, Ariel smiled. This seemed to lighten the mood in the room considerably. The cousins were relieved to have a topic change and although the conversation felt forced at first, things quickly relaxed.

"Maybe you could at least borrow his sword and shield," Aurora said, adding to the prince reference. "I bet Scott would look pretty good storming the prison." She winked in Cinderella's direction.

"Yeah, he saved us last time we were in trouble," Snow White added.

Cinderella forced a smile, but she didn't know how to respond. She hadn't talked to Scott since the amusement park. She was too afraid to ask him about Jenny. And she wasn't sure if she wanted to know what his response would be. But Cinderella was also wanting to call him about something else...she hadn't told anyone about what she saw on those divorce papers. She wanted to confront her mom about them, but she was so confused, had so many questions, she didn't even know where to start! She knew Scott wanted to go to law school and become a lawyer, so Cinderella hoped maybe he could somehow shed some light on the situation.

Suddenly Cinderella jumped up from her seat.

"I gotta go guys. Sorry, but I...uh...I forgot something," she finished lamely.

"I think someone has a sudden urge to call a certain college boy," Aurora snickered.

Cinderella didn't even turn back to deny it. She quickly walked down the sidewalk, back to her own house. As soon as the front door was safely shut behind her, she pressed send on the number she had been staring at on her phone. Cinderella raced up the stairs, her heart thumping wildly in her throat as the phone rang.

"Princess?"

"Hey Scott."

"Hey! It's been awhile, I was afraid you'd forgotten all about me!"

Seems like you're the one who forgot about me, she thought, picturing his hand in Jenny's. Then she quickly shook the image from her mind. *That's not why I called.* "I have kind of a weird question for you."

"Shoot."

"Well...I...um...it started with this project for school," Cinderella stumbled through her words.

Scott cut her off gently. "Princess, it's me. Talk to me."

This is why she loved Scott so much! He could calm her nerves with a few simple words. Cinderella took a deep breath and spilled everything about the family trees, confronting her mom, and the strange writing on the documents.

"So what do you think it means?" she asked, trying not to sound hysterical. "Does that mean my dad isn't really my dad? Am I just the product of some one-night-stand my mom had with some random other guy, and she only told me it was her ex-husband to save face?"

"Well, I'm not actually in law school yet, I'm still just working on my bachelor's. But it seems more likely to me that your mom just didn't know she was pregnant yet when they filed for divorce."

Cinderella had been driving herself crazy all week, going over a million different scenarios in her mind. And in a matter of moments, Scott removed all her horrible, seedy thoughts and replaced them with the most logical answer. "Oh," she wasn't quite sure what to say. "Well now I feel really silly calling you. That's probably all it is."

"I'm actually really glad you called! It's always good to talk to you." Cinderella could feel her cheeks going red, and she was grateful Scott couldn't see her blushing through the phone. But they quickly went back to white when he added, "I've been meaning to talk to you...about Jenny."

"Oh," she hoped to sound casual, but feared it came out too much like a squeak. Either way, Scott didn't seem to notice.

"I just didn't know how to bring it up sooner, I'm sorry!"

"Sorry for what?" she asked, putting all her focus in remaining composed.

"That I didn't mention I was dating her."

"Mm-hmm."

"I just...I didn't know how to tell you. We went out a few times last year, and then when we both stayed at school for the summer, well, we just started seeing each other more and more. And now, well, I guess we're pretty serious."

Cinderella could feel her heart breaking into a million pieces. She fell over onto her side and covered her mouth as a cry tried to escape.

"Are we...okay?" Scott asked hesitantly.

"Yup," Cinderella could feel the tears threatening to escape her eyes in floods. "I need to go," she was barely able to get those last words out before hanging up the phone. She crawled under the covers, forgetting about homework and dinner. Nothing else seemed to matter.

Chapter Thirteen

Snow White slammed the door behind her after getting home from school. "MOM!" she yelled, her face red with anger.

"Honey? What's wrong?" Elizabeth asked, running into the room.

"What did you do?!" Her face twisted with rage as she swore loudly.

"Don't you use that kind of language, young lady!" Elizabeth scolded, waving a finger at her. "Curse words are for hookers and hobos!"

Snow White rolled her eyes, but the reprimand had taken some of her steam. "What did you say to Mrs. Payne? I went to class today, and she told me I had been excused from the family tree assignment. She gave me three books I have to read instead, and a huge book report is due with each one!"

Elizabeth's face went pale, but her daughter was too angry to notice. Then she stood up straight, and with her thin lips in a taut line replied, "I was just protecting you."

"Protecting me from what?!" Snow White could feel the fire that had been building inside her all day threaten to burst out.

"From a man you should never have to know."

"This was actually a fun assignment! I was excited about it! I was looking forward to learning about my ancestors and where I came from. How could you just take that all away from me?"

"I'm your mother. And I will do whatever needs to be done to keep you safe."

"Safe from what?? You won't even tell me who my father was! Today is the first time in my life I've ever even heard you refer to him as a man! Up until now, he's always just been 'the sperm donor'."

"We're done with this discussion," Elizabeth said, walking out of the room.

Snow White followed closely behind her into the kitchen where Elizabeth started to prepare dinner. The yelling wasn't getting her anywhere, so she tried very hard to calm down and speak in an even tone. "How did you even know about the assignment?" she asked. "I didn't have a chance to tell you about it yet."

"I got a phone call from Dana a few days ago, then one from Rachel, then Mary. They were looking out for you."

Snow White couldn't stay calm any longer. "For me?!" she shouted, knocking papers from the counter onto the floor. "You mean for YOU! No one is ever looking out for me! If you were, you'd at least give me a chance to know who my own father is! No," she said, backing away. "My whole life has been a lie to protect you and only you." Snow White turned to leave when Elizabeth grabbed her wrist, hard, and forced her to stay.

"Don't you dare speak to me that way." Her voice was quiet, but her tone was deadly. "You don't have any idea what you're talking about. I have done *everything* for you since the moment I found out I was pregnant, and all of it was to keep you safe."

Snow White was immediately brought back down again by her mom's demeanor. "You're right, I don't know what I'm talking about. But I don't know because you won't tell me. Why won't you tell me anything?"

"I just...can't. I wish you'd trust me enough to leave it at that."

"How can I just leave it alone though, Mom? I don't even know the other half of where I came from. I mean, do you know what it's like growing up, not knowing who your dad is?"

"Actually I do."

Snow White was about to go upstairs and walk away, but this was not the response she was expecting. She paused on the bottom step, her hand resting on the railing.

"I was only four-years-old when my dad left my mom, and I never saw the man again. I don't have any memories of him at all. I only remember my mom and my sisters. They were the ones who raised me, and I've never wondered about him. Do you know why?"

Snow White just shook her head.

"Because the ones who stayed were the ones who loved me, and that was enough."

Snow White was planning on a big, dramatic exit after their fight, but that was taken from her when Elizabeth turned and walked away, leaving her daughter stunned.

***

Cinderella approached her mom's door and tapped lightly with her knuckles.

"Come in."

Cinderella looked down at the papers in her hand, finally ready to get some answers, and pushed the door open. Dana was sitting on her bed reading.

"Hey sweetie, what's up?" she asked, setting the book down on her lap, but keeping a finger in it to save her place.

"I've been looking at these," Cinderella said, holding up the divorce papers. "But there's something I don't understand."

"Okay?"

Cinderella sat down on the bed next to her mom and held the pages open to the spot in question. "What does this mean? Weren't you pregnant with me when you got the divorce?" she asked, pointing to the words that had left her wondering for several excruciating days.

Dana read the document carefully, nodding as she thought back to that day. "Yes, I was pregnant when we got the divorce. But I didn't tell your father, so I didn't want you mentioned in the paperwork."

"Wait...what?"

"By the time I found out I was pregnant, we were already separated and had started the divorce process. I didn't want to complicate everything by throwing you in the mix. Besides, when I found out your father cheated on me, I didn't want you to be around a guy like that."

"So my dad doesn't even know I exist?"

"Well, no."

Cinderella got up from the bed slowly, too stunned to know how to react.

"I grew up with an unfaithful father, trust me, I made the right choice."

"The right choice for who? You?"

"Come on now..."

"No, Mom, you come on! My whole life you've led me to believe that my father abandoned me. That he made a choice not to be a part of my life. And now I find out it was *you* keeping *him* away! He doesn't even know he has a daughter! What if he wanted me? You didn't even give him a chance!"

"Oh, he had plenty of chances," Dana mumbled.

Cinderella didn't want to hear any more. She turned away from her mother, and walked from the room in a daze. She shut the door, despite her name being called, and returned to her own bedroom. Cinderella sat down at her desk, still not sure what her next move would be, when her fingers found the keyboard and she began to type.

She didn't know if it was out of defiance or curiosity, but her fingers seemed to have an agenda as she tried googling "Steven Barnes". When that resulted in too many options, she added Los Angeles, where her parents were married. After turning up nothing, she added "lawyer" which was the occupation listed in the stack of papers Dana had given her. She began following links until she found a profile for attorneys working at the Toppum/Waights firm in California. The photo posted under the name Steven Barnes looked a lot like an older version of the Steven in her mom's wedding pictures. And there was an office number listed.

This was the closest Cinderella had ever been to finding out about her dad, and she wasn't ready to stop. Her hands shook as she typed in the 10-digit phone number. She took one final deep breath before hitting "send."

The phone rang several times before a perky young woman answered. "Law offices of Toppum and Waights, this is Tanya. How may I help you?"

"M-May I speak with Steven Barnes please?" she asked, trying to hide the tremble in her voice.

"I'm sorry, he's already gone for the day. May I take a message?"

"Does he have voicemail?"

"Sure thing, sweetie, just one minute."

After three more rings, Cinderella heard something she never expected: her father's voice. Steven sounded gentle and kind, but his voice also carried an air of authority. After the brief message was spoken, there was a loud beep, which made Cinderella jump. Then she shut her eyes tight, still feeling a little like she was dreaming, and spoke.

"Hi Dad. Boy it feels weird to say that out loud. If you are my dad, I mean. My name is Cinderella, I'm Dana Princess' daughter. And yours too, maybe, if I have the right Steven. So if you were married to my mom, could you please call me back? My number is 801-555-9175. Ummmm...bye."

Cinderella quickly hung up the phone and stared at it, mortified. She knew she had rambled and probably sounded really dumb. Oh well. The only thing she could do now was wait.

Chapter Fourteen

The next day at school, the Princess sisters were sitting around their regular lunch table, but no one uttered a word. Aurora was picking at her salad, stabbing different pieces of lettuce with her fork, but never bringing any of them to her mouth. Snow White sat staring at one of the books she had to report on for History and even though her eyes were focused on the page, her brain wasn't retaining any of the words. Cinderella was nibbling mouse-like bites off her sandwich as she stared at the wall. And Ariel and Belle quickly flipped card over card in a not-so-rousing game of WAR.

When Ariel realized they were turning over cards without picking any up, she stopped. Belle didn't even notice and continued to place cards on the table.

"What is wrong with us?" Ariel finally said, making the others jerk to attention. "This is ridiculous! Why are we letting one stupid little assignment get to us so much?"

"I called my dad last night," Cinderella interjected.

"You what?!"

"When were you going to tell us?"

"What did he say?"

"He didn't answer. I left a really embarrassing message though. Now I guess I just have to wait for him to call me back. If he calls me back..." Cinderella pulled her phone out of her pocket and looked at it for the millionth time that day. It still showed no missed calls.

"He will," Snow White said, placing a comforting hand on her arm.

"What do you mean embarrassing?" Aurora asked.

Ariel shot her sister a dirty look, but she didn't seem to notice.

"I just rambled on about who I was, and whether or not we were related." Her head plopped onto her folded arms. "I must have sounded so dumb!"

"Don't worry about it too much," Ariel comforted. "I'm sure it sounded worse in your head. Plus you were nervous."

"I know, but..."

"Cindy," Snow White said, placing a hand on her arm. "You'll kill yourself if you keep stressing over it! You just have to wait. If your dad is a good guy, he won't care about the message; he'll just be so excited to hear from you, he won't be able to call back fast enough."

"This is what I mean!" Ariel said. "We need a distraction—a night off!"

As if on cue, a flier was placed down on the table in front of them. "Awesome party tonight, Ladies! You should all come." The invitation came from a tall boy with shaggy brown hair. His hair looked to be a little greasy, and his clothes reeked of smoke.

Belle wrinkled her nose and pushed the flier aside. "That was Michael Firth," she said. "I've heard about his parties. We definitely don't want to go."

"Movie marathon at our house?" Ariel asked. The others nodded their agreement. Then they all dispersed to their different classes when the bell rang.

At home that afternoon, Cinderella sat at her desk, working on homework. She normally hated doing homework on Fridays, but she also knew a movie marathon meant staying up late and sleeping most of the day Saturday, so she was trying to get it out of the way. Her phone began vibrating on the desk, threatening to shake right off the edge. Cinderella looked at the incoming call and froze. It was an unknown number from California.

Cinderella's hands shook as she answered the call and held the phone up to her ear.

"Hello?" She was barely able to squeak out a greeting, with her suddenly dry throat.

"Hi, is this Cinderella?" It was a man's voice, the same one she had heard on her father's voicemail.

"Yes." The swarm of butterflies in her stomach were in a frenzy.

"Are you really Dana Princess' daughter?"

"Yes." Her hands began to tremble.

Cinderella could hear him blow out a huge breath of air. "Then you really are my daughter?"

"Yes." Cinderella's face flushed and she felt a little dizzy. *Could this really be happening?*

He chuckled. It was the best sound she had ever heard in her life. "Are you as nervous as I am?" he asked.

Cinderella smiled. "Yes," she choked. "I don't really know what to say."

"Me neither. Why don't we start by how you found me?"

Cinderella began explaining her homework assignment and how it brought up new questions with Dana, and how her mother had finally told her the truth. She found the longer she talked, the more at ease she felt with her dad. She had a dad! Everything around her felt very surreal. She was afraid if she stopped talking and got off the phone, this would all turn into a dream and she'd be back to square one. When Cinderella finally finished her story, her dad was silent for a minute.

"Dad?" She was afraid he wasn't there anymore.

"I just want you to know that I would never, ever have left you behind if I knew you existed." His voice cracked and Cinderella couldn't be sure, but it sounded like he was crying a little.

"You have no idea what it means to hear that," Cinderella said, tears springing to her own eyes as well.

"Your mom and I had problems, but I would have done everything in my power to keep this family together if you had been in the picture." Steven's voice quickly went from sad to angry. "She had no right keeping you from me!"

Cinderella didn't know how to bring up the next part, but she had to know the whole truth. "She told me you cheated on her. That was why you got a divorce. And because of her own father, she kept me a secret. Is that true?" Cinderella hoped with all her heart that Steven would deny everything, or at least add more to the vague story she'd grown up with. She held her breath, waiting intently for him to answer.

Finally, he did. "Partly, yes." Steven swore under his breath, a hint of bitterness in his voice. "I wish I could meet you in person for this conversation. Or I wish you at least knew me better than this one phone call to judge me by. But I guess we better get everything out of the way." Steven took a deep breath and began, "I fell in love with your mom the moment we met, but it took a lot of convincing on her part to even give me a chance. Your mom seemed very...untrusting of men, because of your grandpa, I assume. When I finally convinced her to go out with me and later marry me, she still always had a guard up. It felt like no matter what I did, what I said, she was convinced I was going to leave her. Or cheat on her like her father did to her mother. It put so much stress and strain on our relationship that I...well..."

"You did exactly what she was afraid of." Pieces of the puzzle were starting to fall into place now for Cinderella.

"Yeah...I guess I did. But you have no idea what kind of pressure I was under from Dana! Every time I was two minutes late, I was bombarded with questions! 'Where were you? Who were you with?'"

"So you blame Mom for cheating?" Cinderella could feel a lump rising in her throat. The thrill of having found her father was quickly diminishing.

"She was so convinced I was going to be a bad guy, that she never gave me the chance to prove her wrong!"

"But you didn't prove her wrong." Cinderella's voice was barely above a whisper, hoping Steven would cut her off and contradict her words. "Instead, you gave into all of her worst nightmares. You became her father. Now I understand why she kept me away from you."

Steven remained silent, the guilt twisting around in his gut like a knife. Cinderella took his silence as conceding and she quickly hung up the phone. She paced around her room, her heart so torn with information and emotion that she felt she would explode. She shoved open her sliding glass door and collapsed into a chair on the balcony. She looked up at the darkening sky, tears pouring down her face. Then she glanced across the street and what remained of her heart shattered in an instant. Scott and Jenny were across the street making out on his parents' balcony.

Cinderella's head swam with the night's events as she stumbled back inside and pulled the blinds closed. Her knees wanted to collapse, to force her body onto the bed, never to get up again. But her brain was on overload and she wanted to do something. *Needed* to do something. She paced around her room for several minutes. She really didn't feel like hanging out and watching movies tonight, and she definitely wouldn't be able to focus on homework. Then Cinderella remembered something and she suddenly ran to her backpack. After several moments of searching, and removing half its' contents, she pulled out a paper. Without thinking, she shoved it into her purse, grabbed her shoes, and ran out the door. "I'm going to Snow White's," she yelled over her shoulder and closed the door before her mom could respond.

Chapter Fifteen

"Are you sure you want to do this?" Snow White asked. Her face looked even paler than normal as she glanced over at Cinderella.

"Yes!" Cinderella responded with fire in her eyes. They both stared at the house in front of them. They could already hear the blaring music, even though they were across the street and the car was still running. The extensive weeds surrounding the house had taken over the grass long ago and it was obvious no one spent time on the lawn. The two large windows in front revealed a big crowd inside, even though the curtains were drawn. They could see the shadows of bodies moving to the music. The house was dark, but they could still make out a broken window upstairs, vines running freely up the sides of the house, and shingles falling from the roof.

"This looks like the type of place where people die in the movies," Snow White's voice tremored. "Right now the audience is screaming, 'No! Don't go in there!'"

Cinderella brushed her off with the wave of a hand and started to open her door.

"Where did you get that anyway?" Snow White gestured to the crumpled party flier Cinderella was holding.

"I grabbed it off the table after lunch to throw it away, but then I forgot about it. I found it in my backpack, shoved in with all my books. It's fate, right?" She jumped out of the car and shut her door.

"Or really, really bad luck," Snow White mumbled as she reluctantly followed.

"You don't have to come Snow," Cinderella said, turning around and facing her cousin. "They've probably started a movie by now, but I'm sure if you hurry you can get back before they get too far into it."

"Yeah right, and leave you here to die in your underwear alone?" she said, gesturing toward the house.

"My underwear?"

"Yes! Right before girls die in horror movies they always end up in their underwear first. I don't know how they do it, but it just happens."

Cinderella paused for a moment, then started to laugh. "You're right, they do!"

"Okay, but seriously Cindy, this isn't a joke."

"I know," she said, putting a hand on Snow White's arm, "which is why I'm giving you an out. I just feel...I just feel like I need to blow off some steam tonight. And watching movies is not the way to do it." She held a hand up to the wreckage before them. "This is."

Snow White stepped forward and linked her arm with Cinderella's. "All right then, let's get this over with."

Cinderella felt the knot in her stomach tighten as they approached the front door. A big jock from school, she didn't know his name, stood as a bouncer just inside. They fought the urge to cover their ears as he yelled something to them.

"WHAT?" Cinderella yelled back.

He leaned down and screamed something right in her ear, his breath reeking of alcohol. "DO YOU HAVE AN INVITE?"

Is he kidding? This didn't exactly look like a by-invitation-only party. But the jock didn't crack a smile. "IN

MY CAR!" He opened the door for them to retrieve it when Michael, the greasy haired boy from school showed up. He waved the girls inside and the jock shrugged before shutting the front door again.

Michael threw a smoke-ridden arm over Cinderella's shoulder and pulled her further inside. "I DIDN'T THINK YOU'D COME!" he smiled. "DON'T SEE MUCH OF YOUR TYPE HERE," he added, looking the girls up and down.

"OUR TYPE?" Cinderella asked, trying to shrug off his arm without success.

"YOU KNOW, GOODY-GOODIES," he laughed at his own joke. "IT'S NOT LIKE WE PLAY PICTIONARY AT THESE THINGS."

"THAT'S NOT WHAT WE HAD IN MIND EITHER," Cinderella responded.

Michael grinned wickedly. "THAT SOUNDS LIKE A CHALLENGE." He put both hands on Cinderella's shoulders and guided her into the kitchen. It was strange, but the noise from the rest of the house seemed to be muffled in this room. Cinderella could actually hear conversations instead of just yelling matches.

Lots of kids she recognized, and many she didn't, stood around with paper cups in their hands. They were laughing and moving and spilling a brownish liquid all over the floor as they bumped into each other. A smaller group of kids seemed to be playing some sort of game around the kitchen table. After watching for a few minutes Cinderella figured out that whoever lost each round had to take a shot of a clear liquid that Michael's friend was pouring.

Cinderella found herself shoved into a seat from behind. The kids at the table all welcomed their new player and handed her a shot glass. Cinderella smiled weakly and looked up at Snow White, who looked horrified. Cinderella shrugged and turned back to the boy next to her, who was describing how to play.

Snow White had seen enough! Between the blaring music and the odor of a hundred sweating bodies covered in smoke and booze, she was already feeling dizzy. "Where's the bathroom?" she asked. She got multiple points in different general directions, so she set off to find it. After opening two doors she wished she hadn't, her feet found tile and she quickly closed the door behind her. Then she grabbed her cell phone, hands shaking, and found the number she was looking for.

"Snow White?" the voice on the other end sounded confused.

"You need to come now!"

"What? Where are you?"

"No time to explain. We're at a party and Cinderella is in trouble. I need some..."

Snow White couldn't even finish the word "help" before she was cut off. "Where are you?"

She muttered the address and closed her phone. Now that her mission was complete, she realized just how bad the tiny bathroom reeked. It was worse than any outhouse or port-a-potty she'd ever been in, and this was inside a house! She wanted to splash some water on her face, but one look at the sink told her she could get a number of diseases just by touching it. The amount of hair, grime, and unidentifiable smudges on the counter and sink made her wonder if the bathroom had ever been cleaned before. She saw some green near the faucet and leaned in for a closer look. *Yeah, that's definitely growing something.* Snow White covered her mouth as she began dry heaving. Then she quickly ran from the bathroom and went outside to wait for help to arrive.

Chapter Sixteen

Scott pulled up in record time. Parking on the street was long gone, so he pulled directly onto the lawn and left the car running. He didn't plan on being here long. He reached for the front door only to be stopped by a large, drunken high school kid.

"You can't go in there," he said, crossing his arms and trying to sound tough.

"Yeah? Why not?" Scott asked.

"You go don't to our school, and don't have a tinvination," he slurred.

"I'll tell you what," Scott said, stepping up to the kid and looking him directly in the eyes. "You can either open this door, or you can watch me break it down. But then you'll have a broken door to explain on top of everything else when the cops get here." Scott's shirt tightened over his flexed muscles as he waited for the kid to decide.

The boy's eyes widened and he stepped out of Scott's way. Right then he saw Snow White sitting on the grass, looking pitiful. "Where is she?"

Snow White jumped, then quickly got to her feet. "Follow me," she said, leading the way through the crowded house toward the kitchen. She hoped they weren't too late.

Scott followed close behind, scanning the crowd as they went. When they pushed their way through the kitchen, Cinderella had a cup to her lips and the kids at the table were cheering her on to drink. She looked up and saw Scott, then froze. Michael followed her gaze.

"Hey, what are you doing here? This is a private party."

"Doesn't look like much fun to me," Scott said, making a face at the scene around him. "I'm taking Cinderella and we're leaving," he added.

"She can't go." Michael put a hand on her shoulder, keeping her pinned in the chair. "She promised to play our game, and it's her turn to drink."

"Sorry man, but game's over," Scott said. When Michael wouldn't move his hand from Cinderella, Scott moved it for him. Then he threw Cinderella over his shoulder and carried her out of the party like a sack of potatoes. She screamed and tried to fight him off, but the sight of Michael crying while he massaged his hand kept anyone else from stepping in.

"WHAT WERE YOU THINKING?!" Scott yelled, as he plopped Cinderella down on the passenger seat of his waiting vehicle. Cinderella looked up at his angry eyes and began to cry. Scott immediately softened. "Did you drive?" he asked.

Cinderella nodded and pulled out her keys. Scott handed them to Snow White who accepted them and, with a grateful smile, quietly disappeared. Scott climbed in the front seat and backed the car off the lawn, yanking several weeds down as he did so. He drove a short ways down the road, until they could no longer hear the music, and pulled over. Then he took Cinderella in his arms and pulled her close in a tight embrace. He stroked her hair as she trembled and cried into his strong shoulder.

When she had finally bawled herself dry Cinderella looked into his loving brown eyes. The thought of him and

Jenny on the balcony resurfaced and she looked away, embarrassed.

"What's going on, Princess?" he whispered.

"What do you mean?" she asked, trying to play it cool.

Scott gave her a hard look and she immediately shriveled back into the seat.

"Why were you at a party like that? That's not you!"

"How do you know what's me and what's not?"

"Trust me," he said, gently lifting her chin to make her look in his eyes once again. "I know you, and I care about you. I don't want to see you doing something like that to yourself again. Do you even know what you were about to drink?"

Cinderella shook her head, feeling ashamed.

"Do you have any idea how dangerous that is? Drinking who knows what, given to you by people you don't even know? Forget the dangers of drinking alcohol at your age, what if they had put something else in there? You could have ended up in all kinds of trouble tonight!" Scott hadn't meant to, but his voice got louder with each thought until he was almost yelling again. "I'm sorry," he whispered. "I just can't stand the thought of something bad happening to you." He punched the steering wheel and looked over at Cinderella, who was staring at her hands.

Cinderella could feel her head spinning again. She was beginning to get a headache from all these heavy, confusing conversations today.

"I don't understand," she mumbled.

"What?"

"I don't understand how you can tell me you care about me, you can drive all the way to a party to bring me home, but just a couple hours ago you were making out with someone else!" Her temples were throbbing now, and she began to massage them with her fingers.

Scott was quiet for a minute. "You saw that, huh?"

"Of course I did." Cinderella wanted to yell herself. "It's not like you were hiding or anything! Nope, right there, in plain sight, directly across the street from my bedroom."

Scott took Cinderella's hand between both of his. "I'm so sorry! I didn't mean to hurt you! We had dinner with my parents tonight and I was showing her around their house. We ended up outside, looking at the stars, and kinda got carried away. I wasn't even thinking."

Cinderella shrugged, not knowing what else to say. Then she thought of her father and her anger began to rise again. "You're just like my dad! He said he cared about me, he said he'd do anything for me, and then he went and did something stupid, hurting me twice as bad! My mom was right! You can't trust men!" Cinderella leapt from the car and began walking quickly down the street. It didn't matter that it was the opposite direction from home; she just wanted to keep her feet moving.

"I mean it, Princess," Scott said, chasing her down. He caught up and grabbed her arms, turning her back towards himself. "I made some stupid mistakes tonight, and that was the biggest one."

"What? Kissing your girlfriend in plain site?"

"No. Thinking I could have a girlfriend when I'm already in love with someone else." Scott slid his strong hands down Cinderella's arms and took both of her hands in his, entwining their fingers together. Cinderella felt goosebumps pop up on her arms underneath his soft touch. She couldn't believe what she was hearing! *Did he just say he loved me?*

As quickly as the moment had come, it was gone again when Scott suddenly dropped her hands. He walked a few feet away, pulling his fingers roughly through his hair. "What am I doing?" he whispered to himself, but Cinderella still heard. "This isn't right. I have to wait." Then he looked up and saw Cinderella standing there, watching him. Her gorgeous, chocolaty eyes were all red and puffy from tears. Her long brown hair blew slightly in the gentle breeze. The large moon lit her from behind, creating a glow around her as she stood there, confused.

"Screw it!" he finally said, turning back to her. Scott charged up to Cinderella and with determination he grabbed her around the waist and pulled her in for a forceful kiss. He held her so tight, Cinderella's feet lifted off the ground. But as the kiss continued, he softened both his lips and his grip around her. Her feet slowly returned to the pavement and when their lips finally parted, they were both breathing heavily.

They looked at each other and smiled. Then their smiling turned into a laugh. A year of unspoken emotions had just been sorted out between them. The tension was gone. Scott gave Cinderella's hand a squeeze as he led her back to the car.

"I better get you home before Snow White calls me again, wondering what I've done with you."

"I don't mean to ruin the moment or anything, but where's Jenny?" Cinderella asked, suddenly looking around, expecting her to pop out from the back seat.

"Heading back to Logan, I presume."

"What?"

"We broke up. Seems she didn't like how much I talked about you, or that I was willing to ditch her tonight to come after you."

Cinderella smiled and rested her head on Scott's shoulder.

They spent the rest of the drive home talking about Cinderella's conversation with her father, which was the reason for her sudden interest in attending the party.

"I think you need to give the guy another chance."

"What?!" Cinderella thought for sure Scott would have agreed she was fully justified in her decision to blow him off.

"He made a mistake," Scott said. "A big one, yes, but he's obviously trying to make amends with you."

"But..."

"He didn't have to call you back in the first place."

"Well okay, but..."

"And he didn't have to tell you the truth about what happened between him and your mom. He could have lied and blamed it all on her, but he didn't do that."

Cinderella crossed her arms over her chest, not sure of how to proceed.

Scott glanced over at her sulking and laughed. "I'm sorry I didn't give you the answer you wanted," he said with a grin. "Just talk to him again. He deserves a chance to get to know you. And I think it's obvious he wants to, from everything you've told me."

The car slid into the parking space in front of his parents' house. Cinderella sighed, looking up at her own darkened home. She wasn't ready to say good night yet.

"Now before you go in there, I need you to understand something."

Cinderella looked at Scott and saw the seriousness in his expression. "What's wrong?" she asked.

"Nothing," he answered quickly. "Just...we still can't date yet. You know that, right?"

Cinderella felt her heart drop into her stomach.

"I meant what I said last year. I'm not going to stand in the way of you enjoying high school. I want you to go to dances and meet different guys, and live it up! Besides," he said, "there is no way your mom would be okay with us dating. Not yet, anyway."

"So then you go back to college, I go back to high school and we pretend tonight never happened?" Cinderella could feel her eyes beginning to pool.

"No, not at all! I meant every word I said to you tonight. I'm going to be smarter this time though, and not even try and replace you with someone else."

"So you are going to remain single and wait for me to finish high school, but you want me to still date other guys?"

"Basically," he said, nodding. Cinderella looked at him skeptically and Scott continued. "Look, I know what I want," he said, caressing her chin and then lips with his thumb. "I've had plenty of time to date different girls. You, on the other hand, are just getting started. You might realize in a few months that I'm not the person you want to be with. I'd never be able to live with myself if I knew I was taking that chance or those experiences away from you."

"What if you realize in a couple months that *I'm* not what *you* want?"

"Not gonna happen," Scott said and he pulled her in for one final kiss goodnight.

Chapter Seventeen

Belle waited impatiently outside the school Monday afternoon. All her cousins were in the car, except Cinderella. She stood just outside the building talking to a boy none of them recognized. Belle sighed loudly again before slamming on the horn.

"What's the rush?" Aurora asked.

"I just don't want to sit here a minute longer than I have to. Let's get home already!"

Cinderella finally jogged up to the waiting vehicle and climbed in. "Sorry," she whispered.

"What happened to Prince Charming?" Ariel teased. "Two days later, and you've forgotten him already?"

It took Cinderella a minute to realize what her cousin was referring to. "You mean Brian? No, not in the least! We got partnered for a project in English, so we were just going over some details."

"I think the whole thing is dumb," Belle said, voicing her opinion for the tenth time. "He's not that much older than you. I don't understand why you can't just date now."

"I think it's romantic," Snow White added. "He's waiting for you." She smiled.

"Thank you," Cinderella nodded toward Snow White.

"I say live it up!" Aurora said. "Date around and have fun, just like Prince Charming said. Why waste high school with one guy?"

"You mean like me?" Belle asked.

"I don't mean anything against Craig, but, yeah."

The other three all sucked in a breath.

"So you think even though Craig is amazing to me and completely wonderful, I should ditch him just so I can 'date around'?"

"All I'm trying to say is if the only flavor ice cream you ever ate was chocolate, how would you know that was the flavor for you?"

"You're comparing my boyfriend to food now?"

Ariel frantically shook her head at her sister, but Aurora remained oblivious and continued.

"How do you know you don't prefer strawberry or vanilla or even rocky road, if you don't try them first?"

"So you're saying it's not possible to meet your perfect match on the first try? What if I waste my time trying every flavor in the store, only to realize in the end that chocolate *was* my favorite? And by the time I do, someone else has already snatched him up?" Belle's face was starting to turn red. "Isn't love about taking risks and chances? Don't you think it's better to stay with the person I've found rather than risk losing him over the tiniest chance that someone better will come along?!"

"Whoa! I'm not trying to demean your choice, Belle," Aurora said, putting her hands up in surrender. "I guess everyone is different and they have to do whatever is best for them. I'm just trying to encourage Cindy here. Prince Charming gave her an opportunity to explore the wide world of ice cream, and I think she should take full advantage."

Belle's knuckles were turning white on the steering wheel. She didn't want to agree to disagree. She wanted to win. A smile came across her face when she thought she'd come up with the answer.

"Well what if she does 'taste every flavor' as you're so callously calling it, and it causes a rift in her and Prince Charming's future relationship?"

"How so?" Cinderella asked.

Belle had them now. "Well, when she comes to him after graduation and tells him how much fun she had at dances, and dating, and kissing all these other guys, won't that make Scott jealous? A little hurt even, that she could possibly have fun with someone other than him?"

"But Prince Charming already did all that. He even said so. He had his turn in high school, dating around and getting to know his options. So he *knows* Cindy is the one he wants already. It's only fair that she has a turn to do the same. Why waste high school with one guy? That's what college is for. After you've tried all the flavors in high school, and know what you want, then you can keep going back to chocolate for the rest of your life, because you are certain it's the flavor for you."

"Waste? Waste?!" Belle was shouting now.

"Okay!" Ariel said. "I think we've had enough ice cream for one day. I'm not going to agree with either of you, but I am with Snow," Ariel added. "Besides the fact that it would be illegal," she paused for dramatic effect. "He's proving he's chivalrous! He's way better than any of those toads or frogs we go to school with. You've got yourself a full blown prince!" She patted Cinderella on the back.

Cinderella beamed.

Belle scoffed, but said nothing more. As she pulled the car onto their street her tone went from anger to sarcasm.

"Well does your prince plan on taking you to the prom?" Belle asked, pointing ahead.

The girls had just pulled into their complex, only to find a huge, black limo blocking not only their parking space, but four others beside it.

"What in the world?"

"Who..?"

"Maybe it's a movie star!"

Belle rolled her eyes and jumped out of the idling car. All the windows were tinted, so she couldn't see in as she walked past. She became a little more nervous as she approached the front of the limo and realized just how big the man was standing next to it. He looked just like the bodyguards she always saw on TV: big, bulky, and completely bald, but it looked like that was by choice. He wore a dark suit and dark sunglasses to match the dark expression on his face. His arms were folded across his chest in a menacing fashion and he didn't even glance down at Belle as she approached. *Was this guy for real?*

"Ummmm, excuse me? Do you think you could move your ...car? It's kinda blocking our spot." She motioned toward the multiple spots the limo was consuming.

"Wow! Do you work for the CIA?" Ariel asked, half-jokingly as they approached the man in black.

"What are you guys doing?" Belle asked. "Did you just leave my car running?"

"Like we were going to wait in the car," Aurora said. She dangled Belle's keys in front of her face. Belle snatched them quickly and shoved them into her pocket. Aurora approached the limo and tried to peer in the back window.

"Step away from the car please," the man spoke for the first time.

Aurora jumped back and her cousins laughed.

"It speaks!" Ariel joked.

The giant man looked like he had the hint of a smile on his face, and then it was gone.

The rear door to the limo suddenly opened and this time all five girls jumped back. Out stepped a tall man wearing an equally impressive suit, only his did not make him look scary. The light colored suit accentuated his perfectly tan skin and dark, black hair. His eyes were dark, mysterious even, blanketed by gorgeous dark lashes, which blinked several times as he stepped into the bright sun. He smiled and the dimple in his right cheek winked at them. That dimple usually caused women of all ages to swoon and rush at the man the moment he flashed it, but not in this crowd. The cousins weren't even looking at his dimple; they were all focused on his eyes. The TV didn't do them justice. But here, in the sunlight, there was no mistaking them. Those were Belle's eyes.

Chapter Eighteen

Lucas' charming smile melted into a nervous one as he looked at the five teenage girls standing before him. He chuckled before speaking directly to Belle.

"I was going to ask which one of you was Belle, but after seeing you...I...well...wow," he sighed. "It's really you!" He took a step toward Belle, but she equaled his step by moving backward.

"What are you doing here?!"

"I...well, after getting your letter, I decided I wanted to come see you for myself."

"My letter? But I sent that through fan mail. You weren't supposed to actually get it!"

"I figured," he chuckled again. "But when my assistant saw it, she thought it was worth bringing to my attention. She thought it was a joke at first. I'm glad she showed it to me. I've thought about you a lot the last...what's it been? Seventeen years? Wow."

Belle nodded.

"Look, can we go inside and talk or something? Privately? I have a lot I want to say." Lucas began to shift uncomfortably. This was the first time in his life he was feeling shy in front of an audience.

The girls looked from Belle to her father and, as much as they wanted to stay and gawk at him, they didn't want to get in the way. The four girls made excuses and quickly disappeared into the twins' house. Belle just stared at Lucas, not sure of what to say. *What does he mean he thinks*

about me? He didn't even want me! How dare he come here after
so many years and suddenly pretend to care!

"What is this? Some publicity stunt? You suddenly
pretend to care about your long-lost daughter so the ratings
on your show will jump up? Well I don't want any part of
it!" Belle waved him off and turned away to leave.

"Belle, wait!" Lucas grabbed her wrist.

"Hey! Get your hands off her!" Dave came striding
up, just getting home from football practice. He looked
especially menacing with the sweat and dirt smeared across
his face like war paint. "Didn't you hear her? She said back
off!"

The big guy stepped forward to intervene, but Lucas
waved him away. He immediately dropped Belle's wrist
and smirked at the tough high-schooler. "This your
boyfriend?"

"No!" Belle shouted. Then added with a smirk,
"What? You're the only one allowed to have a bodyguard?"
She took advantage of the stand-off to stalk away and join
the others in Ariel and Aurora's house. She may not exactly
like Dave, but she knew there was no way he would let
them follow her either.

Dave watched her go then turned back to Lucas.
"You're parked illegally you know. You're blocking a lot of
people. I could have you towed."

"Alright tough-guy, stand down," Lucas said.
"We'll move." He motioned for the big guy to get back in
the car and they started up the engine. Dave looked back at
the twins' house, hoping to see some sort of movement, but
they had pulled the blinds shut. He glared into the dark
glass of the limo one more time and walked home.

***

"Is he still out there?"

"Yup." Snow White let the blinds fall back into place as she slid down to a seated position on the couch.

"How long is he going to sit out there?"

"Probably until you agree to talk to him."

"Great," Belle mumbled.

Lucas had pulled his limousine to the side of the building, so it was no longer blocking any parking spots. How they got that huge thing wedged along the building, the girls would never know. But they'd spent the last three hours talking about it, and periodically checking out the window to see if he'd given up yet. A pizza delivery car had pulled up beside them about a half hour earlier, so the prospect didn't look good.

"I don't want to talk to him."

"I know," Cinderella said, even though she didn't believe it. Belle was good at holding onto anger. Really good. But any one of them would have traded her places in a heartbeat. Her dad was here, in front of her, and instead of taking advantage of that she was choosing to be stubborn.

Belle sighed. She stood up, and then sat back down again. Then she stood and paced the entryway. "What would I even say to the guy?"

"Maybe you don't have to say anything," Ariel said. "It sounds like he wants to talk to you." She was having a hard time keeping it together. She had searched out her own father, only to be turned away and left terrified. Belle, on the other hand, had a father searching her out. And she was shunning him. Over what? Pride?

There was a knock on the front door and Belle jumped.

"It's me guys, Mary. Can I enter the super-secret hideout?"

Belle rolled her eyes at her mother's mocking tone and opened the door.

"Hey you," said Mary. "Tough day?"

Belle turned to sit down and noticed her cousins had silently fled the scene once again. The back door was left open a little. *Traitors.* "You could say that," she nodded, looking back at her mom.

"I talked to him," Mary said. "And I think you should too."

Belle's mouth fell open. "What? When?"

"Just now. We had a nice, long chat. He's taking me to dinner tomorrow night to finish our conversation and to, well, catch up. I hope you'll come with us."

Belle was completely floored. "But how can you trust him! He abandoned us a long time ago! He's a jerk!" She jumped to her feet, feeling outraged all over again.

"Honey, just talk to him. I know he made some mistakes, but I did too. We were both very young and very naïve. He's had a long time to regret his decisions. And he does, you know."

Belle looked at Mary, but the firmness in her gaze didn't waver. "Fine."

"Do you want me to walk out there with you?"

Belle gave her mother a look of disgust.

"Alright then, you go first. I'll follow at a considerable distance so as not to cramp your style."

Belle gave her a sideways glare and got to her feet. Then she walked out the door and shut it quietly behind her. There was no going back now.

Chapter Nineteen

Belle tapped on the glass of the rear window with her knuckle.

The window rolled down halfway. "Well look who it is!"

"Look, do you want to talk to me or not?"

"Yes!" Lucas replied, rolling the window back up and stepping from the car. "I'm sorry, please have a seat." He motioned for Belle to climb in first.

Belle paused briefly. Ever since she was a little girl, she'd been taught to never get in the car with a stranger. But Lucas Ferreira was the exception. Even if he weren't her father, his face was extremely well known worldwide. And this wasn't much of a getaway vehicle.

Belle plopped down on the plush, leather seats and was surprised at how comfortable and roomy the interior was. Lucas sat across from her and pulled the door shut. They sat in silence for a couple minutes, neither sure of how to proceed.

"Your mom tells me you recently turned seventeen."

"If you call three months ago recent, then yeah, sure."

"Do you have a boyfriend?"

"Yup."

"But it's not that bodyguard boy?"

Belle scoffed. "Nope. He had his chance, but he blew it."

Lucas tried to hide his grin. "So you're dating someone else?"

"Yup."

"Do you want to tell me about him?"

"Not particularly." Belle scanned the inside of the limo, trying to find somewhere else to gaze so she didn't have to look at her dad.

Lucas sighed and pressed on. "So...your mom tells me you're a fan of the show."

"I used to be."

"Not anymore?"

"Well I was until I discovered the star of the show was a complete jerk." Belle stared Lucas straight in the face when she made her accusation.

Lucas ran his fingers through his thick hair. "I guess I deserve that." He leaned forward, reaching toward Belle who quickly jumped aside. "Relax, I'm just getting a drink." Lucas' reach extended past where Belle had been sitting and he opened a little door she hadn't noticed was beside her. "Do you want anything?" he asked, holding up the bottle of Coke he'd grabbed for himself.

Belle started to shake her head, unwilling to accept anything from this man. But her mouth was suddenly very dry and the ice cold bottle was calling her name. "Yes," she whispered.

"Is regular okay, or are you one of those chicks that always orders diet?"

"I think diet drinks taste disgusting."

Lucas beamed as he popped the top off her Cola and handed it over. "My kind of girl."

Belle took a long swig before setting the bottle down again between her legs. Mary had said Lucas wanted to talk, but he hadn't said anything of real value yet. *Is he*

trying to impress me with his bodyguard, his limo, and his
personal cooler of drinks? Maybe he's one of those guys who
thought I could be bought. Well he thought wrong.

"So did you actually want to talk to me, or did you
come here to make small talk so you could check this off
some list of yours? 'Cause I can help you out right now.
My favorite color is orange, I love spicy Mexican food, and
chick flicks make me cry. Are we done now?" Belle started
for the door handle, but Lucas put a hand on top of hers and
pulled it back.

"You really are direct, aren't you? I guess I should
expect nothing less from the daughter of Mary Princess."
He chuckled to himself and looked back across at Belle, who
now sat with her arms folded across her chest. It was a little
awkward, holding her stubborn pose with a bottle in one
hand, but Belle found a way to succeed. "No, I didn't drive
all the way here from California just to have small talk. I
wanted to see you, to talk to you, to see if you got anything
from me..." he trailed off. "I thought small talk would help
us ease into the more difficult stuff, but clearly that's not
what you want."

Lucas took a long drink from his bottle, wiped his
mouth with the back of his hand and took a deep breath
before continuing. "When your mom and I met, I fell crazy
in love with her from our first date on. She was...is," he
corrected himself, "one of the most amazing women I have
ever met! She's gorgeous, fiery, full of spirit, and she has
attitude like no one I've ever seen. And I work with some
pretty big stars! Best of all, I got to spend every day with
this incredible woman. I felt like life couldn't get any better.
And then one day your mom came to me and told me she
was pregnant. She said she was leaving the show, because
Hollywood was no place to raise her baby. I was crushed! I

had plans of marrying this woman some day and here she was telling me our perfect lives were going to be changed. I wasn't going to see her every day anymore, and she was even thinking about moving back home to her sisters."

Belle knew the details of this entire story already, but somehow, it felt different this time. Lucas' voice grew soft when he spoke of Mary and their lives together, and she could almost see the hint of moisture in his eyes. *Were those for real, or just part of him being a really good actor?* Lucas sniffed, adding to the illusion.

"I was only 21 when your mom came to me that day. I know that may seem old to you, but trust me, I was still completely clueless! And I'll be the first to admit, I was extremely selfish. In my stupid, young boy mind, you weren't an actual person because you didn't exist yet. I was not thinking about you, or your mom for that matter, at all. I was just thinking about me. What did I want? Well, I wanted things to stay the same, so to me, there was only one solution." Lucas cleared his throat. They both knew the word he was referring to, but neither spoke it out loud.

Belle shifted uncomfortably in her seat. It felt weird hearing him talk about "his side." She thought when this subject came up, she'd have some choice words for her father. But in the moment, her mind was a complete blank so she allowed him to go on.

"Your mother was, of course, completely against the idea. I think the thing that hurt her the most was that I would even bring it up as an option. I realize that now. She was devastated. I wanted our "perfect" lives to continue and your mom wanted our perfect lives to change, together. So I did the dumbest thing I have ever done in my entire life, and have regretted it more than I can say for the last seventeen years: I let her go."

Belle didn't realize it, but as Lucas spoke, she had inched forward to the edge of her seat so their knees were almost touching. She let out the breath she had unintentionally been holding and relaxed back into the leather bench behind her.

"I know you already knew all, if not most of that story. And I know what I did, how I handled everything was all wrong. But I want you to know that's not where the story ended for me."

Belle sat up again. "What do you mean?"

"After your mom left, I spent about a year just spiraling downhill, completely lost. I'm not proud to admit this to you, but I want you to know I'm an honest guy. I'm not making anything up to try and win you over to my side, so please just...bear with me."

Belle nodded her consent.

"First I tried replacing your mom, blocking her out with as many women as possible. I was a young, budding actor in Hollywood, so I found plenty of...willing participants at parties and other things. But every time I was with another woman, I found myself longing for your mom even more. So then I turned to alcohol. I partied it up, trying to convince myself that this was the freedom I wanted. I even tried a few drugs. I wanted to completely shut myself off from the life your mother and I had created together. Then one night I hit rock bottom."

Belle scooted closer to Lucas, intent on hearing every word. She thought the lifestyle he was describing was just normal for Hollywood actors, but the way he spoke about his actions with such disgust...she couldn't wait to hear more.

"I was leaving a party and I was completely wasted. I never should have attempted to even walk home, let alone drive."

"You were driving?!" Belle squeaked.

Lucas nodded, his head hung in shame. "I hit a parked car."

Belle sighed a breath of relief.

"Oh that's not all," Lucas shook his head. "There was a mother in the car...nursing her little baby..."

Belle gasped. She quickly covered her mouth with a hand, but it was too late. He had heard. He shook his head, like he couldn't believe the story either. Then Belle actually saw a tear slide down Lucas' cheek. This was not an act.

"The mother and baby were taken to a hospital where they both thankfully survived. But they were hurt, badly so, and it was my fault. My license was suspended, and I spent a couple nights in jail until my agent came and picked me up. He told me my career was in jeopardy. There was talk of writing me off the show if I didn't get some help. But honestly, that experience was enough to whip me back into shape. Do you know what I thought about while I was in jail?"

Belle shook her head.

"You. You saved me, Belle. I thought about that mother and tiny little baby, knowing my own tiny little baby was out there somewhere. And I thought about what I would do if some idiot did what I had done and hurt you. And then I realized what a complete ass I had been. Sorry," he mumbled, covering his mouth. "I thought about you and how I had just let you go. Who would be there to protect you from idiots like me? How were you? Were you healthy? A hundred questions poured through my mind. I didn't sleep at all for two days. Then, after my agent picked me up, I cleaned myself up and took a taxi the four hours to your family's old apartment."

Belle's eyes widened in surprise. *He tried to find us?*

"That was one expensive taxi ride, let me tell you! But by the time I got there, you guys had already moved. Some Asian family was living there, and I think I scared them pretty good, showing up all wild-eyed with no sleep, asking about the former tenants. They knew nothing, of course. Then when I got back to set the next day, I started asking around. I talked to all our old friends, the actresses that Mary used to hang out with trying to find where you'd gone. That's how I found out you were a girl."

Belle had been looking down at her hands, not sure how to take in all this fresh information, but she looked him straight in the eyes again at this new revelation. Lucas smiled at her and, for the first time, Belle couldn't help smiling back.

Chapter Twenty

Belle hated to admit it, but her dad was starting to seem like a pretty decent guy. She finished her drink and accepted another as Lucas continued. "The only information anyone knew was that you were a girl. A few of her closest friends had met you once. They told me how gorgeous you were, as I knew you would be. But they all said the same thing. Mary and her sisters decided to move, to start over, and they cut all ties with California when they did. No one knew where you'd gone. I looked and looked, talked to anyone I could think of, but it was like you had vanished. This was before the days of Facebook, where I probably could have found your mom in a heartbeat."

"My mom doesn't believe in Facebook," Belle interrupted.

Lucas smiled. "That sounds like your mom. Let me guess, she said it takes away from having real face-to-face relationships."

"She said if she wanted to spend all her time talking to a machine, she'd date the TV."

Lucas chuckled and shook his head. He then reached across the seat and put a shaking hand on Belle's. She started to pull away, the intimate gesture catching her off guard. But then she stopped. Belle sat a little more stiffly than before, but she allowed his hand to remain on her own.

"When my assistant brought me that letter you wrote, I almost couldn't believe it."

"Why do you have an assistant?"

"I don't have time to read all my fan mail, so I have an assistant that responds to most of them for me. Although, getting mail is becoming a thing of the past. It's mostly tweets and e-mails now, but she also keeps up with my Facebook and Twitter accounts. She only shows me an occasional letter if it really stands out to her. And, trust me, yours definitely stood out."

"That seems like cheating."

"What does?"

"Having someone else pretend to be you and write posts and respond to e-mails. Isn't that dishonest?"

Lucas slowly removed his hand as he sat back against the black leather seat and pondered her question. "I still send out tweets when I can, and I'll answer an occasional letter every now and then, but I just don't have the time to keep up with it all. Especially since the show has taken off. Between filming, guest appearances, and talk shows, most of my time is accounted for. Isn't it better to have someone I trust acting on my behalf, rather than ignore my fans altogether? This way they get to feel connected to me."

Belle shrugged. "I guess that makes sense." Then she paused for a moment and her eyes grew wide. "Does that mean Bradley Moore didn't actually wish me a Happy Birthday on Facebook? It came from some strange woman sitting behind a desk somewhere?! Oh man, I printed that out and put it up in my locker!"

Lucas laughed again. "Bradley Moore, from my show?"

Belle nodded.

"Not necessarily, some actors are great at keeping up with that kind of stuff, especially the younger ones. I know for a fact that Bradley is always on his phone, doing the social networking thing. It's us oldies that struggle with the technology."

Belle rolled her eyes at his response. "Well I still feel stupid. I'm taking it down tomorrow." She sat back, folding her arms against her chest, the two empty bottles now resting at her feet. "So you actually got to read my letter though?"

"Yes. My assistant didn't know if it was real or not, but she thought I should at least look at it."

"And what did you think?" Belle thought over her bitter words and sarcastic tone. She never thought she'd actually have to discuss it with him face-to-face! Her cheeks flushed a little as she remembered the harsh words she had wanted to use.

"I thought it was my lucky day!" Lucas responded, before Belle could worry any further. "It was clear you didn't want to send it," he said, grinning a little.

Belle looked up to meet his smiling eyes. "I didn't," she said, matter-of-factly. "Now...I'm not really sure what to think."

"Well, do you still want to hear about our family history? I can tell you where my parents and grandparents came from, but that's about it."

"I do, I still need it for school. But not now." Belle didn't think her brain could take on any more new information that night. She suddenly felt very drained and wanted nothing more than to lie down.

"You're going to still be here tomorrow, right?"

"Yes! I'll stay for as long as it takes."

"As long as it takes?"

"For you to trust me."

"I'll have to think about it."

Lucas looked disappointed but said, "Fair enough."

"I better get going," she stated as she slid across her seat and reached for the door.

"I've worn you out, haven't I?"

"I just...I need to think."

"I understand. So will you consider coming to dinner with your mom and me tomorrow night?"

Belle paused and then slowly nodded. Lucas' grin split his face ear to ear. He opened the door for her, then quickly jumped out and turned around to offer Belle his hand. She let him help her out of the limo and then stood to face him.

"Well, good night."

"Good night, Belle."

Lucas moved forward like he wanted to hug her, but Belle quickly turned away and returned to her house. She couldn't believe she was starting to trust him. *After all, he is an actor. Is he just playing us?*

Chapter Twenty-One

Cinderella had escaped back to her own house while Belle spoke with her father for the first time. She sat at her desk, filling names in the little bubbles on her family tree. She stared at her dad's name for a long time. What sat as an empty bubble for 16 years now finally had an occupant. She looked at the remaining empty branches and knew she had to talk to him again in order to fulfill her assignment. She thought about her conversation with Scott and picked up the phone. Then she thought about how her dad hadn't called since their argument and she set the phone back down. Cinderella thought back over the many years she'd spent fatherless and picked up her phone again. Then she thought about how much Dana hated him and she placed her phone back on the desk.

Almost instantly her phone started ringing. She recognized the familiar California number and smiled. "I guess he made the decision for me," she said aloud before answering.

"Well, you answered your phone. That's a good sign...isn't it?" Steven sounded hopeful.

"I was actually just going to call you."

"Really?!" Steven couldn't hide the excitement in his voice.

"Yeah, I still have to finish this assignment."

"Oh." He sounded disappointed.

"Can you just answer a couple questions for me?"

"I'll try my best."

Cinderella asked for names, and he was able to answer each question without a problem. "Well, thanks," she said.

There was silence on the other end. *Did he hang up?* "Dad?"

"I want you to come visit," he blurted out.

"Excuse me?"

"I know I'm going about this all wrong, but I want to meet you! I don't want any more time to go by without knowing my own daughter."

"I...ummm..."

"Give me your mom's phone number."

"Oh, I don't think that's such a good idea."

"But I need to ask her permission and work out details with her. If I just talk to you about it, I have a feeling Dana will see it as my going behind her back. And I don't think that would go over very well."

"I don't think it's going to go over well no matter who brings up the idea."

"I guess I'm getting ahead of myself. Do you want to come and meet me? I know things didn't end up on the best note last time we spoke. I know saying 'I'm sorry' doesn't make up for the mistakes I made. I want you to know I really am truly sorry. The way things went down with your mom, well, that is still my biggest regret."

Despite everything, Cinderella was surprised at how easily an answer came. "Yes. Yes, I definitely want to meet you." She could practically hear his smile through the phone. "But is there any way you could come here? That might go over just a little bit easier with my mom."

"Well you see...it's complicated."

"How so?"

"I'm not exactly sure how to bring this up, so I'm just going to say it. I have two other daughters."

"You...you..."

"Yes, Cinderella, you're a big sister. Monica is twelve and Sophie just turned four."

"So you're married then?"

"I was, but she passed away a few years ago."

"I'm sorry," Cinderella whispered. She wasn't sure how to react to all this news. She should have realized her father had his own life after divorcing her mom, but for some reason she never pictured that life including another family.

"It was cancer." Cinderella was glad he offered the information without her having to ask. "It was really hard on all of us, especially little Sophie. But we came through it and we're getting by one day at a time."

"So they, my sisters, are why you can't come here." It sounded more like a statement than a question.

"Well, we could, but I would really love for you to see where we live. And meet them here, where they are familiar and can show you around. I told the girls about you last night."

"You did? And?"

"And they are so excited to meet you! They were already making a list of all the places they wanted to take their big sister."

Cinderella was completely overwhelmed by the idea. As much as she wanted to meet her dad, she had almost no experience with kids. "I don't know how to be a big sister."

"I'm sure you'll figure it out pretty quick. After all, you do have Dana as your example and she was the best big sister I've ever seen.

Cinderella was surprised to hear a compliment for her mother come out of Steven's mouth. "I think you better let me handle Mom first. Then you can call her and ask permission. I do think it's a good idea for you to ask, but I definitely need to prep her first. I don't think it would go over well if you just called her up out of the blue."

"Alright, give me her phone number and then text me when the coast is clear. Perhaps right after she's eaten some cheesecake. I remember that was her favorite."

Cinderella laughed. "It still is. And that's not a bad idea, actually."

"Well I need to get a few more things done here at the office, so I better say good-bye, but you'll talk to your mom and let me know?"

"I will."

"And soon?"

"I'll do my best." She hung up the phone with a smile on her face. Her dad seemed like a pretty cool guy so far. Now the trick was convincing Dana to let her meet him.

Chapter Twenty-Two

When the girls arrived at school the next day, they were stunned to see several news vans lined up and a crowd of reporters by the front entrance.

"What do you think happened?" Ariel asked excitedly.

"Don't sound so happy. Maybe they're here for a bad reason," Snow White offered.

"I don't think so, Snow," Cinderella said, pulling into a parking stall. "Look at the way they're peering into each car. It's more like they're waiting for something."

"Or someone," said Aurora.

Belle's face went pale. "You don't think..."

"There she is!" a student shouted and pointed in Belle's direction. Then chaos ensued. Belle found herself completely surrounded by blaring camera lights and microphones were being shoved in her face. She was being pulled toward the school by the moving crowd, her feet barely lifting off the pavement. Her cousins had been pushed back into the crowd. Belle couldn't see anyone she recognized.

"Look this way Ms. Princess!"

"Belle, over here!"

The shouts from every direction were completely overwhelming. Belle's head started to spin.

"How long have you known Lucas Ferreira was your father?"

"Did he just recently come into your life?"

"Why the secrecy, Ms. Princess?"

The mob of reporters, paparazzi, and cameramen were relentless. Belle couldn't tell which direction the different questions were coming from. She didn't even know how to respond to most of them. She found herself mostly nodding and shaking her head. She tried to push her way through the swarm, but the hole closed in quickly and she was encircled once again. She started to feel very hot, then the reporters started spinning. Just as she was about to hit the asphalt, an arm reached out and caught her.

Belle's feet left the ground, and she was suddenly bouncing through the crowd in someone's arms. She could hear her cousin's voices around her, but her eyes wouldn't focus on any one of them. She looked up at her rescuer. His strong jaw was clenched tight as he pulled her further and further away from the crowd. The last thing she saw was a pair of piercing blue eyes. Then darkness.

***

"Belle? Belle, are you okay?"

Her eyes slowly opened to reveal a circle of concerned faces. She was lying on a cot in the nurse's room. Her four cousins sat around her on folding chairs.

Belle tried to sit up, but she was pushed back down again by the stern-faced school nurse.

"Don't you dare sit up too fast. We don't want you passing out on us again."

"I passed out?" Belle rubbed her head, trying to remember what had happened. She couldn't believe she'd fainted. How embarrassing!

"Are you okay?" Cinderella asked gently, placing a hand on her leg.

"I'm fine!" she stated, shoving Cinderella's hand back. "I just got really hot is all. Everyone is over-reacting!"

Belle tried to sit up again, despite the nurse's warning. She immediately regretted her decision as her head started to swim, but Belle was not about to look weak again and she pretended to feel nothing.

"How are you feeling?" the nurse asked, as she looked closely into Belle's eyes to check for dilation.

"I'm fine," Belle said. "Really! I don't even know why you're all still here."

"Your cousins are very stubborn girls, Ms. Princess. I tried getting them to go to class, but they all insisted on staying."

"This is dumb," Belle said. "It's probably because I didn't eat breakfast this morning. Just go to class guys."

Very slowly, the other four girls got to their feet and walked from the room. Belle tried to get up again to follow them but the nurse very gently coaxed her back down.

"The police are outside trying to get rid of the crowd, but under the circumstances, I suggest you stay in here for a little while. Your father will be here soon and then..."

"My father?!" Belle barely squeaked the words out. "Why is he coming here?"

"To discuss the situation, I presume."

It was then that Belle noticed the nurse kept glancing at her own reflection in the small wall mirror. She gave her soft curls another pat before continuing, "He caused quite a stir in the school this morning it seems. There are still teachers who haven't been able to start their classes yet from all the excitement."

"There is no need for Mr. Ferreira to come all the way down here. Why don't you just call him and tell him he's no longer required?"

"Sorry, hon, but that's not up to me. Mrs. Grayson is the one who called your mom and your mom called your dad."

Belle laid her head back down on the pillow and crossed her arms over her eyes. *Mrs. Grayson. I should have known!* Mrs. Grayson, the principal, was the biggest *Locker Partners* fan in the entire school, even bigger than all the teenage girls. Of course she was going to turn this silly event for Belle into a chance to meet her idol.

Belle could hear the loud **thump thump** of heavy footsteps as they drew nearer to the door. They were accompanied by a much smaller **clack clack**, as her mother's stilettos drummed on the linoleum.

"Belle?" Mary's dark head peered around the open doorway. "What happened?" she asked, approaching the small cot.

Belle shot up in bed. "It's so stupid! I just got hot from the crowd and passed out. Everyone is making a big deal out of nothing!"

"I'm really sorry," Lucas started to say, but Belle's glaring eyes made him stop mid-sentence.

"You!" she shouted, pointing her finger. "Do you have any idea how embarrassing that was?! I knew it. I knew I shouldn't trust you. I knew you were just using this daughter angle to get more publicity for your stupid show." The last two words were filled with such venom, they sounded more like a hiss.

"I didn't tell anyone, I swear!" Lucas said, raising his hands in defense.

Belle scoffed.

"I really didn't! I honestly don't know how all those reporters and camera people found out about you and where you attend school. But the paparazzi are extremely conniving and resourceful. They have their ways of finding things out to get the biggest story."

Mary sat down on the edge of Belle's cot. "Lucas wouldn't have told anyone, sweetie. He came here to meet you and spend time with you. All that gets ruined once you're being followed around by cameras all day."

"That's right," Lucas said, pulling up a chair. "The last thing I wanted was for the press to get involved in our relationship."

Lucas kept talking. At least his mouth was still moving, so Belle could only assume he kept talking, but she stopped listening. She was too busy focusing on her father's hand which now rested casually on Mary's thigh.

Chapter Twenty-Three

Belle lay on her stomach on top of her pink comforter flipping through a magazine.

"Belle, come on! We're leaving!"

She didn't move.

"Belle, are you coming?"

She continued to scan over the pictures without responding. Her door flew open behind her, crashing into the dresser and knocking over a frame. Belle glanced back at the damage, but didn't budge from her spot on the bed.

"What are you doing?" Mary asked. "Your dad is downstairs waiting for us. Now grab your shoes and let's go!"

"No thanks."

Mary shut the magazine and threw it across the room. "Come on! You were rude to him today, and I will not tolerate you being rude to him again tonight. He's just trying to make up for lost time."

"I can't believe you trust him so quickly already. Can't you see through him Mom? He-is-an-actor!" Belle emphasized each word. "He is just playing us. As soon as his ratings go up, he'll probably be gone anyway."

"In case you don't remember, his show is doing just fine. He doesn't need any more ratings. You of all people should know that, seeing as up until last week, you were one of his biggest fans!"

"Well, not anymore." Belle thought back to their meeting with the principal that morning. Mrs. Grayson was wearing way too much perfume and, despite her being married, she kept shooting daggers at Mary while they spoke. Mary sat quietly with a smirk on her face, pretending she didn't notice, all the while holding Lucas' hand. His hand! Belle couldn't believe in just two days her mom had gone back to holding his hand! To make matters worse, there would now be security guards at all the entrances to the school, at least for the foreseeable future.

"What changed? I thought you guys had a nice visit yesterday?"

"Sure, it seemed fine. Until he started touching you! I think he came back here to get back together with you. The only way for him to do that is by being nice to me. He doesn't actually care about me, he didn't come here to meet me. He came to hit on my mom!"

"You don't like that I was holding his hand today?"

"Not really," Belle said.

"Fine. Stay here and sulk while we go to dinner. But just think of what could happen if we are alone together. All. Night. Long."

With that, Belle jumped up from her bed and ran down the stairs, beating Mary by five steps.

***

Cinderella cut a thick slice from the cheesecake she had just purchased, and placed it on a plate. She gently scooped a big pile of bright red cherries from an open can and placed them on the cheesecake so that a few slid down one side, leaving a trail of heavy syrup. After pouring a tall, cold glass of milk, she set everything out on the kitchen table. Then, setting a fork on top of the folded napkin beside her plate, she called up the stairs.

"Mom! Can you come down here a minute please?"

Dana came down a few steps. "What's up hon?"

"Can you come in the kitchen and sit down with me for a minute? I have something I want to ask you."

Dana walked down the rest of the stairs slowly. When she saw the presentation displayed on the table, she stopped in her tracks.

"Uh-oh. What do you want?" she asked.

"I just want to talk to you for a minute. Will you sit down please?"

Dana laughed and, shaking her head, continued to move towards the table and sat down.

Cinderella sat across from her and motioned for Dana to take a bite.

Dana carefully picked up her fork and loaded it with a large piece of the rich dessert. "It's delicious," she said, setting her fork down again. "But the suspense is killing me. What do you want?"

"Well...I was talking to my dad," Cinderella began.

Dana's shoulders immediately tensed and she picked up her fork again, choosing to focus her eyes on the food rather than her daughter's hopeful expression. When Cinderella didn't continue, Dana motioned for her to go on.

"He wants me to come visit him in California." Cinderella decided to go the band-aid route. Rather than beat around the bush, she ripped off the truth in one quick motion, hoping the sting wouldn't last too long.

No such luck. Dana immediately jumped to her feet, knocking over the kitchen chair she had been sitting on. "Absolutely not! He's practically a stranger! What was he thinking inviting my sixteen-year-old daughter to come visit him without my permission! That selfish, greedy, son-of-a..."

"Mom!" Cinderella had to shout to pull her mother away from her rant.

Dana startled and, righting her chair, settled back down into it. No matter how upset she was, there was no sense in letting perfectly good cheesecake go to waste.

I knew this wouldn't work. Cinderella watched her mother fuming and all the visions she had of meeting her dad began to fade away. "He wanted to ask you first, but I told him not to. I told him to let me bring it up with you first, so if you're going to yell at someone, yell at me okay?"

Dana looked into her daughter's devastated eyes and her anger seemed to melt away a little. "You want to meet him don't you?"

"I really do."

"And you're sure about this?"

"Yes, Mom. Please! I know you didn't like your dad, and I know you don't trust mine, but you have to give me the opportunity to make a decision about him on my own."

Dana nodded, but she didn't say another word. She thought over things carefully as she scooped another bite of deliciousness into her mouth. Then she responded with something that surprised them both. "On one condition. You take Scott with you. I may not approve of him going after my daughter, but that boy cares about you an awful lot and I know he would keep you safe."

Chapter Twenty-Four

Craig lifted his hand to knock on Belle's front door when he heard an eruption of laughter outside. He followed the loud voices around the side of the building and stopped short. The parking lot had been turned into a makeshift BBQ.

"Oh good, you made it." Belle emerged from the crowd and pulled him forward.

"What is this?"

"Well, my aunts wanted to have a good old fashioned BBQ to welcome Lucas." She rolled her eyes. "But since none of our backyards are big enough, they moved it out here instead, ensuring that no one will be able to get into their parking spots tonight. Convenient, huh?"

Craig draped his arm over her shoulder and kissed the top of her head. "Why do I get the feeling you're not really into this party?"

"Look around you." Belle made a face. "We're in a parking lot. This is so embarrassing, why couldn't we go to a restaurant or something?" She covered her eyes with her hand, willing the party to disappear.

Craig removed her hand slowly and peered into her eyes. "It's not that bad. Where is your dad anyway?" He shifted uneasily.

"Wait—are you nervous to meet him?" Belle smiled.

"No, well, I just..." Craig looked around the group, trying to think of a good response.

"You are!" Belle's smile widened. "This party just got good." She pulled Craig over to a circle of lawn chairs where Lucas was talking to her cousins about his show.

"Hey Lucas!"

"Dad," Lucas said, turning.

Belle ignored his correction. It had become a sort of game between them. Belle would not be worn down, she wasn't ready to call him "dad" yet, and Lucas had fun trying to tease her into saying it. "I want you to meet my boyfriend."

Craig gave her a dirty look before stepping forward. Belle smiled sweetly in return. Lucas got to his feet and shook Craig's hand.

"What about Bodyguard?" he asked, looking at Belle.

Now it was Belle's turn to scowl.

"Who?" Craig asked.

"Nevermind," Belle muttered.

Lucas laughed. "It's nice to meet you..."

"Craig."

"It's nice to meet you, Craig." He looked the teenager up and down. "So how long have you two been dating?"

"A little over a year," Belle responded.

"Wow. At seventeen? That must be some kind of record."

Craig wasn't sure how to respond, so he simply nodded.

"Here, join us!" Lucas said, sliding to another chair and offering the one he had just been sitting in.

Craig sat on the edge of the chair, looking uneasy. "So are you okay with your parents dating now, then?" he whispered to Belle.

She shrugged. "I don't love the idea still, no. It really grosses me out when they kiss and stuff. I think they're too old for that." She made a face, and then continued. "But there's not much I can do about it."

"Don't you like having your dad around?"

"I don't know yet. It's just weird, you know? He showed up out of the blue and then we're supposed to suddenly be like a family again? Whatever," she muttered.

Craig could tell she was getting flustered, so he backed off the questions and instead focused on the conversation.

"So you have to film every day?" Ariel asked.

"We work six days a week, usually twelve hours a day."

"Dang! I never knew actors worked so hard."

Lucas chuckled loudly. His boisterous laugh was contagious and soon the others all joined in. "That's only during filming though, then we get a few months off until we start shooting for the next season. Like right now I'm done filming for this season."

"What's it like working with Bradley Moore?" Aurora leaned closer, staring dreamily ahead. "He's so hot!"

"How much do you make for each episode?" Ariel asked.

"How long is the show going to run for?" Cinderella added her question to the pile.

"Whoa, whoa!" Lucas raised his hands in surrender. "Just one at a time, girls." But his smile told them he was loving the attention.

"Belle, can you come give me a hand?" Mary called.

Belle jumped to her feet, eager to get away. Craig followed closely behind.

Mary was standing near the food table, talking with her sisters while they set out dishes, salads, and opened bags of chips. Dana's brow furrowed as she scanned the ancient grill, trying to find a way to turn it on.

"Yeah, Mom?"

"Would you go around and take everyone's orders please? Find out how many hot dogs and how many hamburgers we should grill."

"You're sending me back to the frontlines? But I just got away!"

"Don't be so dramatic. Now scoot."

Belle sighed loudly enough for Mary to hear, then dragged her feet as she slowly made her way back to Lucas and his adoring fans.

When she approached the group, Lucas had her cousins all in stitches. Snow White was laughing so hard, she even fell off her chair.

Belle pretended she couldn't hear them. "Hey Lucas!" she called.

"Dad."

"Hey, Mr. Ferreira, burger or dog?"

Lucas looked at her, eyebrows raised, then just shook his head. "Hamburger please."

"So what was so funny?" Craig asked the question Belle didn't want to as she continued to take orders.

"Lucas was telling us some funny mishaps that have happened while on set," Cinderella explained.

"It's too bad the show doesn't have a blooper reel at the end of each episode," Ariel said.

"Like what kinds of things?" Craig asked, sitting back down.

"Okay Craig, we've got all the orders, let's go tell my mom," Belle cut in. Then she walked away quickly, giving him no other choice but to follow.

He trudged behind Belle, suddenly whipping around when he heard a loud THUD. Lucas was standing over a guy who lay sprawled out on the ground. "Just what do you think you're doing?" he yelled.

The intruder scrambled to his feet. "Just trying to capture the family moment, sir. People are curious to see you as a father figure."

"Well it's none of their business!"

Craig ran up behind the guy, scooping something off the ground. "It would be pretty hard to show off anything without this," he said, holding up the guy's camera.

His face went pale. "Come on, give that back."

Lucas smiled and extended his hands to Craig. Craig returned the smile and tossed the camera high into the air. It sailed right over the paparazzo's head and landed safely in Lucas' outstretched hands.

"Give that back, it's mine! I could...I could call the cops, you know."

"Oh, please do," Lucas' smile widened. "Then you can explain to them how you trespassed on private property, and were peering over the fence at underage, innocent girls. I'm sure you even have a few pictures that could back that up."

"That is not what I was doing!" the intruder's face went from white to red in a flash of anger.

"Well, you see," Lucas said, tossing the camera back to Craig. "That's the funny thing about there being so many of us and just one, little old lonesome you. Did this gentleman make you ladies feel uncomfortable?" he asked, turning to the cousins.

Ariel smiled wickedly. "I think he might be the same guy I saw trying to peer in my window last night while I was changing."

"Oh, come on!" the guy yelled.

Craig tossed the camera back to Lucas, who caught it with one hand. He stepped so close to the man that their noses were almost touching. "Don't ever bother my family again," Lucas said in an icy voice. Then he shoved the camera roughly into the paparazzo's stomach.

The intruder turned and ran back down the street.

"Do you think he'll actually leave you alone?" Belle asked. She couldn't help but be impressed with the way he had handled that guy. It definitely scored some good points with her.

"It depends. The kid looked pretty young. I'm sure he was newer, so maybe he'll sell one of his shots and then change career paths. I can hope, at least."

"Sell what shots? I deleted all the pictures off his camera," Craig said.

"You what?" Lucas asked, turning. He started laughing and soon everyone joined in. All the women clapped and cheered. Belle walked over and threw her arms around his neck, kissing him on the cheek.

"My hero," she whispered.

Lucas approached Craig and gave him a pat on the back. "You found yourself a good man here, Belle. I approve."

Chapter Twenty-Five

One of Aurora's favorite songs came on and before she knew it, she was singing along. Then Ariel started tapping the beat out on her math book. By the time the song ended, both girls were standing on their beds, singing into pencils at the top of their lungs. The homework they had been working on lay strewn across the floor, completely forgotten.

Ariel collapsed onto her bed, laughing. "Man I love that song!"

"Me too," Aurora nodded. "We should totally start our own band!

"Absolutely!" Ariel exclaimed. "We just need to learn how to play instruments...and sing."

Rachel tapped on their door quietly, but it was drowned out by the music and laughter. She turned the handle and stood unobtrusively in the open doorway.

Ariel finally noticed her standing there. "Hey Mom, Aurora and I are starting a band. How do you feel about learning the keyboard?" Ariel smiled, but it quickly faded when she saw the look on Rachel's face. "Mom? What happened?"

Rachel's eyes were red and swollen, but they were also very wide. She stared into the room, but didn't seem to be focusing on anything in particular. Her hands shook and her face was pale. Aurora seemed to notice too. She quickly shut off the blaring music and walked over to their mom slowly.

"Mom?"

"Mom?" They had to say her name multiple times. Aurora finally grabbed her shoulder, which seemed to jumpstart Rachel back to reality.

"Sorry," she whispered. "You girls better sit down for this."

After they complied, she went on.

"I just got off the phone with Warden Turley over at the state prison. It seems your father got into a fight with another inmate..." Rachel trailed off.

"Is he okay? Mom?"

"He's...he died this morning."

Both Ariel and Aurora slumped back in shock. It felt as though they'd just been punched in the stomach, forcing all the air out of them. Ariel knew people died in prison occasionally, she'd seen it in movies, but she didn't expect this. Not in real life. Not that she had any love for the man; he terrified her. Yet her heart still felt torn. After all, he was her dad.

Aurora sat twiddling her thumbs, then she stopped, her face hardening. "Are we supposed to feel sad?"

Rachel jerked, surprised at Aurora's reaction. "Well, no, you don't have to..."

"Good! Because he was an abusive jerk who tried to kill you and us! I don't think we need to be sad in the least. Actually, it's kind of a relief, don't you think?"

Ariel's eyes widened. "Well, he was our dad."

"In what way?" Aurora almost yelled back. "We might as well take a page out of Elizabeth's book and call him the sperm donor. He was never a father to us!"

"Yeah but..."

"But what? This is stupid! Now at least we have a good excuse to tell Miss Payne about why our project is only half done. And now we never have to fear again that he might get out and come after us someday."

Rachel and Ariel both looked shocked.

"Oh stop pretending to be surprised. I know we all had those thoughts at some point, I just voiced them aloud."

"So I take it you don't want to attend the funeral then?"

"Are you kidding?! Is there even going to be a funeral? It seems like a waste to me, for someone who nobody cared about."

Rachel stood quietly and walked towards the door. "There's going to be a memorial on Saturday. I'm going. Let me know if you change your mind."

Aurora scoffed.

"Wait, Mom," Ariel whispered before Rachel could close the door behind her. "I want to come with you."

Rachel nodded and pulled the door closed. No sooner did the latch click then Aurora felt a hard punch on her arm.

"Ouch! What was that for?"

"For being insensitive, you jerk! Couldn't you tell Mom was hurting? He may have been an abusive, horrible man. But Mom still loved him."

"I don't understand..."

"You don't have to! We've only heard all the horrible, nasty things he did, but did you ever stop to think there had to be something good about him? Maybe not in the end, when we met him, but somewhere in the beginning? There had to have been something good for her to fall in love with."

"I guess, but you don't have to punch me over it," Aurora said, rubbing her wounded arm.

"It doesn't matter if you feel no connection to the man and don't care that he's gone. She cares, and that should be enough for you to show some compassion."

"I'm sorry, you're right. I'll go to the stupid memorial thing, and," Aurora added, stopping her sister from a second punch, "I will not speak badly about him in front of Mom. But I'm going for her, not for him."

"You really don't feel bad that our dad is gone?"

"Honestly, I don't know what I feel. Right now I just feel angry at him and a little relieved, but maybe that will change. Do you feel sad?"

Ariel struggled to put the tornado of emotions brewing inside her into words. "I...I'm not sure. I think I still need time to digest everything. Right now I think I feel more...guilty that I don't feel sadder."

Aurora nodded. "That seems to sum it up." Then getting to her feet she added, "Come on, let's go see if Mom is okay."

Chapter Twenty-Six

The small group stood huddled together as the rain drizzled down on top of them. The icy rain chilled them to their bones. They kept moving closer together in an effort to stay warm. The only person who seemed unaffected by the crummy weather was Rachel. She stood stoically at the front of the group. Her eyes, unblinking, stared at the wooden box before them.

The crowd that had gathered for the memorial was bigger than Ariel had anticipated. Originally she thought it would just be the three of them and maybe a priest of some kind. She really wasn't sure; she and her sister had never been to a funeral before. But she was grateful it hadn't turned out that way. Aurora was still putting up a very stiff front, but Ariel felt torn. She was glad for the calming, caring influence of her cousins. She knew if she cried, Snow White would be by her side, crying too. If she needed a shoulder to lean on and a listening ear, Cinderella was right beside her, waiting. And if she felt anger towards her father, she knew Belle would be there to help come up with insults.

Surprisingly though, even with all her aunts and cousins in attendance, there were still a handful of others. A group of four men stood off to the side, shifting uncomfortably. Ariel wondered if they had been former inmates with her dad. The thought made her shudder, and Elizabeth immediately put an arm around her, mistaking the fear for cold. Then there was an older woman who actually seemed to be crying, and a middle aged man stood by her side. Ariel looked at the unusual couple curiously. She wondered how they knew her dad. Rachel had always told them how his parents had died when he was younger, but maybe this was a long lost aunt and cousin she didn't know about who had surfaced. *Strange how some people only show love for a person once they're gone. Although I guess I don't have room to talk.*

Ariel's thoughts came back to the man who was speaking up front. He ended his brief speech and the tiny gathering started to dispel. Ariel turned to walk towards the car, but stopped when she noticed her mom hadn't stirred.

Dana stepped forward and put an arm around Rachel, who barely moved. Without a word of communication between them, Mary and Elizabeth followed suit. The four sisters stood in a row, holding each other. Ariel watched in reverence as they very gently started to move together, pulling Rachel away from the casket. Her heavy eyes finally dropped from the box and she seemed to come back to life. Just as they passed the other couple, the man broke away from the woman and approached Rachel.

"Are you Mrs. McCaw?"

"It's Ms. Princess now," she corrected him.

"Of course, I'm sorry. I'm Warden Turley. We spoke on the phone."

"Oh yes," Rachel said, meeting his extended palm in a friendly handshake. "Thank you for the phone call."

"I'm sorry about your loss, well, for your girls." He pointed his chin in the direction of Aurora and Ariel who stood a few yards behind her.

"He didn't care to be a father; they only met him once."

"Yes, I just..." The warden looked uncomfortable as he stumbled over his words.

"But we appreciate your kindness," Rachel offered.

He nodded and quickly exited the cemetery.

The older woman who had been listening carefully to their conversation got to her feet and grabbed Rachel's arm just as she had turned to leave.

"You're Mrs...McCaw?"

Rachel blew out a small breath and tried not to roll her eyes. "I'm Ms. Princess now."

"But...but you were married to Daniel McCaw?"

Rachel nodded slowly. "I was."

"And these...these young ladies are your daughters? Yours and...*his?*" The woman's eyes filled with tears when Rachel nodded. She covered her open mouth with her small, wrinkled hands as a tiny scream escaped from her throat.

Ariel and Aurora had walked up behind their mom to see what the conversation was about. They were very surprised when suddenly the older woman pushed Rachel aside and threw her arms around the twins in a tight embrace. They exchanged a worried look over her head, but the older woman continued to hold onto them, as if she were afraid to let go.

Dana and Rachel tried to question her, but they were only met by incoherent mumbles.

"Gone...my boy...no other family. He was my only son."

"I think you must be confused," Dana said.

"I'm not confused!" the woman cried out between sobs.

Rachel froze, her eyes wide. "Wait, did you say son?"

"Yes, Daniel was my only son."

Rachel stumbled to the ground and all attention went from the old woman to her.

"Rach? Are you okay?"

Rachel looked up at the older woman, "If you're Daniel's mother then that means..."

The woman looked at Ariel and Aurora, who still seemed confused by the situation. With a huge grin on her face she finished saying what Rachel couldn't. "I'm your grandma!"

Chapter Twenty-Seven

The older woman hugged the girls once again, only this time they hugged her back. Ariel blanched slightly when she heard the word "grandma" and Aurora's mouth dropped open, a tiny squeak escaping past her lips. Dana pulled Rachel back to her feet and turned to Daniel's mom.

"Are you sure?"

"About what dear? That I'm Daniel's mother? Yes, I'm pretty sure that's not something a person forgets."

Dana's face flushed as she realized how her question sounded. "I mean..."

"Don't worry, dear," she chuckled, placing a hand on Dana's arm. "I know what you meant. I was only joking." Then she turned to Rachel. "So when were you and Daniel married?"

"About seventeen years ago. We were only married for two years. We divorced shortly after he found out I was pregnant. After he..." Rachel's eyes widened when she remembered who she was talking to. She tried to brush it off rather than finish the sentence, *tried to kill me and our unborn children.*

"He hurt you." It wasn't a question.

When Rachel wouldn't meet her eyes, his mother's fears were confirmed. "You're the reason he was in prison."

"Wait a minute, it wasn't Rachel's fault!" Mary jumped in.

"No, I didn't mean to offend, or accuse you of anything. I know my son wasn't the good man I always hoped he would be. He took after his father instead." You could see the bitterness still residing in the old woman's eyes as she spoke. "I knew he was in prison for attempted murder, I just didn't know the circumstances behind his arrest. Daniel never told me anything. Well, clearly! I didn't even know the three of you existed!"

Aurora began to shiver from the cold, damp breeze. Her body shook from head to toe and her teeth involuntarily rattled together.

"I'm so sorry! You poor girls are freezing to death out here. Please, can we go somewhere and talk more?"

Rachel looked into the older woman's warm, brown eyes. They were pleading with her not to leave.

"I'm sorry, we don't even know your name yet."

"Of course! I'm sorry, I got so excited to meet you all that I completely forgot my manners. I'm Bertha. It's a horrible name, I know! So please just call me Grandma B." She extended her hand out and met Rachel's in a soft handshake.

"Why don't you all follow me back to my house. I don't live far from here. It's not big, but the couches are comfortable and we can all warm up with some of my famous hot cocoa."

Rachel glanced back at the girls to gauge their reaction. Ariel nodded enthusiastically. Aurora didn't seem as certain, but she was definitely curious about the appearance of a long-lost grandparent. Then she looked to her sisters. Dana urged them to go.

"Go and visit, take your time," she said, waving them forward. "We'll be waiting for you guys at home."

Rachel turned back to Grandma B. "Alright," she spoke softly. "We can stop by for a few minutes. Just tell me where to go."

The excitement radiated through Grandma B.'s bright blue eyes. She clapped her hands together. "Just follow me."

***

The screen door creaked as Grandma B. pushed it open and held it in place for the girls to enter. Her house was very small, but cute and well kept. A tiny, white bullet shot out of a back room and charged straight for the twins. He jumped up on them, licking their legs and barking happily in an attempt to get attention. Ariel knelt down and started scratching his head. In a matter of minutes he had climbed onto her lap, tongue lolling from his mouth.

"That's Eddy," Grandma B. said as she passed through the open room to the kitchen. "He's the only man in my life now, and the only one I trust. Have a seat," she added, nodding toward the little, white loveseat.

Aurora and Rachel sank into the soft sofa, their shoulders touching. Ariel opted to sit on the floor in front of them and continue to pet Eddie, who began drooling on her skirt.

"What kind of dog is he?" Aurora asked, bending over Ariel's shoulder to pat his head. Eddie sat up, excited for the new attention, wiggling like a toddler in search of a restroom.

"He's a Havanese. Isn't he cute?"

The twins looked him over from his short, little floppy ears to the fluffy tail that rolled in against his body. He was all white except for tiny black eyes and a little black nose. He had a short, sweet face that made him look like a puppy even though he was full grown. "Adorable!" Both Ariel and Aurora answered in unison.

"I've never even heard of that," Aurora said.

"I hadn't either," she replied, handing a mug of warm cocoa to each of them. "I discovered the breed with some help from a sweet, young lady at the library. She taught me how to search online for hypoallergenic dogs. I kept looking until I found the right one for me."

Upon hearing those words, Rachel's shoulders relaxed and she released the breath she hadn't realized she'd been holding. Grandma B. looked at her and smiled.

"She's allergic to dogs," Ariel explained.

"I gathered that."

"It's a bummer too, 'cause we were never allowed to have one," Aurora said.

"Well, you shouldn't have any problems with Eddie here."

Aurora stole her gaze away from the sweet ball of fur for a moment and really looked around the room for the first time. For someone who had never heard of Havanese before, Grandma B. had sure caught up fast. There were little figurines around the room, books on the coffee table, framed pictures on the walls, and even a Havanese lamp sat in one corner.

Grandma B. followed Aurora's gaze. "I love my dog," she said, shrugging.

Aurora just nodded her reply and went back to petting him.

Several minutes of silence went by. The girls focused on Eddie, not sure of where to begin. Rachel drained the last drop of hot chocolate from her cup, even though she wasn't thirsty.

"I know this is kind of awkward," Grandma B.'s whisper finally cut through the silence. "I want to know everything, as I'm sure you have many questions of your own. Why don't I start and you can tell me your story when

I'm finished," she said, looking to Rachel. She nodded so Grandma B. continued.

"I met Daniel when I was practically still a kid. Your father was named after his father," she added in response to their confused looks. "I didn't grow up in a great home. Both my parents were alcoholics so they cared more about booze than they did me. Most of the time, I think they forgot they even had a daughter. So I pretty much raised myself. I was skinny and seriously under-fed. I was so starved for attention, of any kind, that I was naïve and very gullible.

"When Daniel came into my life, I thought he was the greatest thing since sliced bread. I basically kissed the ground he walked on, which he loved. Finally, someone paid attention to me! I thought that man was a genius. I would have done anything he asked of me, and did. I was the perfect girl for him; he loved to control, and I didn't know any better so I did everything he told me to without question. He chose what I wore, what food we ate, what meals I was to prepare, how to clean the house, who I was allowed to talk to, everything. I'm sorry," Grandma B. paused, seeing the horrified expressions on both girls' faces. "Should I stop?"

Rachel's mouth also hung open in surprise at Grandma B.'s story so far, but she shook her head. "I think it's important for the girls to know where their father came from."

She nodded her agreement, then took a deep breath and continued. "We were only married a few weeks when he started hitting me. The first time was when I accidentally burned dinner. I thought it was my fault. I thought I deserved the way he treated me. He was always so apologetic the next day. I thought how lucky I was to be married to such a forgiving man. I would mess up, he would teach me a lesson, and then he would apologize and forgive me for my mistakes. **My** mistakes," she repeated, cringing from the memories.

Tears slid down Rachel's cheeks at the familiarity of her words.

Grandma B. didn't notice and went on. "After about a year of this cycle, he asked me why I hadn't given him any children yet. So then we started trying for a baby. Little Daniel Junior was born less than a year later. I had some serious health problems when he was born, and so the doctor had to do an emergency hysterectomy that same day. Daniel was furious! He wanted a big family, but because of my weakness, he was only ever going to have one son." Grandma B. wiped a tear from her eye and continued. "In hindsight, that was the greatest blessing I was ever granted in my life. I thought that because my child was so sweet and so perfect, there was no way his father would ever touch him. But, of course, I was wrong. Daniel ruled with an iron fist. The first time Danny said no to his father in that defiant, little toddler voice of his, he got a fist to the gut."

Rachel gasped.

Grandma B. hung her head in shame, trying to shake away all the horrible memories. "The first time he hurt Danny was when I finally started waking up to reality. Unfortunately by this time I was so scared and so mentally weak, I didn't know what to do. When I actually got brave and threatened to leave, Daniel only laughed in my face. He told me if I ever left, he'd take little Danny somewhere and hide him where I'd never see him again. He even threatened to kill Danny once, if I tried to leave. His own son! I should have been stronger for my son. I should have found a way to get him away from that man, no matter what. But I was scared and alone. Daniel had done a good job of making sure of that. I had no one to turn to.

"As the years passed, Danny grew into a young man and tried to be my protector against his father's reign of tyranny. But his compassion soon turned into pity, and then turned to loathing. He was mad at me for not leaving, and for not keeping him safe when he was younger. When he was sixteen, Danny ran away from home. He would call me occasionally when he was certain his dad would be at work, but I never knew where he was. You can imagine Daniel was furious that his son would take off and so I was forbidden from speaking to him anymore. Three years later, when Danny was nineteen, he came home one night and tried to get me to leave with him. He wanted to save me from his father's dominion." Tears flooded Grandma B.'s eyes and she started to sob. Her shoulders shook from the painful memory of that night.

Rachel stood and wrapped an arm around her. She felt an unspoken bond with this woman. She was practically a stranger, yet Rachel understood all too well the paralyzing fear that came from having a tyrannical husband. Rachel's embrace helped calm Grandma B.'s breathing and she soon regained control.

"I just...I just..."

"Take your time," Rachel soothed.

"I couldn't go with him. I dreamed for years that someone would come and rescue me from the nightmare of my life. And here was my rescuer, standing right in front of me. But all I could think about was how Daniel would react when he discovered me gone. He would know it was Danny, and he would kill him. My son didn't understand this. He thought we could move away and his father wouldn't come after us, but I knew better. I wanted him to have a better life, to be a better person. So I did what I thought was the best for him. I turned him away. But now I know. I know he turned out exactly like his father."

Grandma B. put her head in her hands and all the sorrow from that day came spilling out.

Chapter Twenty-Eight

Ariel and Aurora sat on the floor, crying silent tears. They cried for their grandmother and the horrors she had been through. They cried for their mother, knowing she had lived a similar life. But mostly they cried for their lost father; the suffering little boy, who didn't stand much of a chance, for the man he turned into, and for the man he could have been.

Aurora had slid to the floor during Grandma B.'s story. The twins now sat side by side, holding hands. Eddie lay solemnly between them, nuzzling their fingers and trying to comfort them with gentle licks. The excited, hyper puppy was gone and replaced by a comforting companion. *Dogs really are incredible creatures,* Ariel thought, stroking his back.

"So what happened to Daniel's father, your husband, I mean?" Ariel didn't realize how entranced she was with her own thoughts until Aurora voiced the question, causing her to jump.

Grandma B. looked up, her eyes red and swollen from tears. "He passed away about ten years ago. He got drunk one night and stumbled into the road; he was hit by a truck." The girls gasped, but Grandma B. only shrugged. "Karma, I guess," she replied. "Shortly after that, they transferred Danny to Salt Lake. That's when I moved to Utah, to be closer to my son. I bought this little house, and tried to reconnect with my Danny. He never forgave me for not leaving that night, but he never doubted my love for him either. That's the only part that gives me comfort. No matter how much pain he caused," she glanced at Rachel and then shied away, "he always knew I was there for him. I visited him every week in that awful place, you know. But he never mentioned anything about his life before bars. If I asked any questions concerning his arrest, or what he did with himself, he'd shout at me and stomp back to his cell. We'd sit together and play games, or talk about the few good memories from his childhood, or I would talk about Eddie here." Eddie looked up at the sound of his name, but realizing there were no treats involved, he laid it back down on his paws.

"For what it's worth, I think he was ashamed of the way he treated you, and for turning out just like his father, a man he despised. Men brag about the things they're proud of, but they hide their shame."

"Thank you for sharing your story with us," Rachel spoke in a soft voice.

Grandma B. nodded.

"It's not your fault either. The way he turned out, I mean."

"I know." Grandma B. nodded again. "It took me years of therapy to finally understand that, but I do know. It doesn't do any good to look at the past and wonder, 'what if?' All I can do is look to the future and make good choices for my own life."

Rachel agreed. "It took me a long time to learn those lessons too."

"You got out much sooner than I did."

"Only because my husband got caught."

It was silent again for a while, before Grandma B. spoke. "So can I ask about you and Danny? Daniel, I guess, is how you knew him. Not all the bad garbage. I'm not sure

I can handle that part tonight. But how you met? Is there anything good you can tell me?" Her eyes looked hopeful.

Rachel smiled. "As much bad as there was, I can definitely tell you some good, too. I loved your son." She said it very matter-of-factly. "And I honestly think he loved me too. Despite all the bad, many of the things you've told us about your husband make sense to me. I can see now why Daniel was the way he was."

"I'm sure he did love you, dear. Deep down, I know he had a good heart." The twins shifted uncomfortably. "That's no excuse for the way he behaved. I know that." Grandma B. looked down at the twins. "But your father was a good man once."

The girls nodded and Rachel began her story. "I was coming out of the movie theater one night with my little sister, Elizabeth. This extremely good looking guy was standing across the street waiting for a bus. He saw us and waved. I waved in return and smiled. My sister asked who he was and I told her I didn't know, but it never hurt to be friendly. He crossed the street and approached us. I was a little nervous, but was quickly set at ease by his smile. He was very charming and basically asked me out on the spot. He said he noticed my beauty from across the street and knew he had to find out my name, or he'd regret it the rest of his life."

The twins smiled at this cute little story about their parents. The only stories they had ever been told were the bad ones. It was refreshing to hear something positive for once.

"I gave him my number and we went out the next night. He really was a very sweet man. I could tell he had a bit of a temper. He'd always get upset over little things, but then he'd gain control and everything was okay. But he took care of me. My dad left when I was really little, so I didn't know what it was like having a man around to make me feel protected. But Daniel made me feel protected from our very first date together. He took me to a club where we went dancing."

The girls broke into giggles. They couldn't picture their mother dancing or even at a club, for that matter. Rachel nudged them with her foot and then continued.

"Well, another man got fresh with me and I thought Daniel was going to punch him in the face. He got very angry and forced the other man to apologize. After that night, we fell in love quickly and got married only a few months later. We pretty much eloped; it all seemed very romantic at the time. Then things seemed to change after we got married...I'm sorry," Rachel stopped. "You didn't want to hear any of the bad."

"No," Grandma B. waved her hand. "It's part of your story. I can't expect you to separate the two."

"Well," Rachel swallowed, "the first time he hit me was during a fight we were having. I had gotten home late from work and he didn't know where I was. He was worried I was with someone else. It seemed weird to me that he would be suspicious or jealous. I'd never given him a reason to think that way. But he let his temper get the best of him and...well, just like with you he felt horrible afterward. He brought me flowers and apologized over and over, promising it would never happen again."

Grandma B.'s chin trembled, but she remained composed as Rachel went on. She shared several good stories, highlighting frequent surprises of flowers, treats, and even jewelry. He always took her side in an argument with people at work, neighbors, and even her sisters. She told them how he could make her smile in a way no one else could. But she also noted the good times became more infrequent as the months went by.

"He never wanted kids," Rachel sniffed and wiped her nose. The twins instinctively knew what was coming next. They climbed up on either side of Rachel, squishing onto the tiny couch. Then they each grasped one of their mother's hands in anticipation for the climactic ending. "I knew he never wanted children from the beginning. He made that very clear when we were dating. But, like a lot of women do, I convinced myself that I could change him. That with time, he would change his mind and we could have a family." Rachel squeezed her daughters' hands in return. "I was on birth control. Daniel made certain of that. But one day I started throwing up in the morning, for no apparent reason. After a week of feeling sick when I first got up, and then fine the rest of the day, I grew suspicious and decided to take a pregnancy test. Sure enough, I was going to be a mom. But I was scared to tell Daniel. I just knew I could convince him to be excited about it, but I wasn't sure how to break the news to him, so I waited.

"Unfortunately, my sisters lived in the same apartment building as us. One day one of them asked Daniel if he was excited to be a daddy. They had no idea of his insecurities and that he had no desire to produce offspring. They were all a little leery of him, now I know why. But at the time, I didn't understand their reasons, so I never told my sisters about it. Daniel raced to our apartment in a rage. He was so angry, he didn't even bother to close the front door when he came in. That one mistake on his part probably saved my life.

"He grabbed my arms so forcefully, his fingertips left bruises. He lifted me off my feet and then shook me as he yelled in my face to say it wasn't true. When I couldn't deny it, he threw me across the room. My head smashed into our coffee table then I crumpled onto the floor. I cried out for him to stop, but my voice wasn't loud enough. My head was spinning so much I thought I might black out. I started vomiting on the floor, probably from my concussion, but that just seemed to remind him of the pregnancy. He began kicking me in the stomach. I tried to protect myself by rolling away, but he yelled at me to hold still. I couldn't scream. I couldn't breathe. I closed my eyes and waited to die.

"And then a miracle happened. Because Daniel left the door open, a man who was walking by heard the noise and rushed into the room." Rachel paused and looked at Ariel and Aurora. Her hands were fidgeting with the material on the couch and her eyes kept darting between her daughters and her lap. "It was Steven, actually."

The twins' heads snapped to attention. "Like Cinderella's dad, Steven?"

Rachel nodded, her breath escaping through her lips in short, ragged puffs.

"Why didn't you ever tell us that before?"

"Dana wanted me to keep it quiet, to protect Cinderella from finding out who he was. But I guess I can tell you now, with everything that has happened."

"Whoa," Ariel whispered. She sank back further into the couch.

"I'm not even sure why he was there, he and Dana were already divorced. But I never asked either. It really didn't matter. As soon as Steven saw what was going on, he ran into the room and grabbed Daniel. The two of them fought, but he wrestled Daniel and pinned him to the ground. He called the police and I was rushed to the hospital with a major concussion, a collapsed lung, and several broken ribs. The doctors couldn't believe I was still alive. Even more than that, they couldn't believe I was still pregnant. They had to do X-rays to survey the damage, but they honestly weren't too cautious, even when I warned them I was pregnant. They never thought the baby could survive an attack like that. And then they did an ultrasound. But instead of finding a dead baby, they found two heartbeats instead."

Rachel's hands trembled as she finished her story. It was a miracle that she and the babies had survived the attack. All the doctors said so. Now Rachel sat, wringing her white hands, trying not to burst as she recalled that horrible night. She finally got up the courage to look at Grandma B. and saw that she was sobbing into her own hands.

Grandma B. couldn't speak. She couldn't fathom the monster her own child had become. Rachel sat quietly herself, not sure what to do next. Then Grandma B. pulled her to her feet and they held each other in a tight embrace. Rachel reached for her daughters and the four women stood in the middle of the room, holding each other.

Chapter Twenty-Nine

"So I'm going to be your bodyguard?"

Cinderella could hear the smile on Scott's face, even though she couldn't see his reaction through the phone.

"I know. Can you believe it?"

"Your mom had this idea?"

"Yes."

"**Your** mom?"

"Yes!"

"I don't even know what to say."

"Say you'll come with me!"

"When is this trip supposed to take place?"

"Well, my dad called my mom last night and they talked it over for a long time. We are thinking spring break would be the best time to go."

"Your parents talked on the phone? How did that go?"

"Surprisingly well! There was no shouting, no arguing, it was great!"

"Your mom talked to your dad with no shouting involved?"

"Yes."

"**Your** mom?"

"Are you trying to ruin this for me?"

"Okay, okay, I'm sorry! This just doesn't seem real to me."

"Me neither. I just want to get the flight booked and plans made before she has too much time to think about everything and change her mind."

"Princess, I would love to be your escort! So are we supposed to stay at your dad's house then?"

"That's what they're still trying to figure out. My dad doesn't want you in the house because he doesn't know you and he has other daughters."

"A valid concern from a father."

"You're not mad?"

"Not at all, Princess. He's never met me, he doesn't know what kind of person I am. I hope after he gets to know me, he'll trust me though."

"I do too."

"So you will be staying at the house and I'll be...in a hotel nearby?"

"This is where they aren't seeing eye to eye. My dad wants me to stay at the house, so he can spend as much time with me as possible. But my mom doesn't know if she trusts him yet. She's never known him as a father, so she's worried about how he will be. On the other hand, my mom doesn't like the idea of you and me at the same hotel at night either."

"Well, she can't have it both ways."

Cinderella giggled. "That's exactly what my dad tried telling her."

"Smart man. So, do I need to purchase a plane ticket then?"

"No, my dad offered to pay for our tickets and your hotel. He's so glad my mom is letting me come, I think he would have paid for ten bodyguards!"

Scott chuckled. "Let's not hire ten bodyguards. I don't want to have to fight nine other men for your attention."

Cinderella smiled. "Deal."

"So you'll book the flight then? Or should we drive?"

"Drive?"

"Well, driving takes longer, but that way we'd have a car while we're in California. Otherwise, how would I get to my hotel at night?"

"I hadn't thought of that. I'm not sure. Would you want to drive?"

"I'd be up for it at least."

"Okay, I'll talk to my dad and see what he thinks too. Then I'll call you back and we can get everything finalized."

"Sounds great! I can't wait for April now!"

"Only six more months..." Cinderella's voice trailed off at the thought. It seemed so far away!

"Don't worry, Princess, it will be here before you know it."

"I sure hope so!"

"I better get going, I've got some studying to do. Thanks for calling; you've given me something to look forward to!"

"Me too! I'll talk to you later. Bye."

"Good-bye, Princess."

***

"And action!"

Belle turned around and posed before giving her best killer smile to the camera. "Hi, my name is Belle Louise Princess. Today you'll be journeying with me to discover my ancestry."

"And cut! Okay, let's move things inside the genealogy library now."

When Belle told her dad about the family tree project, and that her teacher had gotten the idea from a television show, Lucas decided to get involved and help. The next day, a small camera-crew had shown up at the condo to film Belle's presentation.

"That show approached me not too long ago, asking if I wanted to be on it," he explained. "I didn't have a lot of time then, but maybe they can use some of what we film for when I'm on it in the future. After all, our ancestors are the same."

Belle wasn't sure about the idea at first, but it didn't take long for everyone to see that Belle and the camera had a mutual love for each other.

She decided to make most of her focus on her father. The assignment was to explore their family trees and discover new things about their ancestors. Belle knew her situation was unique, with the exception of her cousins. She knew nothing about her own father, so she thought a special video on discovering him would be more exciting. Plus she knew the other kids in the class would be so jealous! It's not every day you learn your dad is a movie star. Belle knew the other girls in the class would just die when they saw her project. They all knew he was her dad from the newspapers, magazines, news, and everything circulating online, but she was going to give them an in-depth look at his life.

"Hey Lucas, I think you should be in this scene with me!" she shouted, waving him forward.

Lucas chuckled as he walked towards her. "My daughter is not camera shy," he mumbled to the camera man, who laughed in return. They were all afraid Belle wouldn't know what to do or what to say, but from the moment the little red light started blinking, Belle had taken charge and was directing the rest of the crew on what they should do.

"I've told you to call me Dad if you want," Lucas whispered, once he reached Belle's side.

"Not yet," Belle said, looking back at the camera with an award-winning smile in place. "You have to earn that title from me."

"This doesn't count?" he asked, waving to the camera crew, makeup artists, producer, and director he had hired.

"It's a start, Lucas," she said, twisting the knife a little. "But I need more than a bunch of hired professionals as proof that you're ready to be my dad. Are we ready for the next take?" Belle shouted.

"My job, Belle, remember?" the director yelled back as he talked about the next scene with his producer.

Belle just shrugged and waved the makeup artist over. "Can you do some touch-ups please? I think my face is starting to get a little shiny."

"You know, Belle, I think you would fit right in in Hollywood. Have you ever considered acting?" Lucas asked.

Belle looked at herself in the mirror and, satisfied, sent the makeup artist away again. "Not really," she said. "I always blamed Hollywood for breaking up you and my mom."

Lucas nodded. "You should think about it. I have an agent in mind that would just love you. And I wouldn't mind having you live closer to me either, kiddo," he nudged her playfully.

"Closer or with you?"

"What do you mean?"

"I mean are you asking me to come live with you in California, or get my own place near you in California?"

Lucas responded without hesitation, "Belle, there will always be a room for you at my house."

"Hmmmm." Belle looked a little surprised at his response.

"Alright guys we're ready for this next scene. Do you know what you're going to say, Belle?" the director yelled.

"Yes," she yelled back. Then in a lower voice to Lucas, "I'll think about it."

Lucas smiled as the director yelled, "And action!"

Chapter Thirty

The day had finally arrived. The Princess sisters were excited to share their family tree projects with the class, but more importantly, they were excited to be done with them! The last three weeks felt like an eternity when the girls considered all that had transpired. Belle and Cinderella now had dads in their lives. They both weren't completely sure about them yet, but they had fathers they could talk to and who seemed to want to get to know them in return. Ariel and Aurora now had a grandma they were trying to get to know, and they had met their father and been to his funeral. It had been an emotional roller coaster for everyone! Snow White was the only cousin still left in the dark about where she came from.

As Cinderella pulled into the school parking lot, they all made note of the number of cop cars surrounding the entrances. The school had assured Belle and her family that they would set up security and keep any more reporters from bothering her during school hours. It looked like they were definitely keeping their promises.

The class buzzed with excitement as the girls entered the room. Many of the students were talking animatedly with one another as they held their finished trees up. Snow White grumbled about the project being stupid and stomped back to her chair. She dropped her books on the table with a BANG and pulled out her book reports. Poor Mona, who sat talking with another friend, was so surprised she actually fell off her chair. Snow White didn't even notice as she folded her arms over the books, rested her head on top and closed her eyes.

The other girls exchanged looks and slowly made their way to the back of the room.

"Snow?" Cinderella asked gingerly.

"It's not fair!" Snow White whipped her head up so fast, Cinderella jumped back in surprise. Snow White didn't even notice and charged on. "You all got to make these amazing discoveries about your families and your ancestors, while I was left to read these stupid, boring books." Snow White shoved the books from her desk, letting them crash to the floor.

"Well, it looks like the Princess girls have some tempers on them, don't they?" Mrs. Payne said, appearing behind them. Then, realizing Snow White was not in a joking mood, Mrs. Payne patted her on the back and bent down to pick up the books.

"Sorry, Mrs. Payne," Snow White mumbled. She rested her face on a balled up fist.

Mrs. Payne carefully set the books on the corner of her desk and made her way to the front of the room. Ariel slid in beside Snow White and put an arm around her, but Snow White just shrugged it off.

"I don't want to talk about it right now."

Ariel nodded, then looked forward as Mrs. Payne cleared her throat for class to start. Cinderella, Belle, and Aurora gave Snow White pitying looks as they took their seats, but she looked away from them and frowned down at her reports.

"Now, by show of hands, who did a video for their presentation?"

Belle's hand shot up, along with three others in the class.

"We'll start with the videos first. Mr. Daniels needs the TV for his class today, too. As soon as those are done, we'll move on to the verbal presentations. Who's up first?" she asked, rubbing her thin hands together excitedly.

Belle almost raised her hand, anxious to show off her work, but she decided to hold back and wait. *I'll save the best for last,* she decided.

The first three videos were cute, and a little cheesy. They had poor acting, poor lighting and really poor editing, or so Belle thought. But overall they were done well for a high school project, and everyone applauded their efforts.

"Any last videos?" Mrs. Payne asked, glancing at her watch.

"I have one," Belle said, strutting up to the front of the class. She handed over her professionally made DVD and walked back to her seat, smiling.

Mrs. Payne dimmed the lights and sat down behind her desk. Belle's video began with suspenseful music playing as it showed clips from *Locker Partners* of Lucas Ferreira. Across the screen flashed the words: *Do you know this man?* Then dubbed over the pictures came Belle's voice.

"I knew him too. Only, I thought he was just another good looking actor, like everyone else. Then one night I discovered the truth behind my own family tree. He was–is my dad." Mrs. Payne sat up straight in her chair, all signs of heavy eyelids now gone. The girls in the class started whispering excitedly and a couple even swooned when Lucas smiled at the camera. They had all heard the rumors, of course, that he was Belle's father. But none of them were expecting this special treat of watching exclusive footage of the man.

More dramatic music played as Belle made her first appearance on screen and took the class on a journey of discovering who her father was. She only called him "Dad" on screen for the movie, because the director told her it would have a more emotional impact on her audience. He was definitely right. Belle smiled when she saw most of the girls were sniffling.

When the video ended, the class all cheered loudly. Several of the kids jumped to their feet, trying to ask Belle questions, and it took Mrs. Payne several minutes to get the class calmed down again. Belle beamed at all the attention.

"Well, Ms. Princess, that was quite an extraordinary video! Very well done!"

"Thanks! My dad hired a professional crew to help make it, but I wrote the script all myself."

Mrs. Payne nodded her approval. Then she turned to a boy who had already presented his project and asked him to take the TV to Mr. Daniels' classroom. When Mrs. Payne opened the classroom door, there stood Lucas Ferreira with one hand raised as if he were about to knock.

Mrs. Payne looked stunned and took a step back into the classroom, almost stumbling over a desk leg. Lucas reached out and caught her arm, causing Mrs. Payne to gasp. "You must be Mrs. Payne?" he asked, flashing his famous dimple.

Belle looked from her father to Mrs. Payne, confused. *What is he doing here?* She thought Mrs. Payne looked ready to cry, from a movie star knowing her name.

She seemed to finally catch her breath. "Yes, I am. What can I do for you, Mr. Ferreira?"

"Well, I was helping my daughter with her project and I sort of hoped you'd let me sit in and watch how it turned out."

"We actually just finished watching it." Then in response to the pouty look on Lucas' face, "But we can watch it again. It was very well done. I'm sure the class won't mind."

"You'd do that for me?"

"Of course, not a problem." Mrs. Payne began twirling her hair with one finger as she watched Lucas in awe.

"I've got a couple cameras here, too. They wanted to do a special on my reuniting with my long lost daughter. You wouldn't mind a couple cameramen, would you?" He flashed her another tooth-sparkling smile and brushed her chin with his hand as he spoke. Mrs. Payne turned a deep scarlet.

Was he flirting with her?! Belle could feel her face turning red as Mrs. Payne nodded and held the door open wider for several cameramen to enter the room.

"We're gonna be on TV!"

"This is the coolest thing ever!"

Mona leaned across the table. "Your dad is so hot!" she whispered to Belle with a smile.

Belle shot her a threatening look causing Mona to shrivel back against her seat.

"Poor girl, she's going to think we're all crazy, after Snow and Belle today," Cinderella whispered to Aurora. Aurora agreed, but was soon drowned out by the rest of the class, who were buzzing with excitement again. Belle seethed in her seat while they set up the TV once more and the cameras were placed strategically around the room.

"Flirting can get you anything, my dear," Lucas whispered to Belle when he pulled up a chair behind her.

Belle wouldn't even look at him. She crossed her arms over her chest and stared hard at the TV.

"Honey, I'm kidding. Well, mostly. Belle?"

She pretended not to hear him and was grateful when Mrs. Payne lowered the lights and pushed play.

"Just pretend like this is the first time you've all seen it," Lucas said loudly. Everyone turned their focus to the TV, hoping to gasp, cheer, or sigh at just the right moment so they could get their fifteen minutes of fame and be included on the show.

The cameras slowly panned the room, making sure to zoom in on Lucas occasionally so he could pat Belle on the back or give her shoulders a friendly squeeze. It took all the control Belle possessed to not turn around and deck him.

Lucas and the cameramen stayed for the rest of class, even gaining footage of a few of the verbal presentations. As soon as class ended, Belle jumped to her feet and bolted out the door.

"Wait, Belle! They want to ask a few questions, too. Belle?" Lucas chased her down the hall, but Belle was faster as she weaved in and out of the crowds. She finally reached a dead end and turned to face him.

"I can't believe I was starting to trust you!" She spat the words at him. "You said you wanted to help me with my project, you said you were here for me, but that was all a bunch of bull. Everything has been about you, and publicity stunts, and using me to boost your ratings. Well I'm done!"

"Wait a minute, that's not true."

"Liar." Belle was using every ounce of self-control she could muster to hold back the hot, angry tears that were starting to sting her eyes. Just as they threatened to spill over, someone stepped out from a nearby classroom, coming between them.

"I thought I told you to leave her alone."

"Bodyguard boy," Lucas nodded at Dave. "Look, I just need to talk to my daughter."

"From the looks of it, I'd say she doesn't feel like talking to you."

"Okay, I get it, you're a big tough guy. Now can you move please?"

Belle's control finally broke and tears started spilling down her face. She used Dave's distraction to slip into a classroom and disappear.

"Great, now she's gone. What gives you the right to speak for Belle, anyway?" Lucas asked.

"I care about her."

"Well so do I."

"I don't think using her to parade around and show off is caring about her."

"Look, kid, you're starting to get on my nerves. Now move or I'll make you move."

"Are you threatening me?" Dave laughed.

The cameramen had finally caught up to them and began filming the confrontation. A large crowd had also gathered around the stand-off. Despite the fact that the late bell had already rung, no one moved.

"I just want to go in there and talk to her. This was all a misunderstanding." Lucas reached for the door handle, but Dave got in his way.

"You made her cry."

"Like I said, it was just a misunderstanding." When Lucas reached for the door again, Dave punched him in the chin. It wasn't hard enough to do any damage; it was more of a warning.

The crowd gasped and waited to see what Lucas would do next. He just shook his head and, rubbing his jaw, turned around to walk away. "Fine," he said. "You win."

Dave stood firmly in front of the door, fists clenched.

"Mr. Ferreira, are you going to press charges?"

"Naw, he's just a kid with a crush."

Lucas waved his crew to follow, and the crowd slowly dispersed. Several people voiced their disappointment that there hadn't been more action.

Dave waited until everyone was gone before opening the door to follow Belle inside.

Chapter Thirty-One

Belle sat on the floor of the empty classroom in the corner, wiping at her eyes.

"Now this really doesn't sit right with me. Belle Princess should not be on the floor, looking pitiful."

Belle was not in the mood to fight. She glanced up as Dave approached, but didn't move or say a word.

"Come on." He offered her his hand. "You really probably don't want to be sitting on the floor. Who knows where it's been." Dave winked at her.

Belle couldn't help cracking a grin at his lame joke. Reluctantly, she reached up and took his hand, allowing Dave to pull her to her feet.

"Do you want to talk? Do you want a shoulder to cry on? Or do you just want to forget everything and make out?"

Belle punched him in the shoulder. Hard. "See, I start to think you're being a nice guy, and then you go and say something like that." Belle started to leave, but Dave grabbed her hand.

"Wait, Belle, I was just trying to get you to laugh. I'm joking."

Belle slumped back down onto a table that was leaning against the far wall. "I know."

"That's it? I make a crude joke and you're not going to fight me or anything? What has this guy done to you? You're not the Belle I know."

"Sorry to disappoint, but I've had a really crappy day. I'm just not in the mood to argue. But if you want, I'll write all my insults down and get back to you later."

Dave grinned. "There she is!"

Belle smiled, too. As much as she wanted to hate him, Dave had this ability to make her feel like maybe things weren't as bad as they seemed.

Dave walked over and sat beside her on the table, leaning his back against the wall. His long legs dangled over the table's edge. "Tell me exactly what happened."

"My dad, no, he doesn't deserve to be called that. Lucas Ferreira has been using me, I'm sure, to boost publicity for his stupid show. He pretended to care, he pretended to help me, but it turns out everything was just to make himself look better. He didn't really care. I can't believe I even bought his sob story about how much he's thought about me over the years. I bet he didn't think about me a day in his life. He probably forgot he even had a daughter, until he got my letter."

Dave just nodded. He reached an arm around her waist and pulled her closer to him. "I'm sorry your dad is a jerk."

"Me too. So what happened out there after I left?"

"I punched your dad in the face."

Belle turned her head so sharply, she almost gave herself whiplash. Her jaw dropped. "You did what?"

"Not hard. Just enough to keep him out of here."

"I'm impressed," Belle said, nodding. "And what did he do back?"

"Nothing. He just walked away. I'm sure he wanted to do something, but with a whole camera crew tailing him, it wouldn't have looked good on his part to react."

"Serves him right."

"Do you really hate him that much?"

"I don't hate him, but I just don't trust him either. It turns out my dad is a better actor than I thought."

The door slowly opened and Craig peered inside. "Belle?"

Dave was quick to yank his comforting arm away from Belle. Craig stepped into the room and pulled Belle into a reassuring hug.

"Are you okay? I got here as soon as I heard."

Belle nodded and began describing the situation to Craig as he walked her from the room. She looked back at Dave and smiled, mouthing, "Thank you." Dave simply nodded and then helplessly watched them go.

**

"So you still won't talk to him?"

"Nope."

"Not even to find out what he has to say?"

"I think I've heard about enough from him. I got along fine for seventeen years without a dad. What do I need one now for?"

Mary let out a huge sigh, exasperated her daughter had inherited her own stubbornness. This scene was all too familiar. Belle lay on her bed, reading a book from school this time, while Mary tried to convince her to have dinner with them.

"Aren't you afraid of what might happen if we're alone together all night?"

"I don't care anymore. Do whatever you want."

"But he's leaving to go back to California tomorrow. Don't you even want to say good bye?"

"See ya." Belle mock-waved at the door without taking her eyes off the book.

"Fine. I just don't want you to regret your decision."

"Not a chance."

"You don't know how lucky you are, sweetie. I would have given anything to have my dad come back and make amends when we were growing up. But I wasn't given that opportunity."

"Sucks to be you," Belle said, turning another page.

Mary's face turned red with fury. "Fine! Do whatever you want! I'm done trying to save you from yourself. But don't come crying back to me when you realize the mistake you've made!" With that, Mary slammed the door and stormed down the stairs.

As soon as she was gone, Belle threw the book down and ran to her window. She watched Mary climb into the limo before it pulled away. Belle scoffed. *A limo? What a show-off!* Then she cranked her music up and flopped back onto her belly. She wondered where he had taken Mary for dinner. *I bet it's someplace good,* she thought as her stomach began growling. Belle reluctantly got back to her feet and followed her grumbling stomach to the freezer. *Looks like frozen pizza tonight. Yum.* Belle made a face, then slumped into a kitchen chair while she waited for the oven to preheat.

SIX MONTHS LATER

Chapter Thirty-Two

Cinderella couldn't believe Spring Break was finally here! Scott had been right. The months flew by. As she shoved a sweatshirt into her duffel bag, she couldn't wipe the grin off her face. She would be spending the next eight days with Scott! Eight days! And she was going to meet her dad and two little sisters for the first time! *Does life get any better than this?*

Someone tapped on her door.

"Come in!"

"You all ready to go?"

"Yes!"

"Well you don't have to be so excited to leave me for a week," Dana said sarcastically. Then the grin dropped from her face and her eyes began to water.

"Mom?"

"Please be careful."

"Of course I will!"

"I mean with everything. Drive safe, don't be alone with Scott in his hotel, and take things slow with your dad and sisters. I don't want you getting your hopes up and coming home with a broken heart."

"Mom." Cinderella had to grab her mother's face between her two hands in order to get her attention, as Dana proceeded to list off all her fears. "Mom!"

Dana finally looked at her.

"You worry too much!"

"I know, but that's my job. You're my only baby and I just want you to be safe. We've never been apart longer than overnight. What am I going to do with myself?"

"Live it up! Go out and party!"

"Right..." Dana rolled her eyes.

"Have Mary take you dancing or something."

"Can you imagine me dancing?"

"That's why you should do it! Change things up a little bit."

"Well Mary is going to California to visit Lucas anyway."

"Again?"

"Yup."

"Why is she going over Spring Break?"

"Well, she hoped Belle would go with her."

"And of course she won't."

"Of course. That cousin of yours sure is stubborn."

"So what is that niece of yours going to do while Mary is gone?"

"I said I'd keep an eye on her."

"Oh, so I'm being replaced. Just trading one daughter for another, huh?"

"Yes, basically."

"And you were giving me a hard time."

"It's my job and my right as your mother to give you a hard time."

"Gee thanks."

Dana smiled and pulled Cinderella into a tight embrace. "I'm sure going to miss you kiddo."

"Just put a brown wig on Belle and dress her in my clothes."

"Right. Because you are so similar I wouldn't even be able to tell a difference." Dana released her daughter when the doorbell rang. "I guess that's your ride."

Dana followed Cinderella down the stairs, dragging her feet the whole way. Cinderella swung the front door open and handed her big duffel bag to Scott, who took it out to the car. Then she turned around and, upon seeing her mom's slow progress, rolled her eyes.

"I'm going to need the rest of my stuff sometime this year, Mom." Cinderella walked back up a few steps, and grabbed her smaller bag out of Dana's hands.

Scott arrived back inside before Dana made it to the bottom step.

"Drive careful!" she called.

"Hey Mrs. P! It's good to see you. All set, Princess?"

"Don't call me Mrs.," Dana said, folding her arms across her chest. "I haven't been married for many years."

"Of course. I'm sorry."

"You take good care of her for me, alright?"

"Of course."

Scott took Cinderella's smaller bag from her and swung it over his shoulder. Cinderella picked up her pillow and gave her mom another hug good bye. "Be good," they said to each other in unison. Then they both smiled and Cinderella walked out to the car.

"Oh and Scott?"

He stopped in his tracks before pulling the front door closed. "Yes?"

"Don't touch her."

Scott simply nodded to Dana, then shut the door behind himself. When he got to the car, he was chuckling.

Cinderella looked over at him and the smile disappeared from her face. "Oh no. What did she say to you this time?"

But Scott just waved off her question and started the engine. "You ready for this?"

Cinderella could feel the butterflies having a dance party in her stomach. "As ready as I'll ever be!"

"Let's go then!"

After many long discussions and going back and forth, Scott and Cinderella decided to drive the whole way to California rather than fly. Besides the road trip being fun, they thought it might be nice to have a car while in California. Since Scott wasn't old enough to rent one, this seemed like the perfect solution. The new arrangement also made it easier for Scott to travel back and forth between her dad's house and the hotel, without someone having to drive him everywhere. For Cinderella, it mostly meant twelve hours of uninterrupted Scott-time.

They talked about school and how most of Scott's general classes were a complete bore. They talked about Cinderella's classes and what she was planning on taking her senior year. She revealed her hope to attend Utah State after high school, which brought a smile to Scott's face. But she still couldn't decide what she wanted to major in, or what she wanted to do with her life. Once the subject of school was exhausted, they drove in comfortable silence for awhile.

Cinderella watched Scott as he drove. She loved the way his strong jaw tightened when he was concentrating. A familiar song came on the radio and she smiled when he started mouthing the words. He started drumming the beat on the steering wheel with his thumbs. She wanted so badly to reach up and play with his hair. It had grown out a little since they first met and the soft, brown waves were beckoning her. A sigh escaped through her lips.

"What?" he asked.

"Nothing," she smiled to herself.

"So tell me, what kind of road trip games did you play in the car?"

"Road trip games?"

"Yeah, when you and your mom would go on road trips."

Cinderella stared at him blankly.

"You never went on road trips?!"

"We couldn't afford to go anywhere. I don't remember ever being in the car for more than an hour or two. This trip will definitely be my record."

"Wow. That makes me sad. Our family did road trips every summer. Dave and I would always play I Spy, and the license plate game, you know, things like that."

She stared at him blankly again.

"What?! Okay, we have some serious educating to do."

Scott then explained how to play I Spy and the two laughed heartily when Cinderella's "I Spy something orange" turned out to be a man driving beside them in nothing but an orange speedo. Then Scott taught her how to play the alphabet game, by finding each letter on different road signs. After that, they started looking at license plates to find as many states as they could. During the hunt for Alaska, Cinderella began to doze off.

"Man, Nevada is an ugly state," Scott commented during a particularly long stretch of endless desert. "Don't you think?"

When Cinderella didn't answer, he glanced over and noticed her eyes were closed. He smiled. She looked so amazing! Scott couldn't help but continue to gaze at her. The view beside him was far better than the view out his front window. He was grateful to be driving. The temptation to kiss her beautiful, soft, pink lips was almost too great to bear.

She was very disappointed when she woke up an hour later to discover she had wasted so much valuable Scott-time.

"For the record, you sing in your sleep," he teased her.

"I do not!"

When Scott only smiled in return, Cinderella's face went red.

"Are you serious?"

"Yeah," Scott grinned. "It was adorable!"

"What was I singing?"

"It was very quiet so it was hard to tell, but you were definitely singing a country song."

"Really?" Cinderella's cheeks flushed red again. She seriously needed to figure out a way to keep her blushing under control around him.

"Don't worry about it Princess, it's just me. Plus you made me want to go dancing again. It's been too long."

"That would be so fun! We should go when we're in Logan again, after we get home," she said, hopefully.

"Why wait? Maybe we can find one in California when we get there."

Cinderella laughed. "A western swing club?"

"Sure, why not?"

"In California?"

"Is that so much of a stretch?"

"I think you've been living in cowboy dreamland too long. You forget country and swing dancing aren't as popular in the rest of the world, outside of Cache County."

"Don't spoil my fun. I'll find one! Now that you've doubted me, I must prove it."

"Even if you do find a club that has a western swing dance night, chances are it will be in a bar, and neither of us are twenty-one."

"Oh ye of little faith."

"You want to bet on it?"

"I'd love to! What are your terms, Ms. Princess?"

"The winner gets...hmmmm...how about the loser has to buy the winner a new album of their choice."

"You're on!" Scott extended his hand out so they could shake on it. "I wonder which album I should choose." Scott said with a cocky grin as he rubbed his chin. Then he began humming a familiar tune. The look on Scott's face told her he was lying before. She had definitely been singing loud enough for him to hear, and now he was teasing her by humming the same song.

Cinderella turned red again and tried to cover her face with a pillow. Scott glanced over at her and laughed loudly.

Chapter Thirty-Three

Cinderella held on to Scott's smartphone, guiding him with the navigation as they drew closer to her dad's house. She could barely focus on the small screen as her hands trembled with anticipation. The butterflies that had been gathering in her stomach all day seemed to have formed a conga line. Her stomach twisted and turned until she feared she might actually throw up.

They finally turned down the last street, *his* street, when Cinderella yelled, "Stop the car!"

Scott pulled over quickly and watched with concern as Cinderella leapt from the vehicle. He found her standing on the grass in front of someone else's house, dry heaving.

"Princess? What's the matter?" he asked softly, rubbing her back as she leaned over the lawn.

"I can't do this," she whispered back. She shook her head as tears started running down her cheeks.

"Why? What's the matter?"

"I...I don't know. I've been dreaming about this moment my whole life, wishing, but never actually believing it would come true. Then I spent the last six months talking to my dad and sisters on the phone, planning, preparing, but it was all surreal. This is real now. What if it isn't what I dreamed about? What if things go wrong, or we don't get along, or it's awkward?"

"Cinderella." Scott used her whole name, catching her off guard, but ensuring he had her full attention. "Dreams are not scripted. You can't expect them to go exactly how you have it planned in your mind. Dreams give you the hope you need to attempt something scary. And most of the time, they end up being worth it. But that's why I'm here. If something goes wrong, or you just get tired of being here, I can take you home."

Cinderella nodded and let Scott pull her back to her feet. "Alright," she said. "Let's go meet my dad."

They got back in the car and drove about half a block more before pulling into a long driveway. The yard was green and well cared for, beautiful but simple. They walked up the path, hand in hand, toward the two-story home. It was white with blue shutters and as Cinderella looked at the large windows in the front, she saw the curtains move aside. When they approached the door, they could hear squealing inside.

Scott quickly dropped her hand when the front door swung open and a tiny, pink bullet wearing a tutu and pigtails shot out and wrapped herself around Cinderella's legs.

"You're here! You're here!"

Cinderella couldn't even get a good look at the child's face, as she had it buried between her knees. Cinderella almost lost her balance as the petite little girl clung to her, not allowing for movement.

"Sophia." The voice behind her was kind but firm. "You need to let her breathe. Come here."

The small child looked up and gave Cinderella a huge grin. They shared the same eyes, but her hair was very blonde in contrast with Cinderella's brown.

"Are you a real princess?" she asked, in awe.

"No," Cinderella laughed. "Why would you think that?"

"Because you have a princess name!"

Cinderella squatted down so she could look straight in the little girls' eyes. "My mommy named me Cinderella because she liked the name. So, no, I'm not a real princess. My last name is Princess though."

Sophie's jaw dropped. "Wow! What's a last name?"

Cinderella looked up at her dad for help.

"Just like our last name is Barnes, do you remember?"

"Oh yeah, I forgot!" Then she giggled and ran around her dad, before disappearing back inside. She was almost pixie-like, with her petite features and the way she flitted about. Cinderella smiled after her before standing upright again.

Then, for the first time, she really looked at her dad. His tall, broad frame filled the open doorway. His chestnut hair, newly trimmed, had the slightest hint of gray around his sideburns. He just stood there, staring at Cinderella, as if he couldn't believe she was real. A huge smile split his face and he quickly moved towards her. His long arms enveloped her in a tight hug.

"You're really here," he breathed, not sure whether to laugh or cry.

Steven lifted Cinderella off her feet and twirled her around, like she was a little girl again. She was so caught off guard by the movement, that a squeal escaped her lips. Then Steven released her from the hug, but between the spinning and the excitement, their legs became tangled and they both crashed to the ground. Scott rushed over, only to find them both laughing like little kids as they lay on the grass.

A young girl in a yellow sundress emerged from the door and ran towards the two of them.

"Dad, are you okay?"

"I'm fine, Monica. Now come over here and help your old man up," he said, extending his hand.

Monica reached down for his hand and was quickly pulled off her feet. Steven tickled her as she tried to fight him off, while laughing. Just then Sophie came to the door and, upon seeing the fun, screamed and jumped on top of the dog pile. Her knees caught Steven straight in the chest, causing him to fall back in surrender. Monica quickly righted herself, smoothed her dress, and rolled her eyes at her laughing father.

"So immature," she said, strolling back inside.

Steven stood and lifted the jumping Sophie into his arms. "She's twelve," he explained.

"She's good at it." Scott smiled as he spoke for the first time.

Steven finally became aware of his presence. "I'm sorry," he said, "I didn't even introduce myself. I'm Steven." He extended his hand.

"Scott." He shook Steven's hand firmly as the two men sized each other up.

"Well, let's get inside before the neighbors start complaining about all the noise." Steven guided the little gathering into the house.

"Do you want to see my room? You've never seen my room before!" Sophie pulled on Cinderella's hands.

"Sure! Where is it?"

"This way! But close your eyes, I want it to be a surprise."

"Sophie, why don't we let your sister breathe for a minute, okay?"

"But I want to show her my new bunk-beds!" The little girl's large bottom lip began to pout.

"I don't mind," Cinderella smiled. The moment she said those words, the little girl dragged her up the stairs.

Scott put his hands in his back pockets and looked around the cozy family room.

"Thank you for bringing her here," Steven said.

"My pleasure," Scott nodded. "She's been looking forward to this for a while."

"We have too." Silence. "So how do you guys know each other exactly?" Steven asked.

Here we go. Scott took a deep breath. "Cinderella lives across the street from my parents. She and my younger brother are—were friends."

"Were?"

"It's kind of a long story. They sort of had a falling out last year. But I think things are on the mend."

"Hmmm." Steven nodded. They both looked up at the empty staircase. *How long does it take to look at beds?*

"Dinner is ready!" Monica yelled from the kitchen.

"Dinner, dinner, dinner, dinner," Sophie came hopping down the hall with Cinderella in tow. "Race you down the stairs!" she yelled. Then without waiting for an answer, the child dove for the staircase and plunged down head first.

Cinderella laughed and followed her down, but stayed upright. "Oh man, you won!" she said when she reached the bottom.

"The kitchen is this way." Steven pointed and they all followed.

Monica was standing over a perfectly set table, pouring water into glasses.

"Wow!" Cinderella exclaimed. "You did all this?"

Monica beamed and nodded.

"I'm sorry, I haven't even gotten a real chance to say hi yet." Cinderella approached her younger sister and gave her an awkward side-hug.

Monica looked down, and then slid carefully out of Cinderella's embrace and continued to pour the water.

"Monica is a fantastic cook. You're in for a real treat," Steven said. He pointed to two chairs across from each other for Cinderella and Scott to take a seat. Sophie had already climbed up into a pink booster seat and was making faces at the food on her plate.

"I don't like it," she said, shoving her plate away.

"Yes you do," Monica sat down next to her sister and rolled her eyes. "It's just chicken. We had this last week and you loved it."

"Well I don't like it anymore," Sophie said defiantly, folding her arms across her chest.

"Whatever."

"Sophia, you know the rules. You need to taste your food please. Your sister worked very hard to make this yummy dinner for us."

"Fine." Sophie let out a huge sigh and started picking at her food.

"You made this?" Cinderella asked after taking her first delicious bite.

"Monica is our little chef. She loves to cook." Steven beamed.

"It's wonderful!" Cinderella praised.

"It really is," Scott added, nodding. "And I'm not just saying that because all we've eaten today is road food."

"I want to be a chef," Monica spoke softly.

"You'll be great at it, I'm sure!" Cinderella said.

"Are you guys married?" Sophie blurted out.

Scott coughed on his food. "No," he answered, smiling at the little girl. "We're not married."

Monica glared at her younger sister who seemed completely oblivious and continued.

"I'm going to get married someday," she announced. "And I'm going to wear a big fancy dress that spins really good, and we're going to have a really big cake! **Pink** cake," she emphasized.

"Cool," Scott said nodding.

"Why aren't you married?"

"Because I'm too young to get married," Cinderella answered.

"Why?"

"I'm still in high school."

"Why?"

"Because I'm only seventeen, and that's how old you are when you go to high school."

"Why?"

"Because...I don't know," Cinderella looked to her dad for help.

"That's enough questions for now," Steven said. "Why don't you eat your dinner please."

"I don't like it," Sophie repeated, scrunching her nose and pushing the plate away.

Monica slammed her fork down and stormed from the room.

"Monica?" Cinderella started to go after her, but Steven told her to stay put.

"She'll calm down and come back, just give her a minute. It's hard going from the oldest child to the middle child."

Cinderella hadn't even thought of that. She had forced Monica from her place in the family. Now the somewhat awkward phone conversations over the last six months made a lot more sense. She glanced down the empty hallway but saw no sign of her. Then her attention was drawn back to the table and she smiled as she watched her dad try and coax the little girl into taking a bite. *So this is what it's like having siblings.*

Chapter Thirty-Four

Belle walked into the kitchen to find her mom standing there, leaning against the counter. Her large suitcase was set at her feet, but Mary didn't move. Belle walked past her and opened the fridge, pulling out their water pitcher and pouring herself a glass.

"Aren't you supposed to be leaving?"

"I want you to come with me."

"Mom, seriously, we've been through this. I'm not going anywhere."

"It's been almost six months, Belle! This is ridiculous! I think you've done your freezing-him-out stage long enough. He gets it. You're mad. Now act like an adult and talk to him. You guys need to work this out."

"Well, Mom, that's the great thing about being a teenager. I'm not an adult, so I don't have to act like one."

Mary pounded her fist on the counter. "Belle! Why won't you even talk to him?! You have no idea what really happened, or why he did the things he did! Your father loves you, and he's been trying to prove that since the moment he stepped back into our lives! Why won't you let him?"

"Because I don't care what he has to say! He sold me out for some extra camera time. Period. That's not love!"

Mary clenched her fists. It took every fiber of her being not to strangle her sassy daughter. "You are so stubborn, girl!"

"I learned from the best."

Mary reached under the counter's edge and yanked out a barstool. She sat down hard, her shoulders hunched. "Fine. You win."

"What?" Belle asked.

"I won't go. I won't see him again. I can't live my life torn between the two people I love. And when it comes down to it, I will pick you." Mary kicked her suitcase forcefully, knocking it over. Then she walked up the stairs, crying.

Belle looked from the fallen suitcase back to the empty hallway where her mom had just disappeared. *Now what?*

***

Upstairs, Mary sat on her bed, unable and unwilling to move. She wiped her eyes, but the tears kept coming back. Then, taking a deep breath, she pulled out her phone. Mary felt her dread building more and more with each ring.

"Hey Babe, you at the airport already?"

"I'm not coming."

"What?"

"It's Belle."

"What's wrong? Is she okay?" The panic in his voice was evident and very real, making this that much harder.

"She's fine, but she still won't accept us. I just can't keep living two lives. It's tearing me apart!"

"Can I talk to her?"

"You've tried, Babe! That girl is so stubborn, I swear! Sometimes I just want to wring her neck! But she's my daughter. We've always been a team, but lately I feel like I've just been the referee between the two of you. It's tearing my heart in half!"

"I know. And you're right, I can't expect you to choose between us. I just hoped she'd get over this and we could actually start being a family."

"I did too. I wanted to be a family more than anything in the world! But I can't marry a man my daughter won't even speak to. I'm not strong enough to do this anymore." Mary's voice had grown softer as the tears poured down her already dampened cheeks. "Good bye, Luke. I love you!"

"I love you, too."

Mary fell down on her pillows, moaning loudly. She felt her dreams shatter with the click of her phone.

Belle stood outside her mom's bedroom door, ear pressed against the wood. When her mom's sobbing got louder she assumed the conversation was over and pulled away. Then she began pacing the hallway, going over the half of the conversation in her mind that she had overheard.

Belle didn't mean for this to happen. With her mom in close contact with Lucas, it was easy to stay mad at him because she knew he was still around. But that phone call and the loud sounds of agony coming from her mom's room made it seem pretty final. She kept thinking that someday she'd forgive him and finally allow him to speak to her again. Then as time passed, it had become easier to just stay mad. But now her dad was gone, and it was all her fault.

Belle quietly slipped into her own room and leaned against the bedroom door. *What have I done?*

Chapter Thirty-Five

Cinderella stood on her tip toes, wrapping her arms around Scott's neck as they hugged good bye.

"Thank you for driving me here," she whispered.

"You're welcome, Princess. Now get some rest. I'll see you in the morning." He started walking to his car when Sophie began to weep.

"Sophie, what's wrong?" Cinderella knelt down by her sister.

"I'm going to miss him!" she sobbed.

Cinderella had to try not to laugh. "We'll see him tomorrow, sweetie."

She sniffed. "We will?"

Cinderella nodded.

"Oh, okay." The child skipped back into the house, all signs of tears gone.

Cinderella stood back up and waved as Scott drove to his hotel.

"Your boyfriend is really cute," Monica said, blushing.

"Well, he's not really my boyfriend. We're just good friends."

"Have you ever kissed him?"

Now it was Cinderella's turn to blush. But she was saved from having to answer by her dad clearing his throat behind them. Monica jumped and ran up the stairs to her room. Steven chuckled as he watched her go.

"You better get to bed too," he said. "I want nothing more than to sit down and talk with you all night, but that would be selfish of me. I know you've had a long drive, so I'll save more of my questions for tomorrow."

Cinderella stretched her arms and yawned. "Thank you." She smiled up at him. "Good night...Dad." *Wow, that felt weird!* She had been calling him "Dad" for nearly six months now during their talks on the phone. But actually saying the word to him in person was a whole new experience. She hesitated for a moment and then gave him a hug before following her sister up the stairs.

Monica had two twin beds in her room, so Cinderella was sharing with her, much to Sophie's dismay.

"But I have bunk-beds now!" she had whined. "She could sleep in my room!" Her four-year-old tantrum would not be subdued until Cinderella promised to have a sleepover one of the nights in her room. Sophie thought about it for a moment before deciding that option would suffice.

Cinderella was finally able to close the door and get ready for bed. "Whew!" she sighed dramatically. "She is a character, isn't she?"

Monica laughed. "That's a nice way of putting it." She climbed into her own bed and pulled up the covers.

Cinderella hefted her suitcase onto the bed. She searched for a minute until she found her pajamas. Then she glanced around the room, unsure of where to change. She had always been an only child, so this had never been an issue before. If it were one of her cousins in the other bed, she wouldn't think twice. *But what is the protocol with a newly discovered younger sister?* She glanced at Monica's form and was relieved to see her head facing the other way. She then changed quickly and crawled into the bed on the opposite side of the room, reaching up to turn off the light. It was amazing how tired her body felt after a day of travel. She didn't exert much energy, other than reaching up occasionally to change the radio station, yet she felt exhausted!

Monica began shifting in bed and making an occasional noise like she was about to talk, and then she'd get quiet again. Cinderella smiled inwardly at her sister's shyness. Her two sisters were complete opposites!

"Monica?"

"Yeah?"

"Is there something you want to ask me?"

"Well...earlier when I asked if you had kissed Scott your face kinda went red. But then Dad interrupted and you never answered me."

"Shoot. I was hoping you'd forget."

"Sorry."

"I'm just teasing." Cinderella sat up on one elbow so she was facing Monica's bed. "Yes, Scott and I have kissed. But we aren't dating. At least not yet. He thinks I'm too young for him, so we're just friends right now."

Monica seemed to think this over for a little while. "So what was it like?"

"What?"

"Kissing a boy."

Cinderella smiled at the memory. There were a lot of words she could think of to describe how she felt when Scott kissed her, but she wasn't sure how much detail she should be sharing with a twelve-year-old. "It was nice," she said.

"I wonder if I'll ever kiss a boy."

"What? Of course you will!"

"I don't know."

"Why do you say that?"

"Because boys don't really like me. And I'm too shy. I don't know how to talk to them."

"Well, I can tell you I used to be exactly like you. And not that long ago. I was pretty shy and I didn't think a boy would ever look my way. But then I met this really cute guy named Dave."

"What about Scott?"

"I'm getting there!" Cinderella smiled, and Monica grinned back. She loved that they were finally connecting. "So Dave became good friends with me and my cousins and he really helped me learn how to talk to guys. I started to feel more and more comfortable around him. Then I started realizing guys really aren't that scary. And most of them are just as scared to talk to a pretty girl as you are of them. One time I was hanging out with Dave and I met his older brother, Scott."

Her eyes had become adjusted to the darkened room now, so Cinderella could see the smile on Monica's face.

"Scott was super cute and a super flirt! We just kind of clicked right away. I can tell you, when you meet the right guy, he won't be scary to talk to forever. You become a lot more comfortable around each other. Scott still gives me butterflies in my stomach every time I see him or talk to him, but I'm not shy with him either. He is my favorite person to talk to in the whole world."

"So when did he kiss you?"

"Well, I ended up kissing both brothers on the same night. It was part of this tradition they have at the school where Scott goes." Monica raised an eyebrow so Cinderella explained further. "They have this big stone 'A' on his campus, where if you stand on it and kiss someone at midnight, it makes you both 'True Aggies'. It's just something a lot of the kids do to say they've done it, but it actually goes back a long time too. Anyway, the only way to become a 'True Aggie' is by kissing someone who has already done it. That's why I had to kiss both brothers. Scott was already a 'True Aggie' so he kissed me, and then I kissed Dave, making him one. Does that make any sense?"

Monica still looked a little confused, and then a lightbulb seemed to have clicked. "So...it's kind of like kissing tag?"

"I guess. Kind of."

"So you got to kiss two guys? In one night?!"

"I did. But you know what? It wasn't all that cool. I wish my first kiss had been more meaningful...and private. I mean, I liked them both, but at the time kissing them was more of a game."

Cinderella left out a lot of details from that night, especially about lying to her mom. She also tried to emphasize that kissing just for the sake of kissing was not worth it. She had only met Monica a few hours ago, yet she felt a need to be her teacher and protector. She was finding it easier than she thought it would be to step into the big sister role.

"Scott has kissed me one other time since that first night," she continued. "It was after we had gotten to know each other really well and I knew how much I cared about him. I can tell you, there was a huge difference! It's so worth it to wait and make sure you really like a guy before kissing him. The kiss was way better the second time around!"

Again, Cinderella left out the details surrounding the second kiss. The fact that it had taken place after he rescued her from a bad party wasn't exactly information she wanted her little sister to know. *Man, both kisses took place*

surrounding events I am not proud of. And those are stories I
definitely don't want my little sisters finding out about.

"So do you love him?"

Cinderella was taken back a little by her bold question. "I...I...I care about him a lot. He's one of my best friends in the whole world. But I haven't had enough experience dating him to say if I'm in love with him yet."

Monica seemed satisfied by her answer. She rolled over a short while later and was quickly asleep. Cinderella, on the other hand, was still physically exhausted, but her mind was now racing with questions.

Chapter Thirty-Six

OOMPH! Cinderella was awakened by pointy, little knees colliding with her chest. She tried to sit up, gasping to catch her breath, but a squirmy four-year-old body held her down. She finally managed to open her eyes and saw a smaller set of her own eyes only inches from her face.

"Wake up, Cinderelly! Dad made French toast!"

As quickly as the munchkin appeared, she scooted off the bed and was gone. Cinderella stretched, rubbed her sternum, and groaned, only to discover a smiling Monica watching her.

"I'm glad you enjoyed the show," Cinderella said.

"Better you than me!"

"I take it she's gotten you before."

"Are you kidding? I've had so many hits to the chest, I'll be amazed if I ever grow boobs."

Cinderella laughed. "Well, I'll only be here a week, then you can have your alarm clock back."

"Oh goodie," Monica said sarcastically.

"Guys! Come on! Dad put cimanon in the French toast. Hurry!" Sophie stuck her head in the room, encouraging her older sisters to get up. When they didn't move quickly enough, she made a grunting noise in frustration and then left again.

"What's the plan today?" Cinderella asked, plopping down on one of the wooden kitchen chairs.

"We're going to the zoo!" Sophie yelled, throwing her arms up in the air.

"Indoor voice please, Sophia."

She stuck her tongue out at him before trying to shove half a slice of French toast in her mouth at once.

"Yes," Steven said, "I let the girls each choose a place to take you on your first visit here. Sophie chose the Sacramento Zoo for today. I hope you don't mind."

"Of course not! I haven't been to a zoo in ages."

"Good! Well let's eat quickly and get a move on, it's supposed to be hot today. I want to get to the zoo before it gets too miserable outside. I assume Scott will be joining us?"

"Yes!" Sophie yelled.

Steven put a finger to his lips, signaling the child to quiet down.

"Yeah, I better give him a call so he can get here." Cinderella excused herself from the table and went back upstairs to retrieve her cell phone. She noticed her dad didn't say anything, but his face looked grim as she walked away.

***

"I want to ride on the lion!" Sophie jumped up and down, pointing to the carousel as they stood in line for a turn.

"We'll have to see, honey. There's a lot of people in line in front of you, so don't get upset if someone else takes the lion first."

"Does telling her that actually work?"

Steven shook his head and mouthed the word, "No". Cinderella looked down at her little sister who was pretending to be a great lion, stomping about on the cement. She had her shirt pulled up around her head, like a mane, and would occasionally growl or roar at passersby. As soon as the carousel slowed, her head snapped up in attention.

"Lion! Lion! Lion!" she sang as she twirled in circles between the turnstiles.

"Keep your fingers crossed," Steven said, looking down at his daughter.

Cinderella and Scott, and then a reluctant Monica, all crossed their fingers as they moved forward in line. The second Steven handed over their tickets, Sophie was off like a bullet, weaving in and out of people to get to her precious lion. She scrambled up and, reaching over as far as she could, Sophie patted the dolphin beside her.

"Come on, Scott! Come sit by me!"

"I think someone has a crush," Cinderella whispered from behind him.

Scott smiled and whispered, "I hope it's you." His warm breath in her ear sent chills down her back.

"Hurry!" Sophie yelled in desperation, even though no one appeared to be making a grab for his reserved dolphin.

Sophie was patting her lion's head and explaining to it how fast she wanted to go, when Scott caught up. He climbed atop the dolphin and Cinderella rode on what she guessed was a hyena. The three of them sat in a row and clipped their buckles into place. Monica, insisting she was too old, sat several rows in front of them on a peacock bench. Steven stood in front of the trio, snapping pictures. Then he moved forward to get a snapshot of Monica, grumbling at the camera.

"Giddy up, lion!" Sophie yelled as the carousel whirred to life and began moving around in circles. The soft organ music was mostly drowned out by giggling and happy screams.

"I'll race you, Sophie!" Scott leaned forward on his dolphin, pretending to urge her forward.

"Sco-ott!" Sophie said, exasperated. "We can't race them, they all move the same!"

"Oh right, I forgot."

Sophie laughed.

"You look pretty good on that dolphin," Cinderella said, smiling.

"Oh yeah?"

"Mm-hmm, very...manly!"

Scott leaned down, hugging his dolphin tight and giving Cinderella a super cheesy grin.

She had it timed just right and was ready. The carousel was coming to a stop, so she quickly snapped a picture of him with her cell phone, then jumped down off her hyena-thing and ran.

Scott tried to hurry after her, but he forgot to undo the belt first and ended up falling off his dolphin. This made Sophie and Cinderella laugh even harder than before. Scott got back to his feet, lifted Sophie off of her lion and then used her to chase Cinderella down. He held her out in front of himself as she growled and squealed. The two of them caught up to her and Sophie began tickling her sister. Then Scott picked Cinderella up like a sack of potatoes and directed Sophie to snag her phone. Sophie did as she was told.

"Hey, I thought you were on my side!" Cinderella protested.

Sophie giggled harder as she handed the phone over to Scott. He opened it and deleted the embarrassing image from her camera roll.

"Good job, Soph!" he said, putting his hand out for a high five. She returned it with a hard slap.

"Yes, you two do make a great team. It's just too bad I already posted it to Facebook!"

Scott's face dropped for a brief moment, then he continued his pursuit. When Steven and Monica finally caught up to them, Sophia was sitting on top of Cinderella's back, dumping cold water on her from a water bottle. Cinderella laughed and yelled, while Scott recorded the whole thing using her own phone.

"Payback," he said. "Now the Facebook world knows you were captured by a four-year-old."

Sophie grinned at them. "What does capture mean?"

"It means we caught up to Cinderella, and you wouldn't let her get away.

"I'm a good capturer!"

"You sure are!"

Monica watched the three of them laughing together and scowled.

"Don't waste your water, Sophia, you need that for drinking to keep you hydrated," Steven admonished.

Sophie climbed off her sister and allowed Scott to help her up. Cinderella brushed the dirt off her pants and tried to flatten down her damp hair with her hands. Then Scott lifted Sophie up onto his shoulders as they walked on to the next exhibit. Monica trailed behind.

Chapter Thirty-Seven

They ended up spending almost the entire day at the zoo. By the time they had seen all the animals, watched all the shows, took a break for lunch, rode on the rides, and done some souvenir shopping, it was late afternoon. Once they piled into the car to leave, the group realized two things. They were exhausted and they were all starving! So Steven took them out for an early dinner.

When they finally arrived home that night, Sophia was sound asleep, her head dangling off Steven's shoulder.

"You two better call it a night," Steven whispered as he walked past with the sleeping girl. "I'm just going to lay Sophie down then I'll be right back." Monica yawned as she walked through the front door after him.

"G'night, Scott," she waved without looking back.

"I think I'm being kicked out," Scott smiled. "Who knew you'd have a curfew of," he looked down at his watch and his eyes widened. "7:30!"

"Is that all?!" Cinderella grabbed his wrist to look for herself. Then she gave him his arm back. "I can't believe it's only 7:30! It feels like 11:00!"

"I know! We have time for a movie, and I'd still be gone before your curfew back home."

Cinderella was about to respond when she was cut off.

"Not tonight," Steven said, reappearing down the stairs. "If you don't mind, Scott, I'd like to spend some one-on-one time with my daughter tonight."

Cinderella bristled. She didn't like the way he was being so domineering.

"Of course," Scott said, nodding. "Good night, Princess." He turned to Cinderella and quickly kissed her on the cheek before backing out the door and disappearing for the night.

"You don't want to get to bed, too?" she asked, stifling a yawn.

"Naw. Besides, I've had to share you with too many other people today. I feel like we still haven't really talked much." Steven waved her into the living room, where she sank onto the nearest couch. "That is, if you're up for it," he added, suddenly very aware of how quiet the house felt.

"I am." Cinderella nodded, then had to cover another yawn. "Sorry, I promise you're not boring."

Steven smiled. "Well that's good to know!"

Cinderella looked down at her hands, waiting for Steven to say something. When he said nothing, she looked up at him again. He was looking all around the room, not making eye contact, while fidgeting with his hands.

"Dad?"

"Yeah?" he finally looked in her eyes, then moved away quickly once again.

"You okay?"

"I just...how long have you and Scott been seeing each other?"

Cinderella could feel her cheeks turning red. *First he was bossing me around, and now he wants to know all the private details about my life?* "What?"

"It's pretty clear you're into each other. How long?"

"We aren't dating. We're just friends."

"Hmmm. Friends with...benefits?"

"Dad!" Cinderella could feel her blood start to boil.

"What? There is definitely something going on between you two."

"Why can't we just be friends?"

"Boys don't look at girls the way he looks at you when they're 'just friends'." Steven used quote marks in the air.

"I didn't realize this was the kind of talk you had in mind tonight. Maybe I will go to bed after all."

"I just want to make sure you're being...careful. Your aunt Mary got pregnant by mistake and..."

Cinderella jumped to her feet. "Number one, don't ever call my cousin Belle a mistake!"

"That's not what I..."

Cinderella cut him off. "And number two, I can't believe you would think that low of me! I'm barely seventeen years old! That's...gross! I do have morals, you know." Cinderella stomped out of the room and grabbed her cell phone as she raced through the front door. She could hear Steven calling after her, but her rage pushed her forward and she didn't look back.

***

Dana could hear her phone ringing, but it was in the bottom of her purse somewhere, and her arms were loaded down with grocery bags as she frantically tried to unlock her front door.

"Hang on!" she kept yelling, even though the person on the other end couldn't hear.

She finally got the door open and dropped the pile of bags at her feet before rummaging for her phone. She grabbed it just as the call went to voicemail. "Of course," she said, plopping down on the sofa. The phone almost immediately started ringing again. This time, she answered it quickly.

"Hello?"

"Hey, it's me."

"What's wrong?"

"Nothing's wrong...well...I just..."

"Steven. Tell me what's wrong."

"I think I ruined it."

He sounded so disheartened, Dana actually felt bad for him. "You ruined what? Is Cinderella okay?"

"Yeah, she's fine. At least...I'm pretty sure she's fine, but she's really mad at me. She stormed out of the house and took off with that kid, and now I don't know when or if she's coming back."

"What?!"

"We sort of got into a fight and she called him to pick her up and I'm afraid she's not coming back here."

"So she's with Scott though?"

"Yeah," Steven sounded annoyed.

"I can't believe you let this happen."

"Look, I know you hate me, but I didn't have to call. As much as it pains me to admit this...I need your help. But if you can't be civil..."

"Fine," she cut him off. Dana let out a breath to calm herself. "If she's with Scott, then she should be fine. I'm sure she just needs to cool down, and then she'll come back. How long has she been gone?"

"Almost an hour! How do you know she'll come back?"

"Did she leave her stuff at your house?"

"Yeah."

"Then she'll be back. A woman never abandons her shoes."

"Wait...are you making a joke?"

Dana grimaced. "Yes, Steven. I'm trying to lighten the mood."

He grunted. "How do you know she and that...boy aren't heading straight for his hotel room?"

"Because I know my daughter."

It was Steven's turn to sigh. "Teenagers are hard. How do you do this?"

"One day at a time. Now tell me what happened."

"Well, I wanted to talk to her about that boy."

"You mean Scott?"

"Yeah..."

"Wait, let me get this straight. You brought up the guy she likes? It's only the second day!"

"I know, I just don't like the way he looks at her."

"What way?"

"Like he..." Steven couldn't bring himself to say the word. "Like he really likes her."

"You mean loves her?" Dana smiled as she imagined Steven squirming. These feelings were all too familiar. It was kind of fun having someone else to go through it with.

"No!"

"He loves her, you know."

"Don't say that!"

"Why do you think I sent him with her to visit you?"

"Because you're sick."

Dana laughed out loud this time. "I know it's hard to deal with, trust me! But Scott is in love with our daughter."

Steven groaned.

"As much as I don't like him, or any boy for that matter, I know he's trustworthy. I sent him along because I didn't know how things would go with you and I knew he would keep her safe."

"So do we hate this kid?"

"Unfortunately, no. It would be a lot easier if we did! You're free to hate him. I've tried, but he's just too darn...likeable."

"I've noticed," Steven said, sounding defeated. "So we don't hate the guy who is after our seventeen year old?"

"Sorry, but no. He treats her very well, and respects her. I can't help but respect him in return."

"I can't believe you're okay with all this. The Dana I knew would have thrown the kid out on his butt for even looking at her daughter."

"Trust me, I tried! But the dumb kid kept coming right back! And he kind of made me like him in the process. The little punk."

This time Steven had to smile.

"But don't you dare let him know I like him! Do you hear me?"

"Loud and clear. So he's not...taking advantage of her in any way?" Steven asked.

"Absolutely not! He would not still be around if anything like that was going on!" Dana closed her eyes, trying to push those thoughts from her mind. Then something clicked. "Wait, is that what you approached Cinderella about tonight?"

"I just wanted to make sure."

"Oh, Steven."

"Well, she's my daughter!"

"Yeah, you were right."

"About what?"

"You ruined it."

"How do I fix this?"

"Start with chocolate chip pancakes for breakfast. They're her favorite. Then pray she'll at least acknowledge your existence by the end of the day."

"That's it? That's your advice?"

"No, my advice would have been don't bring up Scott with Cinderella. But unfortunately you called about an hour too late."

"Great..." Steven mumbled. Dana started to speak again when she was quickly shushed. "Shhhh, I think she's home."

"You do realize she can't hear me right?"

But Steven ignored her. He sat up straighter on the couch, his ears perked as the front door slowly opened. Cinderella appeared around the corner, stopping dead at the sight of her father.

"I thought you'd be asleep."

"I was waiting up for you. Please don't ever take off like that again, you scared me to death!"

"Gee, I'm sorry. Did I make you feel uncomfortable?" With that, Cinderella turned and walked from the room.

Steven could hear his phone laughing as he returned it to his ear. "Wow, sounds like you really ticked her off!"

"I'm glad you're enjoying this so much," he said through gritted teeth.

"I'm sorry, it's just funny to hear someone else on the receiving end for once." Then Dana's voice softened. "Look, Cinderella is a very good kid. She has a huge crush on Scott, but he won't date her while she's still in high school."

"So he really is a good guy?"

"Yes."

"Dang it."

"I know. But you need to understand, not only did you bring up a sore spot, but then you questioned her morality."

"So I...?"

"Need to apologize."

Steven let out a huge sigh. "I keep thinking this parenting thing will get easier at some point. Does it?"

"With girls? No."

"That's what I was afraid of."

Chapter Thirty-Eight

"Come in, come in!"

Ariel and Aurora stepped into their grandma's living room and looked around. The scene was familiar this time and it brought back a flood of memories from that first night. Eddy raced into the room and by jumping on top of the couch, was able to lunge at them for attention. Ariel thankfully caught him mid-jump or the poor puppy would have gone right over the edge and smashed to the ground.

"Eddy missed you two," Grandma B. said with a smile. "Have a seat," she motioned toward the couches.

The girls stepped further into the house and sat down. They hadn't seen their grandma in over six months, but they had talked to her on the phone plenty of times since their first meeting.

"So how are you? Is it nice to have a break from school?"

Ariel nodded enthusiastically and Aurora let out a huge breath. "For sure!"

"How much longer?"

"The last day of school is the first week in June. The...third, I think?" Ariel looked to Aurora for confirmation, but Aurora just shrugged her shoulders.

"So are you girls going to prom? That's coming up after the break, right?"

Aurora's face lit up at the mention of the dance. "I'm nominated for royalty!" she exclaimed, her face glowing with pride.

"Wow! That's fantastic, sweetie! So do you have a date then?"

"Not for sure yet, but I've been flirting with three guys in particular. I expect to get an offer soon."

Grandma B. laughed. "Three? Wow!"

"Well, you have to keep your bases covered. I've hinted to them all that I don't have a date yet. We'll just have to wait and see which one takes the bait first."

"And what about you?" she asked, turning to Ariel.

"I'm not expecting to get any offers. I haven't had much luck with guys this year."

"It's because you don't put yourself out there enough," Aurora commented.

"Thank you, Mom, but I'm okay with not going. Snow and I have already talked about having a movie marathon night, and I'm totally okay with that."

Aurora rolled her eyes. "But don't you want to be there to see your only sister get crowned?"

"I do, but I just don't see it happening, I'm sorry."

Aurora folded her arms across her chest and began to pout.

"Uh-oh, did I start something here?"

"No, Grandma B., it's okay. She just wants me to find a date so I can be there. But I don't want to ask a guy to prom. I think that would be tacky."

"Well I agree with you on that one. Call me old fashioned, but I think the guy needs to be the pursuer."

"Thank you!" Ariel looked meaningfully at Aurora.

"Fine, fine, fine. I'll have Belle record it on her phone and you can watch the video later," Aurora said. "But it would be more exciting to see it live," she mumbled.

Ariel pretended not to hear her sister. "So, Grandma B., what have you been up to?"

"Oh, this and that. Nothing too exciting in my life."

"Where do you work again?" Aurora asked.

"I work as a secretary—excuse me, an administrative assistant for an engineering company in Salt Lake. I work for a group of a dozen or so engineers, taking notes, keeping track of things, filing, etc. It's basically glorified babysitting is what it is," she said with a smile.

The girls both returned her smile. It was nice visiting with Grandma B. Even though they still hardly knew her, she had a very easy way about her that made the girls immediately feel at home. It was still hard to believe this sweet woman was the one who raised the horrifying man they had met at the prison less than a year ago.

"So tell me more about this dance camp you are participating in this summer."

"It's super cool!" Aurora started.

"Yeah," Ariel added. "It's kind of like one of those reality dance shows on TV."

"Dance shows?" Grandma B. asked.

"Yeah haven't you ever heard of..." Aurora trailed off and her jaw dropped. She hadn't noticed it before, but as she looked around the small room she realized for the first time that there wasn't a television anywhere to be seen.

"Don't you have TV?" Ariel asked, equally shocked.

"I just don't see much use for it."

The girls froze momentarily, not sure of how to proceed. But Ariel decided to just continue the conversation as if she did have one.

"It's only, like, one of the best shows on television!" Ariel exclaimed. "Basically dancers from all over the country try out for a panel of judges. Then the judges pick the top 20 dancers and from there they have to perform different types of dance each week and America votes for their favorite one."

"Oh, sounds interesting. People at work are always talking about a singing show like that. Oh what's it called?"

"There are lots, but this show is for dancers," Aurora replied.

"So you girls are going to be on TV?"

"No, no, no, we're just participating in a camp this summer. The camp has a bunch of different guest teachers, who teach different genres of dance. So we get to focus on and learn a new style of dance every week for ten weeks."

"This is going to make me sound so ignorant, but what do you mean by different styles of dance?"

"You know, like ballet, jazz, hip-hop, contemporary, ballroom," Aurora counted them off on her fingers.

"Salsa, swing, western-swing, break-dancing, animation," Ariel added to the list.

Grandma B. looked confused. "I've heard of two of those," she chuckled. "So what is animation?"

Ariel got to her feet and tried to do her best impression of a robot. Aurora pulled out her phone and turned some music on to join her. Neither was very good at localizing their bodies to animate properly, but since Grandma B. didn't have anything else to compare it to, she didn't comment.

Then the older woman surprised them both by getting on her feet and moon-walking the length of the room.

"Go Grandma!" Ariel exclaimed.

They both clapped for her, as she did a turn and came back the other way. The girls both laughed as Grandma B. fell back into her seat.

"Phew! I am too out of shape for that!"

"Here, let me show you some good animation," Ariel said, pulling out her phone and searching the internet.

"What's this?" Grandma B. asked, coming around to the side of the couch and looking over her shoulder.

"Please don't tell me you don't know what YouTube is," Aurora stated.

"Oh, I've heard of it! The guys at work talk about funny things from here all the time."

The girls exchanged a surprised look. "We have some serious educating to do," Ariel said.

All three of them were crammed onto a tiny couch, staring at Ariel's small phone screen. Then Ariel and Aurora took turns showing their grandma video after video for the remainder of the afternoon.

Chapter Thirty-Nine

The next morning at breakfast, Cinderella would not even make eye contact with her father. She felt both angry and embarrassed by their unexpected conversation. Monica seemed to notice the change in their behavior, and kept looking between the two of them, searching for clues. But Sophia remained in her own world of oblivion and happily chatted endlessly while they filled up on pancakes.

"I'm going to head back upstairs," Cinderella said, after eating as quickly as possible.

"Cinderella, wait!" Steven said, standing. "Can we go in the other room and talk please?"

"Fine." Cinderella headed toward the family room without looking back.

"Wait! I wasn't done talking yet!" Sophie cried after them.

"We'll be right back, Baby, I promise. Why don't you tell Monica about it until then, okay?"

Sophie smiled and turned to her sister.

"Great," Monica mumbled, but pretended to be interested anyway.

Cinderella stormed into the room and sat on the far corner of the couch furthest away from her father. "What do you want to accuse me of now?"

Steven put his hands up in surrender. "I want to apologize."

Cinderella's ears perked, but she pretended to look at a parenting magazine beside her.

"I am so sorry, sweetie! I should have known better than to question your relationship with Scott. I'm not trying to excuse my behavior, but you have to understand, I'm scared to death of losing you!"

Cinderella put the magazine down and looked at him.

"I just barely found you, and after seeing the way you and Scott were together yesterday and seeing the way he looks at you, well, I freaked. I didn't want to find you, only to have you taken away by some guy. Does that make any sense?"

"Yeah, I guess. But Scott and I aren't even dating! We like each other, but we're just friends."

"I know that now, and I'm sorry."

"Okay."

"So are we okay?" Steven earnestly looked scared to hear her response.

"Yes," Cinderella smiled. "We're okay." She walked across the room and gave her dad a hug.

"Please talk to me next time before leaving. I'm responsible for you while you're here. I would hate to lose your mom's trust and have her not let you come back."

DING-DONG!

"Was that your doorbell?"

Steven looked confused. "Yeah, it was. But who would be here at 8:00 in the morning?"

Cinderella and Steven got to the front door just in time as Sophie threw it open. "Uncle Lucas!" she screamed.

Cinderella's jaw dropped as the little girl wrapped herself around the movie star's legs. There was Lucas Ferreira standing on the front porch, dressed in black leather and looking hotter than ever.

He'd clearly ridden his motorcycle to the house. His hair was smashed down from the sleek black helmet he carried under one arm. Lucas set his helmet down on the entryway table before scooping up the bouncing four-year-old, making her giggle.

"Hey Cinderella," he said, setting Sophie down. "It's good to see you again. Nice p.j.'s." He smiled.

Cinderella looked down. She had completely forgotten she was still in her pajamas with mussed hair. How embarrassing! "But how do you..? What are you..?" Cinderella couldn't find the right words.

Steven reached out and warmly shook Lucas' hand. "What are you doing here? It's been awhile!"

"I know, sorry it's taken me so long to get out this way again. Life has been busy. For you too, I see," Lucas added, nodding toward Cinderella.

"Yeah," Steven smiled. "So it looks like you two have met."

"We did," Lucas nodded. "On my trip to Utah."

Cinderella still stared blankly at the two men.

"What can I do for you?" Steven asked. "Here, why don't we all go in the living room and sit down."

"Hi, Lucas!" Monica suddenly entered the room with a bright smile on her face. She had somehow managed to dress, pull her hair up, and even add a small touch of makeup before making her appearance.

"Hey kiddo!" Lucas put an arm around Monica and pulled her in for a hug. He kept his arm draped over her shoulder as they followed everyone else into the living room.

"I'm sorry, but how do you two know each other?" Cinderella finally managed to find her voice.

"Well, we used to spend a lot of time together back when your mom and I were still together, and when Mary and Lucas were dating."

"Yeah, we'd double date all the time," Lucas nodded. "We thought we were going to be brothers-in-law one day."

"After everything happened and we both split up, well, we had become really good friends and we just stayed in touch."

Cinderella put her head in her hands. This was just too much to take.

"Is something wrong?" Steven asked.

Cinderella shook her head. "It's just so weird to think about. All these years we were all living together in Utah, and you guys were together here. But we didn't know about each other."

"It is crazy how everything happened. Lucas and I even roomed together for a little while after the divorce."

"So did you guys hang out with Daniel, the twins' dad too?"

Lucas and Steven both shifted uncomfortably. "Daniel...didn't really like doing things with other people. He was super...protective."

"Controlling," Lucas murmured.

"Of your Aunt Rachel."

Cinderella nodded. She got to her feet and walked around the room. It just seemed too weird that her dad and Belle's dad were best friends.

"I'm sorry, we've gotten off subject a bit."

"So what brings you out this way?" Steven asked, turning to Lucas.

"I need your help, man."

"Anything. What's wrong?"

Lucas shifted uncomfortably, looking at the girls.

Steven got the hint. "Why don't you girls head upstairs and get ready for the day?"

"I'm already ready," Monica smirked.

"Then help your little sister," Steven said. "Now." His tone was firm and left no room for argument.

Monica begrudgingly waved goodbye to Lucas and helped guide Sophia from the room. Cinderella followed them slowly, trying to catch a snippet of the conversation. But Lucas waited until the girls were all completely out of sight, with the door shut before he began talking again.

Their voices were too muffled to be heard through the door, as Cinderella quickly found out while attempting to push her ear against it. She started to walk upstairs when she heard her name called.

"Cinderella?"

"Yeah?" She cupped her hand over her mouth, trying to sound further away from the door.

"Why don't you stop eavesdropping and come back in."

Cinderella's face turned red and although she wanted to run upstairs and hide, her curiosity won. She slowly pushed the French doors open and then quietly shut them behind herself.

"I could actually use your opinion too," Lucas said. "We mostly wanted the young girls out of the room, but since you already know Belle and the entire situation, there really isn't a point in kicking you out."

Cinderella took a seat beside her dad on the couch and waited for Lucas to explain.

Lucas took a deep breath and began. "I'm sure you know that Belle won't talk to me. And I'm sure you know what went down at school and *why* she won't talk to me."

Cinderella nodded. Oh boy, did she! Every time Lucas was brought up, it resulted in Belle going off on one of her rants and Cinderella, unfortunately, was forced to listen to the details of that fateful day over and over again.

Lucas turned back to Steven and continued. "Belle has not spoken to me since that day. Every time I try and get her on the phone, she just hangs up on me. She won't give me even a second to explain myself. But that's beside the point. I can't lose her! When Mary left with Belle, it killed me inside! I know I've made a lot of mistakes. A lot. And I know I don't even deserve to have them in my life. But this is one area where I want to be selfish. I want my family back, but I don't know what to do!"

Lucas got to his feet and began pacing the room. He ran his hands through his hair so many times, it was sticking up in every direction. "Mary was supposed to come up and spend this Spring Break with me. We both hoped that Belle would come with her and finally agree to see me again. Well, she didn't. Mary called me up in tears and told me we needed to stop seeing each other. She couldn't handle being caught in the middle between me and Belle."

Lucas fell back into the large armchair in the corner, where he had been sitting. He slammed his fist into the soft leather armrest. "I...I don't know what to do anymore! What hurt even more than Mary breaking up with me was listening to her cry while she did it. If she wanted a clean break from me, as much as I would hate it, I would let her go. I can't force a woman to love me. But she was sobbing, Steven. She could barely even get the words out. I know she loves me! Only God knows why, but she loves me, dang it! I can't let her and Belle disappear from my life again. I won't!"

Lucas seemed to sink even deeper into the chair as he put his face in his hands. His shoulders began to shake.

Cinderella didn't know what to do. She wasn't comfortable enough with Lucas to hug him, but patting a grown man on the back and telling him everything would be okay seemed a little silly, too. Maybe she should have just gone upstairs and gotten dressed with her sisters.

Steven crossed the room in two long strides and stood firmly beside Lucas' chair. He placed a hand on Lucas' shoulder and continued to stand there, without uttering a word. Once Lucas regained his composure, he patted Steven's hand, and then Steven silently returned to the couch. Cinderella watched the whole interaction in awe. These men definitely knew each other well. They obviously knew how to communicate and how to gauge and react to the other without words.

"I agree, you can't let them go," Steven spoke softly. "I think you need to go back to Utah and, I don't know, stand on their porch until one or both of them will talk to you. They can't stay inside forever."

"Do something big." It was the first time Cinderella had opened her mouth since coming into the conversation, and both men turned to her, surprised. It was almost as if they had forgotten she was even there.

"What do you mean?" Lucas asked.

"Belle is stubborn, ridiculously so. But she also loves to be the center of attention. The reason she had such a hard time with you being there is suddenly she wasn't the main focus anymore. She will never admit it, because she's never wrong either, but the biggest reason she was so mad about you interrupting class was not because she felt like you didn't really care. You stole her limelight."

Lucas nodded. "That makes much more sense to me. Belle is definitely a lot like her mom." He smiled at the thought of Mary and the number of times they'd gotten in a fight. Every single time he would back down long before she would. Lucas would get tired but Mary was super stubborn and wouldn't back down for anything.

"If you do something that draws attention to her, not you, it would definitely get you closer to winning her over. I don't think Belle actually dislikes you at all. But backing down now would admit to being wrong. And she won't do that."

Lucas jumped up and came towards Cinderella. He completely caught her off guard and before she realized what was happening, he'd pulled her to her feet in a tight hug. "Thank you! I have to go see them. I'll leave now."

It was definitely awkward, especially when Cinderella realized very quickly that she was still in her pajamas and wasn't wearing a bra.

"Don't just rush out to Utah without a plan," Steven said. "You need to be organized. You need to know what you're going to say, and what you're going to do. Otherwise, you'll just end up right back here on my couch, in tears."

"Tears?" Lucas tried to scoff, but after his display moments earlier, he knew denying it wouldn't do any good. He took a deep breath and stretched his arms. "What on earth am I going to do?"

Cinderella and Steven followed him back to the front door.

"You just got here! Don't you want to stay for a little while and rest? It had to have taken you a couple hours to get here."

"No, thank you though. I'm actually in the area today for a promo and should probably get back. Besides, I have too much planning to do." Lucas grabbed his helmet off the table and used it to smash down his muddled hair. He then gave them each a quick hug again and thanked them for their help.

"Remember," Cinderella called after him, "think big!"

Lucas gave her a thumbs up. Then he hopped on his bike and drove away.

Chapter Forty

Scott came walking up the steps just as Lucas left.

"Was that..?" he asked, pointing his thumb over his shoulder.

"Lucas Ferreira, yeah."

"Wow, I can't believe I missed him! What was he doing here?"

"Long story," Cinderella said. Scott grinned at her and for the second embarrassing time, Cinderella realized she still needed to put on a bra. "Be right back!" she yelled, dashing up the stairs two at a time.

"How are you, Scott?" Steven asked, patting his back.

"Uh, pretty good," Scott said. He wasn't sure how to react to this sudden interest.

"I just wanted to say thank you for taking care of Cinderella last night." He didn't make eye contact with Scott as he spoke. Both men seemed fascinated with something on the ground instead, as they spoke.

Scott nodded. "Of course." He wasn't sure how Steven was going to react to him today. Part of him had feared Steven would tell him to leave.

"Today is Monica's turn to pick where we take Cinderella, and she chose a basketball game. Do you like basketball? We'd love to have you join us."

Scott smiled. "I'd love to. Thanks for inviting me." *Basketball? I can't wait to see Cinderella experience that!* He tried not to let his eagerness show, but Steven noticed.

"Something funny?" he asked.

"Oh, nothing, sir," Scott replied. *Basketball?!* He chuckled this time and when Steven gave him a questioning look, Scott tried to hide it behind a coughing fit.

***

Cinderella covered her ears for what felt like the hundredth time. Basketball stadiums were loud! After a somewhat quiet day of walking around and window shopping at the mall, nothing could have prepared Cinderella for the night that awaited her.

"I can't believe you've never been to a basketball game before!" Monica yelled over the screaming fans.

"My mom really isn't into sports," Cinderella shrugged.

She looked down the row at her family and Scott. They were all decked out, head to toe in Kings gear. Monica had even pulled out some makeup before they left the car and painted little purple crowns on each of their cheeks. Cinderella was mostly surprised when Scott joined in as well, and bought a Kings shirt at the mall. She knew he liked basketball, but she'd never watched it with him before. Only fifteen minutes into the game and Cinderella had already seen a whole new side to Scott she'd never seen before.

"Is this what sports do to guys?" she asked Monica, pointing at her dad and Scott who were both on their feet, yelling at the team below.

Monica laughed. "Yeah, usually." Then she looked a little hurt. "Do you not like this? Aren't you having fun?"

Cinderella quickly remembered it was Monica who had chosen their destination and she tried to recover her words. "No! I mean, yes, I am having fun! This is just all very new to me. I've never been to a basketball game, or any kind of sports game for that matter. I just didn't know what to expect."

"Well, I don't get as crazy as my dad, or Sophie." Both girls looked over at the four year old, who was standing on her seat and yelling at the top of her lungs, "Come on ref! That was traveling! If you aren't going to make the calls, then just go home!" They looked at each other and burst out laughing.

"I guess that's what happens when you're raised by a dad," Monica said.

"And what about you? What made you choose this for our activity tonight?"

"I don't yell like my family does, but it really can be fun and exciting to watch. And it's tradition." Monica shrugged. "We used to have season tickets and come with my mom all the time." Monica looked down at her hands.

Cinderella put an arm around her little sister and hugged her. "I feel honored that you would bring me to a place that's so special to your family."

"You're our family now, too, I guess."

"Well, maybe you can teach me what's going on. I'd ask Scott, but somehow I think that might be dangerous right about now."

Monica beamed. She seemed to come to life as she began describing the players and the rules of the game.

***

The rest of the week seemed to go by in a blur. Before Cinderella knew it, Scott was loading up his car and it was time to say their good byes.

Sophia stood on the porch sobbing. She grabbed Cinderella's hand, and kept trying to pull her back inside the house. "You can't leave me!" she choked out amidst huge, salty tears. It took every ounce of control for

Cinderella not to start bawling right along with her. Sometimes she wished she could be like a four-year-old again, and just wear her emotions on her sleeve. If Sophia's over-dramatic demonstration wasn't so comical, she knew she'd have a hard time keeping her own tears in check.

Monica stood stoically, leaning against the front door with her arms folded across her chest. Cinderella guessed she was wearing her sunglasses to hide her own red, puffy eyes. But she knew better than to accuse her of such. Instead, she gave her sister a warm hug and told her to text as often as she wanted. Monica simply waved and made an excuse to get back inside the house.

Cinderella reached forward to hug Steven good bye, but suddenly Sophie was between them declaring, "Sophie sandwich!" They hugged tight, making the little girl squeal as she became smashed between them.

Scott could sense a need to intervene. He began chasing Sophie around on the grass so Cinderella could have a private moment to say good bye to her dad. They hugged tight, both afraid to let go first. Neither knew when they would be seeing each other again.

"Please visit this summer?" Steven asked, his eyes pleading.

"I'll talk to Mom and see what we can work out."

"I love you, sweetie! I'm so glad you reached out and found me!"

Cinderella nodded. She couldn't control the floodgates much longer. "I love you too, Dad!"

After shaking Steven's hand and hugging Sophie tight, Scott put an arm around Cinderella and slowly guided her toward the car. Her feet felt like lead, she could barely get them to move forward. Her head spun as she looked back one last time at her new family. She waved, trying to be brave, but as soon as she sat back in her seat, she finally lost all control. She looked back in the side mirror and watched helplessly as Sophie tried to chase after them. Steven caught up to her about halfway down the street and carried her back to the house, kicking and screaming.

Cinderella knew she was doing the ugly cry now, but she didn't even care. Her body shook with sobs as the feelings of despair and loss washed over her.

After a long period of silence in the car, Scott reached over and took her hand. "Are you okay?" he asked.

"I just miss them so much already!"

"I know," he whispered. "Your family is pretty great."

Cinderella leaned against his arm and continued to weep until she didn't have tears left. Her body felt completely exhausted. She tried stretching out in the cramped seat.

"You tired?"

"Yeah, my dad and I stayed up really late talking last night." She sniffed.

"Oh yeah? What did you talk about?" Scott was trying to be super sweet by distracting her, but the images of them laughing late into the night sprung tears to Cinderella's eyes all over again.

"Everything." Cinderella yawned. Between the lack of sleep and the intense amount of emotions, Cinderella was suddenly drained of all energy.

"Why don't you lay your chair back and get some rest?"

Cinderella gave his hand a squeeze before lowering the chair and closing her eyes. Maybe sleep would make her aching heart stop hurting, at least for a little while.

Chapter Forty-One

Getting back to reality was hard. Cinderella slept most of the drive home, since she had stayed up the entire night before talking to her dad. She felt bad Scott had practically driven home by himself. But, in Scott fashion, he said he understood. Sometimes Cinderella wondered if he really was a prince who just threw on a pair of jeans one day to blend in with the commoners.

Unfortunately, he didn't have a lot of time to talk when he dropped her off. He helped carry her bags inside, and then she found herself saying good bye yet again. He wrapped his arms around her, pulling her in close.

"Thanks for a great trip!"

"Thank you for being my bodyguard," she managed a smile.

"Princess, if I could be your bodyguard as a fulltime job, I'd be livin' the dream." He winked and turned to walk away.

"Hey, you still owe me an album," she yelled after him.

"What?"

"We never did find a country swing club."

Scott nodded his head, remembering. "You're right. I'll bring it with me next time I come down to visit."

"You better not take too long, or I might charge interest."

Scott laughed. "I'll be back soon then. It's a date."

He beeped his horn twice and waved before pulling out onto the road to return to school.

***

Monday morning came far too early, and far too soon for Cinderella. Walking through the halls, she felt like a sleep-deprived zombie. Suddenly being home and back in school again with her cousins made the California trip feel like a dream. As Cinderella stumbled towards her locker, she saw a crowd of people. *Now what?* Then as she got even closer, she saw the crowd was not just near her locker, but looking directly at it.

The outside of her locker was covered with a neon blue poster board that said "It would be purrrfect if you went to the dance with Me-ow." The poster was covered with cut-out magazine pictures of cats.

"What the heck?"

The crowd closed in as Cinderella went to open her locker. She had no idea what to expect, but something told her to open it slowly. She was glad she did! As soon as the locker was open enough to see inside, dozens of cat stuffed animals spilled out onto the ground. Several people laughed, some cheered, and then the crowd began to move away, their curiosity satisfied.

Cinderella noticed each of the cats was wearing a tiny little collar. When she picked one up to examine it closer, she began laughing.

"What's so funny?" Ariel asked, peering around Cinderella's shoulder.

She pointed out that the name "Brian" was written on all the little tags hanging from the cat collars.

"What's with all the cats?" Belle asked.

"And who is Brian?" Aurora inquired, eyebrows raised.

"Brian, he's in my English class. We worked on a project together at the beginning of the year. I can't believe he remembered," she said, smiling.

Cinderella's cousins all looked at her quizzically.

"I made a joke once about growing up and being a crazy cat lady one day. I guess he's just trying to help me get there." She picked up handfuls of the stuffed kitties and crammed them back into her locker. "I'll have to clean these up later, I'm going to be late."

"That's really cute," Snow White cooed. She bent down and helped Cinderella gather the rest of the cats. Their cousins followed suit.

"I think it's kinda weird," Belle added. "When Craig asked me to prom, he used flowers and chocolates."

"Yeah, but you guys are already dating," Ariel pointed out.

"You know this means he likes you, right?" Aurora said, looking smug.

"What?" Cinderella asked. She carefully closed her locker again and turned to face her.

"Oh please! Let's examine the facts here. First, he remembered an inside joke between the two of you from months ago. Then he obviously spent a decent chunk of change to purchase all these cats and individually write his name on each one. Then," she said, pausing for effect, "he found out where your locker was and figured out a way to get inside. He put a ton of time and effort into asking you out. Looks like Prince Charming has got himself some competition!"

Cinderella rolled her eyes and pushed past Aurora to get to class. "We're just good friends," she said over her shoulder.

"Yeah, isn't that what you tell people about Scott, too?" Cinderella didn't answer. Aurora was right and she didn't know what to say, so she just kept walking. Cinderella's ears turned pink as she could hear Aurora laughing behind her the rest of the way down the hall.

After school, Cinderella, Belle, and Aurora went dress shopping for prom. Aurora ended up getting asked by two different guys during the day and still had not decided which one she was going to say yes to. One of them asked her by leaving a giant teddy bear at her desk in second period. The bear wore a sign that read: "I would be beary excited if you went to prom with me." She found the name Ryan Jenkins slipped under the big red ribbon that was tied around the bear's neck. Then she was asked again during lunch. When she went through the line and ordered food, the cafeteria lady handed her a huge bowl full of fortune cookies, instead. It read: "I would be very fortunate if you went with me to prom." She had to crack open all 114 cookies to find the name Ethan Spelling written on the back of one of the fortunes.

Aurora tried convincing Ariel to take one of her dates so she could attend, but Ariel wasn't terribly thrilled with the idea of dyeing her hair red and pretending to be her sister all night. Aurora accepted that response, but wouldn't take no for an answer when it came time to head over to the mall.

"You have to come with us!"

"Why? I'm not even going to the stupid dance."

"Because I need your opinion!"

"You'll have Belle and Cinderella with you."

"But I want you to come! Pleeeease!" she begged. "Come on, you won't even be there to see if I become royalty. The least you can do is help me look as stunning as possible."

Ariel rolled her eyes, but the guilt trip finally worked and she reluctantly agreed to tag along. Snow White flat out refused, and could not be swayed. So the four of them walked into the first dress shop and began looking around.

"What about this one?" Ariel asked, trying to keep a straight face. She held up a dress that was not only about five sizes too large, but she couldn't even name the color. It wasn't quite brown, it wasn't quite red, but it was lost somewhere in between the two.

Aurora immediately pulled a face and then ripped the dress from her sister's fingers and slammed it back on the rack.

"Can you just be serious for once in your life?"

Ariel sighed. "Oh come on, that takes all the fun out of it."

Aurora turned and stomped away from her.

"Okay, okay, okay!" Ariel chased her down. "I'll be helpful, I promise."

Aurora gave her another glowering look, but it quickly faded into a smile as she began considering the elegant gowns before her.

"So who are you leaning towards?"

"What?"

"Well there has to be one boy you'd rather go with over the other."

"Oh. I was going to pick my dress first, and then decide by which guy matches my dress the best."

Ariel had to turn back to the racks quickly, using the gowns to hide her laughter. She began scanning the dresses again, pulling out ones she thought Aurora might like. She had to quickly occupy her mind before she said something she might later regret.

"Have you guys found anything yet?" Cinderella called across the small shop.

"Nothing that really jumps out at me," Aurora said.

Belle walked over, shaking her head. "I think I'm ready for another store."

"Me, too."

Two stores and three hours later, the girls had finally each picked out a dress and were ready to go home.

"Definitely Ethan," Aurora nodded, holding up her newly purchased evening gown. It was a strapless, sweetheart neckline with rhinestones covering the entire bodice, making it sparkle. The dress was a soft red, which accentuated her hair very nicely. It was floor length, with just a little bit of a train in the back. It was a very elegant choice, and made Aurora look absolutely stunning.

Belle picked a dress that was a lot sassier, fitting with her personality perfectly. It was a baby pink hi-low dress, that started at her knees in front, but hung much lower in the back. The top was spaghetti straps with a straight neckline covered in sparkly beading. There was a small, pink bow at the waist, and the entire skirt was covered in ruffles.

Cinderella went the simple route, with a form-fitting slender gown in turquoise. It had capped sleeves and a little bit of scattered beadwork. There was one gather on her left hip, which gave the dress a little bit of flare, but it was a much simpler gown in comparison with the other two.

Chapter Forty-Two

Right after school, Snow White went over to the library while her cousins headed to the mall. She had no desire to listen to them all gush about the upcoming dance, when she had no chance of going. She claimed she didn't care and it wasn't a big deal, but the truth was she didn't want to get emotional and cry in front of them. The outing would have turned into everyone pitying her instead of just having fun and being able to get excited about the dance. She removed herself from the equation and tried desperately to focus on homework instead.

Snow White also didn't want to go straight home because she knew her mom was there and she didn't want to answer a million questions about where her cousins were and why she wasn't with them. After staring at the computer screen for twenty minutes and getting nothing done, she decided to play solitaire instead.

"Who's winning?"

Snow White jumped. Her eyes had been so focused on the cards, she didn't even hear Dave come up behind her.

"Sorry," he laughed. "I didn't realize you were so focused."

Snow White turned and laughed with him. They got shushed by the librarian sitting nearby so she lowered her voice. "I was just completely zoned out."

"So where's your whole crew?"

Great. I don't go home to avoid these questions and here they are, coming from him of all people. "They're out dress shopping for prom." Snow White turned back around and began clicking cards again.

"Then why aren't you with them?"

"Are you kidding me? Do I look like the type of girl who gets asked to prom?"

"This feels like a trap."

Snow White smiled. She hated that after everything they'd been through together, he still made her face flush and her pulse quicken. "It's okay. I know I'm not tall, I know I'm not skinny, and I'm definitely not outgoing like the other girls are. Guys just don't notice me." Snow White sniffled, but quickly tried to cover it up by coughing.

"Hey," Dave said, placing a hand on her shoulder. "Do you want to go for a walk with me? It's stuffy and quiet in here, but I bet it's really nice outside. Let's go see."

Snow White picked up her purse and followed after him. They walked around the library twice, in silence, before settling under a large oak tree.

"So who are you taking to prom?" Snow White asked.

Dave shrugged. "I dunno yet."

"Oh, come on!"

"No, really. I haven't asked anyone yet."

"But you're nominated for prom king. Doesn't that mean you have to go?"

"Yeah, I guess. The problem is the only person I actually want to go with already has a date. And even if she didn't, I don't think she would go with me."

"Belle." She didn't have to wait for his reply to know she was right.

Dave rolled onto his back, resting his head against his folded arms. He didn't respond to her, but the way he avoided eye contact told Snow White she had guessed correctly. Then he suddenly sat up so fast, he caused Snow White to jump again. "I have an idea!"

"Oh yeah?"

"Why don't you go to prom with me?"

"What?" Snow White's face flushed crimson.

"I'm serious. You want to go, I have to go, why not go together?"

"I never said I wanted to go..."

"Oh please. Every girl wants to go to her junior prom."

Snow White couldn't think of a comeback. Her face still felt abnormally hot and her heart was racing. The truth was she did want to go. She really wanted to go! And she didn't even care who she went with, she just wanted the experience of going. Snow White smiled at him.

"Is that a yes?"

"Belle might kill me."

"That sounds like a yes."

"Sure, I guess."

"Great!" Dave clapped his hands together and then laid back down.

He seemed to ponder for a moment before opening his mouth again. "So we're friends, right Snow?"

"Uh-oh, that sounds like a loaded question."

"Actually, I was wondering if you would help me out with something that night. And I promise, this is not why I asked you! I've just been racking my brain, trying to figure out a way to get her back."

"She has a boyfriend, you know."

"I know, and I even like Craig. I just want to be part of her life again, even if it's just as friends! But right now, she won't even acknowledge me, at least not in public." Dave thought back to the few times Belle had needed rescuing this past year, and how he had been her shoulder to cry on for a few brief moments.

"She doesn't let go of things easily."

"I know. But I gotta at least try, right?"

"So what's the plan?"

Dave explained his idea to Snow White and then waited for her response.

"It could work..."

"Yeah?" His voice sounded hopeful.

"Or it could backfire horribly."

"I know I'm taking a chance, but it's kinda my last shot."

"Alright, I'll help you."

Dave threw his arms around her, catching Snow White off guard. Her heart skipped a beat again. It wasn't even that she liked him or anything, but having Dave, or any guy for that matter, this close to her always caused the same reaction.

When Snow White returned home a few minutes later, she couldn't keep the smile off her face. She was so glad now that she had decided not to go to the mall with her cousins! Completely lost in her own thoughts about the dance, she skipped right past the unfamiliar car parked in front of her house.

Snow White almost burst through the door, ready to tell her mom the good news, when she heard yelling from inside. Snow White froze, her hand on the doorknob, and listened.

"But I don't understand why you won't!"

"I have my reasons, and none of them are your business!" Snow White was shocked to hear her mom's voice. She had never heard her yell like that before.

"Please, Ms. Princess! I really didn't come here to upset you, but we need your help! You're the only one who can…"

"I don't want to hear anymore," she said, cutting him off. "I said no. Now I'd like you to leave, and please don't ever contact me again!"

The doorknob was ripped out of Snow White's hand as the stranger yanked from the other side. Snow White didn't have time to react. She stood frozen in the doorway, face-to-face with a young looking man who was dressed in a nice business suit.

He looked equally surprised to see someone standing in front of him. Then as he looked at Snow White, from her flaming red hair down to her blue sneakers, the anger on his face softened. He glanced back at Elizabeth, who was standing in the family room with her arms folded, and gave her a knowing look. Then he shook his head, and walked past Snow White and out onto the sidewalk.

"Who was that?" Snow White asked, closing the door behind him.

Elizabeth was visibly shaking with fury. "What are you doing here?! You're supposed to be out with your cousins!"

"I just…"

"He's nobody! I want you to forget you ever saw him, and don't you dare ever talk about him again!"

Elizabeth stormed up the stairs, leaving Snow White completely speechless.

Chapter Forty-Three

"You traitor!" Ariel pretended to be upset, but she had a huge smile on her face. "We were supposed to spend prom night together, eating chocolate and watching chick flicks!"

Snow White shrugged. "I'm sorry! Do you want me to tell him no?"

"Of course not!" Ariel said. "But you should have come with us. Now we're going to have to go shopping all over again." She groaned.

"Yay!" Aurora clapped her hands together and bounced with excitement.

"Oh, I saw a dress today that would look perfect on you!" Cinderella added.

Snow White was glowing with excitement. She was afraid her cousins would be upset that she was going to a dance with Dave, aka the enemy. But they all seemed genuinely excited that she would be joining them that night. Belle remained tight-lipped and unusually quiet while the others gushed over Snow White, but at least she didn't yell.

"I think it's really cute how he was your first kiss and now he's the first guy to ask you on a date. Awww!"

"He's not my first kiss."

"What?!" Everyone snapped their attention to Snow White. Even Belle sat up straighter and looked to her for clarification.

"I decided I'm still going to claim my lips as virgin. Unlike the rest of you, when Dave kissed me, I didn't kiss him back. I think a kiss has to be consensual to count as losing your VL."

Ariel laughed and patted Snow White on the back. "You would make a great lawyer," she said. "Always very nitty-gritty about the details and getting the facts right."

Snow White jumped. "Oh my gosh, that reminds me!" She pulled a crumpled business card out of her back pocket and held it up. "I think there was a lawyer here today, talking to my mom."

Snow White then described the conversation she overheard and the strange man she saw leaving her house when she got home.

"Elizabeth yelled at you?" Aurora's jaw dropped.

"I can't picture your mom yelling like that!" Cinderella added.

"I couldn't either, until today. Now I know she can. Boy, she can!"

"What makes you think he was a lawyer?" Belle asked. "Just by what he said?"

Snow White shifted her position on the floor. "After my mom went upstairs, I ran after him."

"You what?!" Her cousins were all stunned.

"First you score a date for the prom, then you chase down a strange guy to talk to him? Whoa! Big day for Snow!"

Snow White smiled shyly. "I just asked him who he was and why he was talking to my mom. To earn a reaction like that from her, I wanted to know what it was about! Then there was the look he gave her after seeing me, I dunno, it was just all really weird."

"So what did he tell you?"

Snow White passed the card around. "He handed me his business card and told me I needed to talk to my mom about it. Then he said if I had any other questions, I could contact him later."

"Bizarre!"

"I know, right?" Cinderella handed the card back to Snow White, who set it on top of her dresser. She wasn't sure if she wanted to ask her mom about it, especially after the last reaction she got. *Maybe I'll talk to her after she's had time to calm down.*

***

When Aurora had to tell one of her prom dates no because she had already been asked, she very slyly mentioned that her sister hadn't been invited yet. She may have also used a few hair-tosses to help sway him, but no matter how it happened, Ariel had a date by the next day. The other three had to drag her and Snow White out to buy dresses, and insisted they come out and model each one.

Ariel made faces in the mirror when her cousins forced her to walk, turn, and pose in each dress. Picking out a dress was usually fun and exciting, but she felt a little weird going to the dance with one of her sister's leftovers. She finally chose a fun, flirty lavender dress that came right to her knees. The skirt was layered with a thick ribbon, accentuating her tiny waist. The short, A-line dress rested on one shoulder with a thick strap, leaving the other shoulder bare.

Snow White, on the other hand, smiled shyly in the mirrors and turned slowly while her cousins oohed and awed. Her cheeks went crimson when Ariel let out a loud whistle over a particularly low-cut one. After much debating between the girls over their favorite, Snow White ended up choosing a dress that surprised everyone. She wore a long, dark blue gown that was completely covered in sequins from top to bottom, causing her to shimmer as she walked. The dress was more form fitting than any one of them would have picked out for her, but it hugged her curves in all the right places.

Over the next couple days, the girls spent a lot of time discussing hair styles, makeup options, and which shoes to wear on their special night. It didn't take them long to notice a significant difference in Cinderella. She seemed to have changed since her California trip.

"Are you guys coming over after school?" Belle asked at lunch one day. "My mom bought some fake eyelashes and I wanna see how they look."

"Don't you have prom committee?"

"Not till 5:00."

"Do you need some help?" Snow White asked.

"Yes!" Belle exclaimed, throwing her hands down on the table. "This prom is going to be completely fabulous, but I think it's going to be the death of me first."

Snow White patted one of her hands. "Just don't die before the decorations are done."

When Belle glared at her she responded with, "Of course I'll come help. As long as you can give me a ride from your house."

"Yay!" Belle clapped her hands together and looked at the twins expectantly.

They both nodded. "Yeah, we'll come. I wanna see what you've been working on anyway."

They all turned to Cinderella, who was staring at her phone and typing furiously.

"Earth to Cinderella," Ariel tapped her shoulder. Cinderella held up her index finger, telling her to wait. "Did you just see that?"

"And the phone wins again," Snow White rolled her eyes. "Are we surprised?"

"Can you help with prom decorations?" Belle asked.
"We're only days away now, so this is crunch time."

Cinderella smiled at her phone and continued to type, oblivious to her cousins. Belle tried waving a hand in front of her face, causing Cinderella to look up.

"Hey look at that, you can still hear!"

"What?" Cinderella looked at them all, confused.

"What now?" Belle asked, crossing her arms.

"I'm helping Monica with her math assignment. Hey, do you guys want to hear the funniest thing Sophie did last night? My dad just sent a picture."

"So the prom decorations?" Belle asked.

"Here it is," Cinderella held up her phone, completely ignoring Belle's question.

"Fine. Whatever. I gotta go anyway. I'll see the rest of you, who actually care, later tonight." Belle left the table in a huff.

"What is with you?" Snow White asked.

"What?" Cinderella was typing on her phone again.

Snow White looked at the twins, who shrugged in return. Then they got up from the table and slowly walked to their own classes. Cinderella looked up a few minutes later to share a joke Scott had text her.

"Where'd everybody go?" She jumped to her feet and quickly left the cafeteria.

***

Prom night had finally arrived! After going to an array of dances throughout the school year, the Princess sisters had getting ready down to a science. All the dresses and shoes were laid out nicely on Ariel and Aurora's beds, ready to be put on. Then next door, they visited the makeup station at Belle's house. Mary helped them each apply stylish makeup to go with their gowns. Then it was on to

Snow White's house where Rachel and Dana helped curl hair and create some fabulous up-dos. The girls talked excitedly as they got ready for the night. Ariel didn't know much about her date, Ryan; she had only met him a couple times. She kept trying to ask Aurora for details about him and his interests, but the only details Aurora could supply were about his features.

"Seriously," she whispered to Snow White. "I don't care about his super toned arms, his curly brown hair, or his radiant green eyes. I want to know what movies he likes, the bands he's into, even his favorite subject in school. I swear if a rock had dimples and a great smile, she'd flirt with that too."

Snow White snickered, but she had worries of her own. "How are Dave's friends going to react to him bringing me?"

"They'll take one look at you in that stunning dress and they won't even care if you're popular or not."

Snow White tried to smile, but the nerves were preventing her from feeling excited.

The girls finally ended up in Cinderella's family room, where Elizabeth waited with the camera for pictures and some final spritzes of perfume. They created a rotation so they weren't all doing hair at once, but they all ended up at Cinderella's house for pictures and to be picked up by their dates.

Dave arrived first, simply walking across the street to collect Snow White for the evening. Belle conveniently had to use the restroom when he arrived and excused herself from the room. For Snow White's sake, they were all very cordial to Dave, but Dana and Mary did have to work hard not to lunge across the room and strangle him. After a few snapshots and lots of, "Mo-om please!" Elizabeth was satisfied and let them be on their way. Craig and Ariel's date, Ryan, were on the basketball team together. They were in the same group, sharing a limo, so they arrived together next. Belle and Ariel hammed it up, creating lots of fun poses for their foursome. They pretended to pin their boutonnieres on the wrong date, then since the guys stood so much taller, they got a picture of them holding the corsages over the girls' heads. Finally after they got a shot of the girls giving the boys piggy back rides, Elizabeth proclaimed her camera was about to die, so they gave up and hurried out the door.

Ethan had borrowed his dad's fancy sports car to take Aurora to the dance.

"Don't you need more batteries first?" Aurora asked, when Elizabeth held the camera up.

"No, I was just getting done with their antics, so I said the camera was dying. It still has plenty of life."

Cinderella and Aurora both laughed. Then Aurora took Ethan's arm and guided him over to the fireplace. Elizabeth snapped one picture of Ethan sliding the corsage onto Aurora's wrist, and one of Aurora pinning on his boutonniere. Then she put an arm around his waist and he placed an arm around her shoulder for a more traditional pose. After they left, Cinderella peered out the window. She didn't see any sign of Brian's arrival. After a few minutes passed, and several glances at the clock, Cinderella checked her phone. Sure enough she had a missed call and voicemail.

"So where is he?" Dana asked.

"He had some car trouble on the way over, so he's running a little late." She sat down carefully on the couch so as not to mess up her perfect hair.

"I gotta get going, but have fun tonight sweetie!" Mary waved and left.

Elizabeth followed shortly, handing her camera off to Dana before she did.

"You guys can go to dinner," Cinderella said. "I know you had plans tonight."

"I'm not leaving until I capture some memories of you and your cute date."

"And we've got all night to eat food. There's no rush," Rachel added.

Across the street, Scott was watching all the traffic going in and out of Cinderella's house. He came into town to visit his parents for the weekend, not realizing it would be prom. Before Dave had left the house, Scott stopped him. "Does Cinderella have a date?" he tried to ask casually.

"Yeah, she does."

"Who with?"

"Why? It's not like you'd know him."

"Oh, I'm just curious." He shrugged and pretended to flip through one of his mom's magazines.

"Yeah right," Dave rolled his eyes. "If you want to go see Cinderella, why don't you just man up and walk across the street? You look like a creeper sitting here, peering out the blinds at her." Then he had left.

Scott watched as Dave went inside and then left a few minutes later with Snow White. He drummed his hands on the coffee table, but found himself looking out again when he heard another car pull up. But Cinderella didn't leave the house with either of the next two boys. A few moments later his heart plummeted when a gorgeous, red convertible stopped in front of her house. A tall, good-looking kid got out and approached the door. Scott picked up another magazine and pretended to flip through it, but kept his peripheral view out the window. When Aurora emerged moments later, Scott let out a sigh of relief.

He counted quickly on his fingers and when he realized Cinderella was the only one left, he dashed into his kitchen. Scott grabbed a bag of popcorn and whatever movie his parents had been watching earlier then raced outside.

There was a knock on the door. "That must be him!" Dana got to her feet to answer it. But instead of finding Brian on the other side, there stood Scott.

"Oh, hey Scott. What are you doing here?"

"Is Cinderella home?"

Cinderella walked over to the front door to see what was going on.

"Hey Princess, you didn't have to get all dressed up for me!" he winked.

"What are you doing here?"

"Well, I'm in town for the weekend and thought I'd stop by to see if you wanted to watch a movie." He held up a DVD and bag of popcorn that were tucked under his arm.

"I have prom tonight."

"Yeah, I can see that. Sorry! Guess I should have called first."

Cinderella fidgeted. She hated to send Scott away, but the thought of Brian seeing him here when he came to pick her up made her feel nervous, too. "My date is actually going to be here any minute now."

"I can take a hint. I'll make myself scarce. Well, have fun tonight!" He gave her a hug goodbye and whispered, "You look stunning!" before he left again.

"Well," Dana said, "That was awkward."

Scott walked back across the street with his head down. He felt so stupid! But seeing her look so gorgeous had been worth it. As he reached his parents' front door, a car pulled up behind him. Scott watched as a young man knocked on Cinderella's door, and then went inside. His heart ached when he watched them emerge together a short time later. They both had huge smiles on their faces and seemed to be laughing about something.

Scott knew he only had himself to blame for being in this position. But it really sucked watching another guy place his hand on the small of her back as he guided her towards the car. He could feel the hot fury building inside him, and he unconsciously balled his fists when her date opened Cinderella's door for her. Then her date climbed into the driver's seat and they were gone. Scott gathered his stuff together and decided to drive back to Logan that night. He knew if he stayed home, he would constantly be checking out the window for her to return that evening, and Scott really didn't want to be one of those creepy stalker guys. As soon as he had his duffel packed, he said goodbye to his parents.

"But you just got here yesterday!"

"I know, I'm sorry Mom! I just remembered there are a few things I need to take care of this weekend."

"You're sure they can't wait for tomorrow?"

"Yeah, sorry! But I'll be back soon to visit again. I promise!" He kissed her on the cheek and left.

This patiently waiting thing was going to be a whole lot harder than he thought!

Chapter Forty-Four

The prom was held in a large building at the local college. Cinderella and Brian pulled up next to a long row of limousines and fancy cars.

"Sorry I didn't have anything nicer to drive," he said.

"Oh, I don't care!" Cinderella tried to reassure him.

She had been to all the girl's choice dances during the year, going in a group with her cousins. But this was the first date where she really found herself alone with another guy. Cinderella had only ever been in dating situations like this with Scott. She had become so comfortable with him, she wasn't sure how to act now. It also didn't help that she kept having images of Scott standing there on her porch, running through her mind. She wondered if Brian took her home early enough, if she could still fit in a movie with Scott. Then she quickly pushed those thoughts from her mind. *Tonight I am with Brian.*

Brian handed their tickets over at the door and they walked into a beautifully decorated room. There was silver and blue material draping down from the ceiling, with a large chandelier in the center. Then the walls had material of the same color running down them, with tiny white lights behind the folds of the fabric. It gave the illusion that the walls had water running down them. Cinderella felt like she was inside a waterfall.

"Wow!" Brian looked around in amazement.

"I know!" Cinderella let out a huge breath she hadn't realized she'd been holding.

"Your cousin did a fantastic job."

"My cousin?"

"Yeah, Belle. Didn't she and her boyfriend head up the committee that planned this whole thing?"

She felt like a complete jerk. Now Belle's absence the last couple weeks, since Cinderella returned from California, made complete sense! She had been bringing up prom and how busy she was constantly, but between school, Scott, her dad, and her sisters, Cinderella had been really preoccupied and never paid much attention. She spotted Belle dancing with Craig in the center of the room and headed over, pulling Brian along.

Belle saw them coming and stopped dancing. "There you are! We were starting to get worried."

"Brian had some car trouble, but we're here now. This place looks incredible, guys!"

Belle looked up at Craig and they both smiled. "Thanks! It's nice of you to notice."

"I'm sorry I've been so spacey lately! I should have helped you with all this." She waved an arm around the room.

"Well, every time I tried to bring it up, your sister would text you, or your dad would call, or Prince Charming had something funny to share. It just seemed like you had this new family in California and we didn't really matter anymore."

Brian shifted uncomfortably and quickly excused himself to find a drink.

Cinderella threw her arms around Belle and gave her a big hug. "I'm so sorry! I was trying to figure out how to fit these new people into my life, but I guess I wasn't doing a very good job of keeping everyone balanced."

"Well, you're the only one of us who has a dad now, so I guess I don't know what that's like."

"You could have a dad too, you know?"

"No, I already burned that bridge. My mom broke up with him. He's probably found a great new Hollywood family by now." Even as Belle said the words, she hoped they weren't true. But she didn't know how to make things right. After putting up such a fight against Lucas, she wasn't sure if she could go back on her words without making herself look like an idiot.

Cinderella desperately wanted to tell Belle how untrue that was. She wanted to tell her how he'd driven all the way to her dad's house in Sacramento, practically in tears, over the thought of losing her and Mary. But Cinderella knew she couldn't say a word without ruining everything, so she simply hugged Belle again.

"Now I better go find my date. I think I scared him off."

Belle laughed and nodded her understanding. Cinderella looked around the crowded room until she spotted him by the refreshment table, looking lonely.

"Sorry," she said, walking up to Brian. "Should we dance now?"

Brian didn't know how to do western swing like Scott did, but he was surprisingly good at hip-hop! Cinderella even asked him to teach her a few moves. They spent a lot of time hanging out with Brian's friends, who all danced together in a big group. Brian was really easy to talk to and they had a lot of fun together. Now she couldn't figure out why she had been so nervous in the beginning. As the night wore on, Cinderella found herself thinking about Scott less and less and just having fun in the moment with Brian and his friends.

***

Snow White was worried about spending the evening with Dave and all his football buddies, but so far everything was going pretty smoothly. When he first showed up with Snow White on his arm, his friends couldn't hide their shock. She was met by several open, gaping, mouths and blank stares but the group was making an effort to have her feel included. At first no one seemed to know what to say to her, but as they all relaxed, words came more easily. Snow White found herself lost in conversations about classes and teachers with people she never realized she would have anything in common with. She and Dave were having fun together, too. Then as the time grew closer for announcing prom royalty, Snow White could tell Dave was getting tense.

"Don't stress about it. Everything will work out."

"Will it?" he asked.

"Well, I can't make any promises, but at least she'll know how you feel. Then you can either finally have her forgiveness, or you can know for sure and move on."

"You make it sound like moving on is an option."

"It might have to be."

Dave sighed. He knew Snow White was right. Why couldn't he just go back in time and not make those stupid mistakes? Now, it was over a year later, and he was still paying for his poor choices. He had liked Belle a lot, but then he'd let those stupid seniors convince him to make a bet he could never win. That stupid bet! Even after he'd technically won by kissing all the cousins, he'd lost their friendships and, most importantly, Belle's trust. He was actually surprised Snow White was even allowed to go out with him after everything that happened. He was afraid when he went to pick her up, he'd be met by pitchforks! But her mom and aunts had been very cordial.

"Here we go." Snow White grabbed his arm.

Dave looked up and noticed Mrs. Hightower, the vice principal, was stepping up to the podium. As soon as the song ended, the music was turned off and everyone turned their eyes towards the small stage.

"It's time, everyone!" she said in her sing-song voice. "Are you ready to find out who your king and queen will be?"

The crowd cheered loudly.

Aurora squeezed her date's hand in anticipation. Across the room, Dave did the same to Snow White, but his anticipation was for something else entirely.

"Before we reveal your results, let's give a round of applause to your junior class officers and their dance committee for putting on this fabulous night for us, and for these amazing decorations!"

Everyone cheered loudly, and several people whistled. Then Mrs. Hightower waved her hands in a flourish as she held up the results card. She cleared her throat dramatically before speaking again.

"She wants to be a game show host so badly, she can taste it," Ariel joked. Her date laughed loudly, resulting in a stern look from the vice principal.

"Your princesses are: Heather McCall, Aurora Princess, and Amber Justenson!"

The crowd cheered enthusiastically. Aurora's face fell at first, but she quickly recovered with a bright smile and walked on stage to claim her flowers. She looked down into the crowd and saw Ariel giving her a thumbs up. Then when she had Aurora's attention, she pulled a face. Aurora

       Frogs & Toads

smiled even brighter. Leave it to her goofy sister to make the situation seem light.

"And now, your junior prom queen is: Miranda Chatwin!"

The applause grew even louder, and many catcalls were made as Miranda walked onto the stage for her crown. Snow White knew Miranda only from sight; she'd never actually talked to her before. She was a bubbly little cheerleader who had a permanent smile on her face, one of those who would make you guess cheerleader the moment you met her, even if she wasn't wearing her outfit. She accepted her crown graciously and hugged each of the princesses in turn. Snow White looked over at Dave to see his reaction.

"It's cool," he mouthed. "We're friends."

Snow White nodded and waited for the vice principal to continue.

"And now for your princes." Mrs. Hightower cleared her throat again. Ariel rolled her eyes amidst several groans.

"Okay, okay!" she said, putting a hand up to stop them. She then rattled off the names of the three boys who had almost been crowned king, but not quite. Snow White only recognized two of the names, and even then she didn't know them well. "And your king is: David Prince!"

The crowd erupted into cheers and applause. Many of Dave's buddies gave him a pat on the back as he walked toward the front. "Here goes nothin'," Dave whispered to Snow White. Once on stage, Dave had a crown placed on his head. He turned and gave Miranda a hug of congratulations. Then he whispered something in her ear. Miranda smiled and nodded. The moment passed so quickly, no one else would have even noticed it, but Snow White was watching very carefully.

"And now, the traditional dance of this year's prom king and queen," Mrs. Hightower announced. Very quickly, Dave reached for the microphone.

"Actually, no disrespect to you, your highness," he said, looking at Miranda, "But there's only one girl I want to dance with tonight. Belle Princess, will you dance with me?"

Belle wasn't sure she had heard right. She looked at Craig, who looked just as stunned as she felt. Belle stood frozen for a moment longer, until people started chanting her name. She made her way toward the stage and was met by Dave in the center of the dance floor. He held his hands out to her and she hesitated for a moment before clasping them. He pulled her into a waltz position and guided her around the room gracefully. The students had all spread out along the edges of the dance floor, giving them ample room to move about freely. Miranda grabbed her own date and joined them for the slow dance.

"What are you doing?" Belle finally asked.

"Dancing with you."

She rolled her eyes. "I mean, you're supposed to be dancing with Miranda."

"But I wanted to dance with you."

"Why?"

"Because I love you, Belle. I told you that last year and it's still true today. I'm not giving up on you, or on us."

Belle stopped dancing. She looked up into Dave's sapphire eyes and saw the hope residing in them. She closed her own eyes and for a moment she was taken back to that first kiss outside McDonalds. He made her whole body flood with warmth when he kissed her. The hair on the back of her neck stood up, and she opened her eyes just in time to see Dave leaning in for a kiss. When their lips came together, the warmth washed over her and her body tingled with the familiarity of his touch.

The room erupted with cheering and catcalls.

Then she pulled away. "No. I'm sorry, Dave, I'm so very sorry! I do care about you, I really do. And you've helped me several times this year when I needed someone most. But I care about Craig, too, and I can't do this to him."

The crowd around them clapped as the song came to an end. Then the other students flooded the dance floor again as the tempo picked up. Several people came over to offer Dave their congratulations. Belle used the opportunity to slip away. She had to find Craig. She only hoped that he hadn't seen the kiss and decided to leave her. Dave was left standing in the middle of the dance floor, alone, and completely crushed.

***

Belle found Craig standing outside, leaning against the brick wall of the building. She approached cautiously, standing beside him and the wall.

"You didn't leave me."

"No, part of me wanted to though. I guess it's a good thing we came in a big group. I didn't think it would be fair to take the limo just for myself."

"I don't even know where to start."

Craig turned to finally face her. "How about why you left me standing there to go dance with a jerk?"

"He's not a jerk."

"Oh really?! Because you've spent the last year and a half talking about what a jerk he is! So obviously I'm missing something, or there's something you're not telling me!" Craig couldn't keep his voice down any longer. A couple students standing nearby quickly moved away.

"I know I did. I was just so mad at what he did to me! But the truth is, I was hurt because I cared about him last year. I thought he cared about me, too."

Craig stiffened. "If you're trying to make me feel better, this is not the way to do it." He was still seething, but had managed to bring his voice down to a normal level again.

"I'm trying to be honest with you. I don't think I've always been completely honest, so I'm trying to fix that." Craig didn't say anything, but he didn't walk away either, so Belle went on.

"When you first asked me out, I was so furious about the whole stupid Dave thing that I jumped at the chance to make him jealous. With you. But then I fell in love with you." Belle gently grabbed his face, and turned it so Craig was looking straight into her eyes. "I love you, Craig!"

"Then what happened tonight?"

"I think I needed to see if anything was still there. I needed to know once and for all if Dave and I had a future together, or if my future is with you."

"And?"

"And when he kissed me..."

"He kissed you?!"

Belle flinched. "You didn't see that part?"

"No, but I'm going to go punch that punk in the face!" Craig moved toward the door, his fists tight. Belle held him back.

"I'm sorry, I thought you saw. I just wanted you to know that when he kissed me, I pulled away because I was thinking of you. I'm choosing you!"

Craig still faced the door, but he had stopped pulling under Belle's grasp. His tall, broad shoulders slumped in defeat. He knew he wouldn't be able to punch Dave and get away with it. But at least he could get away with the girl.

He suddenly turned and grabbed Belle's face in his hands. He kissed her like he had never done before. His lips dug into hers with such force, Belle forgot to breathe. His fingers ran through her hair and raced down her back as he pulled their bodies together. Her heart raced and her head swam in the comfortable scent of his cologne. He smelled incredible! Her body filled with a familiar warmth and she knew she had made the right decision. When he finally released her, Belle felt dizzy and stumbled a little. But Craig caught her in his arms and held her tight.

"Promise me you're done with him."

"I feel like I could be friends with him again now."

Craig pulled back and looked at her, his brow furrowed with concern.

"But I am done with dating him. I promise! You're the one I want to be with."

Craig kissed her again, gently this time. "I guess since we're the ones throwing this party, we should probably get back inside. What do you say?"

"Can you handle going back in and being in the same room as him?"

"I can't promise my foot won't accidentally get in his way if he walks too close to us, but otherwise I promise to behave."

Belle laughed and they walked back inside together, their arms around each other.

Chapter Forty-Five

The next morning Belle woke up to someone knocking on the front door.

"It's Saturday morning, go away!" she yelled, even though she knew they couldn't hear her. Her mom had gone to work, so when the knocking persisted, Belle finally rolled out of bed.

She threw the door open, ready to yell at whatever annoying solicitor was pestering them so early in the morning. Instead, she jumped back at the sight of the large, dark man who stood before her. Her heart stopped for a brief moment. Then she looked at him closer, from his dark glasses to his grim expression.

"Hey! Don't you work for my dad?"

"Belle Princess, you're to come with me."

"I'm to come with you?" she mimicked his serious tone. "Are you for real? Of course I'm not coming with you!"

"Your father sent me to pick you up."

"If you haven't noticed, Colossus, I'm still in my p.j.'s. I'm certainly not going anywhere with you, in my p.j.'s, for my father. I haven't even spoken to him in months." She started to close the door, but the giant man forced it open again.

"Hey!"

"I was told to use force, if necessary."

Belle looked him up and down and then, deciding he must be joking, she started to shut the door again. He moved toward her suddenly. That's when Belle decided it was time to take him seriously.

"Okay, okay! Geez! Can I at least get dressed first?"

"Clothes will be provided at your destination."

"Clothes will...what?"

When he moved towards her again, Belle scampered around him and ran outside. There, in front of her house stood a sleek, black limousine with the door open. She hurried inside to find four messy-haired, sleepy-eyed girls clad in their pajamas as well.

"What's going on?" Ariel yawned.

"Are you kidding me? If I had known you all were being kidnapped too, I might not have put up such a fight! Stupid Goliath out there almost gave me a heart attack."

The other girls all laughed.

"So where are we going?" Snow White asked.

"Beats me!"

"But he's your dad. Didn't he tell you what was going on?"

"Yeah, the father I haven't spoken to in months gave me a detailed plan of our day." Belle rolled her eyes.

"You're nasty when you get woken up early," Aurora prodded.

"So we all just willingly got into an unknown vehicle headed for an unknown destination. Why do I feel like this is going to end with all of us dead in a gutter somewhere?"

"Ariel!"

"Well, seriously guys! Watch a crime show! This is how they all start out."

"Somehow I don't think a serial killer would go to all the trouble of ordering us a limousine. Here, ride in style to your death." Belle was in a sarcastic mood.

A short time later the limousine pulled into the parking lot of a large, beautiful building.

"Where are we? Can you tell?"

The girls pressed their faces against the glass, trying to get a peek at their destination. They sat back and started talking excitedly.

"A spa!"

"Your dad can kidnap us anytime!"

The back door opened and the girls stepped out into the bright sunshine. Their captor led them inside the building. They walked past a beautiful fountain feature up to the front desk.

"The Princesses have arrived for their appointment," he said in a gruff voice.

The slender woman behind the desk looked up and smiled. "Oh, of course! Right this way, we're ready for you."

"Excuse me," Aurora spoke up.

"Yes?" She turned to face them.

"What exactly are we having done today?"

"Oh, Mr. Ferreira asked for the full package today. You'll start with a full body massage with your choice of aromatherapy, followed by a special moisturizing facial, then we'll move on to your pedicures, and we'll finish off with a hot towel hand massage. Does that sound alright to you?"

The girls all squealed in response. The lady smiled and waved them forward.

"I'll be here to pick you up in a few hours."

"Okay, bye Hulk! Don't miss us too much." They all waved, but still got no response from him.

"I honestly think he might be a robot," Ariel said.

"Who cares? Let's go get pampered!" Aurora pranced down the hall, the others following close behind.

The girls were first led into a large, dimly lit room with several comfortable couches and chairs lining the walls. Soft, water features trickled down the walls and made for a very relaxing ambience. A small table sat against the far wall, with a pitcher of cold, cucumber water and a bowl of soft peppermints. In a very soft voice, the front desk lady told them to take a seat, enjoy some water and their masseuses would be along momentarily to take them each back for their massages.

"Umm, excuse me?" Cinderella whispered before she left. "Are we supposed to be...naked for our massage?"

Snow White blanched. The woman smiled kindly.

"You are given the option to undress to your comfort level."

The clacking of her heels echoed off the stony walls as she returned to her post at the front. As soon as she stepped out of earshot the girls whispered feverishly.

"There is no way I'm taking my clothes off for a stranger to touch me!" Snow White looked like she wanted to get up and run from the building. Sensing her thoughts, Cinderella placed a hand on her arm.

"You don't have to. You can stay in your pajamas. I'm sure the massage will still feel just as nice."

"I'm taking it all off! I want to experience the massage on my skin. Who knows, maybe my masseuse will be hot!" Aurora waggled her eyebrows, making the others laugh.

"It's probably going to be a chick anyway," Ariel said. Aurora scowled.

"You can do whatever you want Snow, but just remember, they're professionals. I'm sure they are mature about it and don't even think about us as being naked."

"I'm still not gonna do it. Are you guys?"

Snow White looked around at the others, who all nodded. Then she looked at Cinderella. "You too?"

"Yeah, but I'll probably keep my underwear on at least."

Two women entered the room, and the girls went silent. They were young, probably in their early-twenties. They were dressed in black slacks and black shirts, with their hair pulled up in a loose bun. The blonde one smiled sweetly, "Belle?"

Belle stood and, head held high, followed her from the room. The brunette looked at a paper she was holding and called Ariel's name. Ariel jumped to her feet and waved like a beauty queen in a pageant as she strode away, leaving the others chuckling. In turn, Cinderella, Aurora, and Snow White were all led from the waiting area by their individual masseuses clad in black. Much to Aurora's disappointment, they were all female.

The individual rooms were small and quaint. They were very dark with only a small, soft glow emanating from a lamp on the little counter. The rooms were just large enough to fit one massage table, and a counter which held the only light in the room, as well as an array of aromatherapy candles. Soft, instrumental music came through a speaker just above the counter. The girls were shown the aromatherapy candles and asked to choose a scent. Then they were told to undress to their comfort level, and climb beneath the sheet on the massage table. The masseuse explained she would return in a few minutes.

There were several hooks along the wall by the door where the girls could hang their clothes. With the exception of Snow White, they quickly undressed and climbed beneath the soft blue sheet. They then placed their faces in the hole at the end of the table and waited for the soft knock from their masseuse, signaling her return.

It was an interesting experience to have someone else rub and massage their bodies. But once they got over the weirdness factor of having a stranger touch them, the cousins all felt very relaxed. Even Snow White, who almost fell asleep during her massage, admitted it was a wonderful experience. When their hour was up, and they had been massaged everywhere from their necks to their fingertips, and down their legs to their feet, the masseuse covered them back up with the sheet. She then explained they could return to their pajamas or, since they were having other treatments, they could put on the robe that was hanging on the back of the door.

The girls came together again in a larger room, with five high-backed chairs lined side by side with pedicure tubs attached. They were all wearing the soft, fluffy robes.

Cinderella looked at Snow White, surprised. "You changed!"

Snow White smiled shyly. "Not until after my massage was over. But yeah, I decided it looked comfy enough to wear while they work on my hands and feet."

They climbed into their chairs, soaking their feet in the hot, frothy water. Another woman dressed in black approached the girls with a tray of nail polish colors to choose from. They each selected their colors and then leaned back in the chairs and closed their eyes. Several ladies, older than the masseuses, came in and began working on their feet. The girls were so relaxed, they barely spoke during their pedicures. When they were finished, the cousins' feet were clipped, rubbed, and polished to perfection.

The cousins were excused for a bathroom and water break, before being led to the next room for their facials. Almost every person who spoke to them, from their masseuse to the lady carrying the nail polish tray, reminded the girls of the importance of drinking a lot of water that day. The girls were split into two groups where they were guided to two rooms containing three beds each. Just behind each bed was a stool for their esthetician to sit. Beside the stool sat a small silver tub and a strange looking white machine with a long arm attached. They were told this machine produced the steam for their exfoliation. The Princess sisters then laid down on their beds and immediately had their hair pulled back and wrapped in a warm towel. Their estheticians then began cleansing their skin with cotton pads. The steam exfoliation was an interesting experience, almost like looking directly into a humidifier. Once they were properly cleansed, exfoliated, and moisturized, the girls were told to remain in the room for their hot towel hand massages.

Almost four hours after their arrival, the girls felt as though they were floating in heaven. They were so comfortable and relaxed, the thought of taking off their robes and returning to normal clothes was completely unappealing. When they were led back to their original massage rooms, the girls were surprised to find their pajamas were gone. Laid out on the tables were their own jeans and a comfortable shirt from home.

"Where did these come from?" Belle asked.

But her masseuse just smiled slyly and shrugged her shoulders, before leaving the room so she could dress.

"Can we live here?" Ariel asked the lady at the front desk as they walked out.

She didn't respond, but merely smiled and thanked them for coming in.

"I think she might be a robot, too," Ariel whispered, "only she's the perma-grin kind."

The sun was blinding after being in the darkened rooms for so long. They quickly climbed back into the limo and settled into the soft leather seats, wanting nothing more than to give into their relaxed bodies and fall asleep. But their escort had other plans in mind.

"Wait, this isn't the way back home." Cinderella spoke up when the limousine turned the opposite direction.

"You're not going home," came the brusque voice from the front.

"See, we are being kidnapped! He just wants us good and relaxed so we don't put up a fight!"

"If I was going to kill you all, I wouldn't waste so much money on you first."

"Why I do believe Titan here just made a joke!" Cinderella laughed. Then the others all joined in.

"Where are we going for real?" Belle asked.

"To get you some clothes."

"Pampering first and now he's taking us shopping?! Belle, you have the coolest dad on the planet!" Aurora exclaimed.

Belle tried not to smile, but the sucking up to win her back was blatantly obvious and, for the time, she would take it!

"So, do our moms know about all this? How long are we going to be gone?"

"Everything has been arranged." He wouldn't give them any more clues than that.

The girls were provided lunch in the limo as they drove, and they ate ravenously after skipping breakfast that morning. The car ride was much longer this time, ending up in downtown Salt Lake. They stopped in front of a line of very nice store fronts. There were trees and a large, ornate, circular fountain in the center of the stores. It looked like an extravagant, outdoor mall.

"Wait, is this City Creek?" Aurora asked the driver as he held the door open for the girls.

He simply nodded his head, and offered a hand to each of the girls when they exited.

"Wow! I've wanted to come here since I heard it opened," she giggled with glee.

The girls all looked up in amazement at the tall, two-story buildings.

"You have two hours to each pick out a nice dress and shoes for this evening." He handed a credit card to Belle, and then shut the car door behind them after the last girl climbed out.

"Is he serious?!" Ariel took the credit card from Belle and examined it. "It looks real enough!"

"What are we waiting for?!" Aurora exclaimed, practically jumping in the air.

"Wait," Belle paused. "How nice of a dress?"

"Something formal."

"Where are we going?" Snow White asked. But the driver got back in the car without so much as a grin.

The girls went into one store after another, laughing and talking excitedly while they tried on new styles. Their time at the spa was the quietest the group of girls had ever been, and now they were making up for it.

"I would feel a lot nicer if my hair wasn't such a mess," Belle stated, stepping out of the dressing room in a floor length crimson gown. She tried to tame her masses by brushing her fingers through her hair, but it still stood up in strange places from all the events of the day. "Why couldn't my dad let us bring our makeup, or a brush at least?"

"Oh, come on!" Cinderella exclaimed, standing next to her. She looked at their reflections side-by-side in the full length mirrors. "It would have made the day a little less exciting if we'd gotten ready first. Besides, you can't wear makeup for facials, and the massage would have messed up anything we'd done with our hair anyway."

"I guess you're right." Belle frowned at their images. "Well, we definitely can't wear these, or we'll look like Christmas!"

Cinderella laughed. It was true. With Belle in her deep crimson dress, and Cinderella in the emerald green one, they looked like they were trying to celebrate the holiday together.

Two hours later, as directed, the girls stood on the curb each holding a small bag with their new heels, and a larger dress bag draped over their arms. It had been a very successful outing. The girls couldn't wait to find out where they were headed next! The limousine pulled up to the curb and the oversized driver helped them load up their spoils.

Cinderella smiled a few minutes later when the limo parked outside a nice salon. "Looks like he read your mind."

Belle looked out the window and grinned in return. "It's about time! I think this is the longest I've ever gone without makeup in my life!"

"Really?" Ariel asked, giving her a hard time. "How about the first twelve years or so of your life?"

"Not so," Belle responded. "I came out of the womb wearing lipstick and mascara."

Ariel rolled her eyes and then followed Belle out of the limo. They stepped through the glass doors of the salon and were immediately greeted by a bouncy, excited woman of about fifty.

"You must be the Princess girls! We've been waiting for you! Come in, come in, don't be shy!"

She grabbed Cinderella and Belle by the hands and pulled them over to some chairs. The other girls followed closely, trying not to laugh as the overzealous salon owner spoke with a flourish, drowning them all in perfume each time she lifted an arm.

"You two will start with makeup. These are Anton and Angelina," she said pushing Belle and Cinderella into chairs. "You're in good hands with them; they'll have you stunning in no time! As for you three, come, come!"

Snow White and the twins almost had to run to keep up with her prancing as she turned a corner and guided them to the back of the salon. She shoved them down into the chairs lining the back wall, to first have their hair washed. She introduced the stylists who would be working on them and then bounded away. The stylists all did an incredible job, wrapping, curling, and twisting the girls' hair into elegant up-dos. Then they swapped with Belle and Cinderella, who looked like supermodels in their gorgeous new makeup. After hair and makeup were complete, the girls felt fresh and alive!

"I think this has been the best day of my entire life!" Aurora gushed.

"Me too!" Ariel said. "But I'm starting to get awfully hungry!"

Snow White and Cinderella nodded their agreement.

As if on cue, the limousine pulled up and their escort informed them that they were headed for an early dinner.

The girls were instructed to change into their formal dresses and then they would continue on their way.

The limousine took them to a large building in the heart of downtown. The restaurant was located up on the tenth floor, with huge windows lining the walls to show off incredible views of the city. The girls had only ever heard of the place, and they gasped at the elegance when they walked inside.

"I can only imagine how gorgeous this must be at night when the city is all lit up!" Snow White exclaimed.

The girls ate from the ritzy buffet until they felt they might burst.

"I knew I shouldn't have picked such a tight fitting dress!" Ariel complained, grabbing her stomach.

"Oooooh! I'm so full!" Cinderella moaned as the elevator started to go down.

The golden doors opened and the girls stepped out. They started walking toward the exit when Belle spotted a familiar face.

"Dave!"

He turned his head at the sound of his name and it was obvious he wished he could go the other direction. His face clearly displayed dread.

"I'll catch up in just a second," Belle said, and she rushed toward him before she could chicken out. She had wanted to talk to him since abandoning him on the dance floor last night. She just wasn't expecting the opportunity to present itself so soon. "Hey," she said, approaching him cautiously.

"You guys go ahead, I'll be right there," he spoke to his parents who smiled and waved at Belle. Clearly he hadn't told them about the prom, or they probably would have done something with their fingers other than wave.

"We're here for a wedding reception. Family friend." Dave offered the information without being asked. "Is there another dance tonight I don't know about?" He nodded toward Belle's formal dress.

"No, it's a gift from my dad. He's trying to make up or something." Belle abruptly leaned forward and wrapped her arms around Dave. "I'm so sorry!" She pulled back and looked him in the eyes, letting her arms drop when he didn't return the hug.

Dave nodded. "I guess I kind of deserved that. I had my chance last year and blew it."

"Maybe if things had been different...I don't know. I just want you to know that you really do mean a lot to me. I know I've been a brat to you for a while now, but I really don't want to push you away for good."

"Yeah I'm sure Craig will love that, after I embarrassed him last night."

"We talked about it. He knows you're my friend."

"So we're friends again?"

"Of course." Belle hugged him again.

It wasn't what Dave had been hoping for, but it was definitely a start.

"Belle! We gotta go!" Ariel called to her. "Monstro is expecting us outside like right now!"

Belle smiled at Dave and then quickly followed her cousins outside. She felt good! She knew things with Dave might be a little awkward at first, but their relationship was definitely on the mend.

Chapter Forty-Six

The girls screamed when the limousine pulled up to a small landing strip and they saw a private plane ahead of them.

"No freaking way!"

"Are you serious?!"

"Is that for us?"

"I can now reveal your final destination. You will all be meeting up with your mothers in California for Mr. Ferreira's new movie premiere."

The girls stood frozen in place. Had they heard him right?

"You better get a move on. You don't want to miss your red carpet entrance."

Belle's jaw dropped. She couldn't believe all this! Her dad was making it impossible to stay mad at him with this extravagant day. She shook her head to try and clear it, but no clarity came. *Is he really trying to win me back because he cares, or just to impress my mom?* Belle lifted her long skirt a little and stepped toward the small plane. The others watched her closely and then followed suit. They carefully climbed aboard the aircraft and after meeting the pilot, quickly found their seats for takeoff.

The ride started off very quietly, with the cousins all feeling a little nervous, never having ridden on a plane before, let alone a small, private plane. But once they were in the air and flying smoothly above the clouds, the girls began talking excitedly again about what lay ahead of them.

"He said our moms will be there, right?"

"I think so."

"Does that mean they had a day of pampering like we did?"

"I don't think so. My mom had to work."

"Ours, too."

"I wonder if my mom will be there too. I thought they broke up."

Before they knew it, the captain was telling them that they were about to land. Snow White squeezed her eyes shut as the plane bumped to the ground, and the twins clasped hands, but they landed safely without incident. Another limousine was waiting for them just outside the plane.

"Boy your dad knows how to live in style!" Aurora exclaimed, sliding across the leather seat to make room for the others. Their California escort was also big, but he greeted the girls with a warm smile and excitedly told them all about the area as he drove through the city.

"I'm starting to miss our Ogre friend," Ariel whispered, as their new guide continued to chatter incessantly. The others stifled giggles behind their hands, but he was too busy talking to notice.

Time seemed to be traveling at warp speed. Just as they were feeling settled with their surroundings, the limousine began to slow and they could see flashing lights ahead of them.

"Are you ladies ready for your time in the spotlight?"

They scrambled to look at their hair in the mirror, adjust their dresses, and check each other's teeth for any clinging food particles. Then the limo door was opening and their driver extended his hand to help the first girl step out. The sound from the crowd was deafening and Belle was tempted to cover her ears as she emerged out onto the red carpet. Then what felt like a thousand flashes went off and Belle wanted nothing more than to shield her eyes. Instead, she put on her most charming smile and pretended it didn't bother her.

"Who is that?"

"That's Lucas Ferreira's daughter!"

"What's her name? Bella?"

"No, Belle."

"Belle! Belle, look this way!"

"Belle, what's it like having one of Hollywood's hottest actors for a father?"

Unlike the time when she had been caught off guard and bombarded at school, Belle was ready for this. She politely answered questions, posed for the cameras, and flirted a little with the reporters. She glanced back to see her cousins trailing behind her, looking a little lost and unsure. Then another limousine pulled up behind them and Lucas stepped out, looking dashing as ever in his black tux.

He saw Belle through the crowd and his face lit up with excitement. She looked at him and returned his smile. Her eyes began to water a little at the sight of him. It had been months since she had actually seen him, and the last time they were together she had treated him horribly. But one look at his glowing face, and she knew he was sincere. Belle looked from her dad to her cousins in their beautiful, expensive gowns. She thought over how much he had spoiled them all that day, and the way everything was planned perfectly, and she knew it was all for her. Now she understood how very wrong she had been about him. Belle suddenly turned around and ran past her cousins, as fast as her heels would allow, straight into his arms.

Lucas caught her and hugged her tightly back.

"I'm so sorry!" he said.

"I know."

"I just want you to know, all those cameras I brought with me to your school that day, they weren't for me. Honest! I was trying to make a video of you to show to my agent friend and see if he was interested in signing you. I shouldn't have been so stupid, and just explained what I was doing first...or even asked you if you were interested. But I got so excited about the idea, I kind of just took off with it, without ever consulting you. I'm sorry!" he said again.

"I'm sorry, too!" Belle exclaimed. "I don't know if you've ever noticed, but I can be a little stubborn sometimes."

Lucas laughed loudly. "I love that about you! Don't ever change."

Belle smiled and dabbed at her eyes.

The reporters ate up their emotional reunion and continued snapping pictures like crazy. Lucas was very good with the crowd, stopping to take pictures with Belle, to sign autographs, and answer questions about his new film. But it was obvious he would rather just hurry inside and be able to talk to his daughter in peace.

When they finally did make it inside the building, Lucas guided them through the lobby into a smaller room. The room was brightly lit with ceiling lights and offered plenty of privacy with no windows. The long, mahogany table standing in the center suggested the room was typically used for conference meetings. But tonight, it had been converted into a party room for their use. The chairs which normally surrounded the table were gone, creating more space for Lucas and his guests to mingle. Ornate flower arrangements decorated both ends of the large table, with a buffet of desserts and appetizers in the center. Several posters stood on easels around the room, displaying still shots from the movie. As the girls glanced around they were greeted by smiling, familiar faces.

"Mom!" Belle called out to her, excitedly. "You came!"

"Are you kidding me? Of course I came!" Mary hugged her tight.

"But I thought you and Lucas broke up?"

"We did, honey. But when he called with this crazy plan to win you over, I decided to play along."

"I'm glad." She smiled.

"Where did you get this dress? It's stunning!" Belle exclaimed, taking a step back and noticing the form-fitting violet gown for the first time.

"You like it?" Mary spun around, causing the diamond beading along the bottom of the dress to sparkle in the lamplight. "Unlike you, I've known about this for a couple weeks, so your aunts and I went shopping."

"That's dangerous," Belle smiled.

"I know, right?"

"So did Lucas pay for all of you too?"

"He offered, but we didn't take him up on it. And I did all our makeup, see?" Mary leaned forward, displaying the brush stroke and pink sparkle eye shadow she had used on a couple of the girls for prom the night before.

The other girls greeted their dressed-up moms with hugs as well and excitedly told them the details of the day. Cinderella was telling Dana what they had for dinner, when she was almost knocked over from behind.

"Cinderelly!"

Tears sprung to her eyes as she bent down and scooped up her baby sister. "What are you doing here?"

"Uncle Lucas invited us to watch his new movie. Cool, huh!"

Cinderella looked around and saw Steven and Monica walking towards her with huge smiles on their faces. "Surprise!" Monica said, giving her a hug.

"Lucas thought it would be fun to get the whole gang back together." Steven answered her question before she could even ask it. "Hello, Dana," he added, through gritted teeth.

Dana gave him a curt nod, but was visibly uncomfortable. Talking on the phone, she had almost become relaxed with the idea of him. But seeing him in person again was very different. She shifted from one foot to the other then turned her focus to Monica and Sophie as Cinderella introduced them. Dana smiled and thanked the girls for making Cinderella's trip so wonderful.

Cinderella then went around the room making sure all her cousins and aunts got to meet her new family. When she brought them over to the twins, Steven looked at Rachel warmly. Rachel surprised everyone when she threw her arms around Steven, hugging him tightly.

"I'm glad to see you too," he said softly. "I'm glad to see you're doing so well."

"I never got to thank you," Rachel whispered, tears springing to her eyes. "Thank you!" She hugged him again and then turned to her girls. "Aurora, Ariel, this is Cinderella's dad, Steven."

Overcome with emotion, the girls both hugged Steven as well. His cheeks reddened slightly. Cinderella's mouth dropped open.

"Am I missing something?" she asked, glancing between them.

They told a little of the story about how he had rescued Rachel to a confused Cinderella and Monica, without giving too much gruesome detail. Thankfully Sophie had wandered away during their boring grown-up talk, and was busy at the dessert table trying to see how many cookies she could fit into her mouth. While they continued to visit, Cinderella slipped away to find Lucas. She then threw her arms around him and gave him a huge hug. It didn't feel awkward this time.

"I thought the plan was to win Belle back. You didn't have to spoil the rest of us, too!"

"Yes, but I knew the best way to win Belle over would be to win you all over as well. If her best friends all like me, it will be a lot harder for her to keep ahold of a grudge. I'm very devious that way."

"Well, thank you!" Cinderella said. "For everything today, but especially for bringing my dad to me."

"I couldn't have done this without you."

Cinderella smiled and gave him a high five. "Way to think big."

"The night's not over yet." Lucas winked at her.

Cinderella couldn't even imagine what else he had in store.

Lucas guided the group from their small party room to their seats in the large, open theater a little while later. They took up an entire row near the back.

"The movie is about to start, but I have to welcome everyone first," he said. "So take your seats and I'll be back in a little bit."

The lights began to dim, signaling to the rest of the crowd that the show was about to start. One of the producers stood and welcomed everyone to their premiere. He spoke about the film for a few minutes and then he welcomed Lucas Ferreira, the star of the show, to come up and say a few words. Lucas walked over to the mic and told a funny story that happened during filming, causing the crowd to laugh. Then he pulled the microphone from the stand and began speaking from the heart.

"About six months ago, I was introduced to one of the most amazing people I have ever met: my daughter, Belle Princess."

Belle's stomach flip-flopped and her heart began to beat faster. *What is he doing?*

"I fell in love with Belle's mom back when we were both still kids and I knew I had a daughter, but because of my own stupidity, I lost them both. When I tried to track them down, I couldn't, and it seemed like they would be lost forever. Then one day, almost seventeen years later, I received a letter in my fan mail. It was my daughter writing to say she needed some information about my family's history. I went out to meet her and after spending about a week with her and her mother, I knew what had been missing from my life all these years. My family."

Belle looked over and saw there were tears in her mom's eyes. She grabbed Mary's hand, and they sniffled together as Lucas continued.

"Well, because I'm not a very smart man, I made some more stupid mistakes along the way and I almost lost my daughter again, this time for good. But they are both thankfully here tonight, supporting me."

The crowd cheered loudly and several began looking around, scanning faces for his family.

"In fact, Belle, Mary, would you both join me on stage for a minute?"

The crowd cheered loudly again, and the people nearest them began waving them forward.

"You wanna?" Mary asked, eyeing Belle carefully.

"I guess we better," Belle said.

Her face turned pink, but she tried to act casual as she walked the long distance from the back of the theater up to the front. They walked hand-in-hand and received several pats on the back and cheers as they continued to move forward. Lucas hugged them both when they reached him and then he dropped to one knee right in front of Mary.

She covered her face with her hands, completely shocked. "Lucas?"

"Mary, I have loved you since the day we met, in that tiny, crowded audition room. You give me a reason to live, you make me want to be a better person, and you make me laugh like no one else can. Without you, my life feels completely empty and pointless. These last couple weeks without you have been hell! I don't ever want another day to go by where I can't see your beautiful, smiling face, or listen to your sweet voice. Please, will you marry me?" Lucas pulled a ring out of his pocket and held it out to her. Even the people on the back row could see the huge, sparkling diamond.

The crowd was completely silent as everyone waited in anticipation for her response. Mary was crying, her hand resting over her mouth. She looked to Belle, who nodded through her own tears.

"Yes!"

The crowd erupted into cheers. Lucas got to his feet and he and Mary kissed. Then he turned to Belle and dropped to one knee again.

"Ummm, what are you doing?" she whispered.

"Belle, I want you to know that you are one of the two most important people in my life. I love your mom, but even if things didn't work between us, I will always want you a part of my life. I love you more than words can even express. I have thought about you every single day from the moment your mom told me you were coming. Even for all those years we were apart, I still cared about you and wondered what you were like. I hope you will forgive me for all my stupid mistakes. And I promise I will try every single day to be the dad you deserve."

He pulled out another ring box and the crowd hushed to see what was going to happen next. He opened the box to reveal a beautiful ring with a pink, heart shaped diamond in the center and several smaller diamonds around the band. "I love you Belle! I want to show you with this ring, that I am equally committed to you and I want you a part of my life, just as much as your mom."

"I love you too, Dad!"

The crowd erupted again into loud applause while he slipped the ring onto Belle's finger and got to his feet. He and Belle hugged and then he put an arm around each of them. "Sorry to take up so much of your time. You can all watch the movie now." He started to walk away and then quickly turned around again. "Enjoy the show!" he added.

The audience laughed as the three of them walked back up the aisle toward their seats. The lights went completely out and the huge screen in front jumped to life. Belle couldn't really focus on the movie. She looked down the row at her family and how much they had grown since that stupid assignment from Mrs. Payne. Before the assignment, the girls had always assumed their dads were all big fat toads, and not worth having in their lives. But the last several months had proved their assumptions were wrong. Or perhaps, more accurately, that their opinions could change.

She looked clear down at the other end of the row where Aurora and Ariel sat on either side of Rachel. Aurora glanced over at her and the two shared a smile. The twins' dad was a toad. That was fact. He was a nasty, horrible man who didn't deserve them. But in trying to make a connection with their father, they discovered a sweet, loving grandma they never even knew existed. She loved them and was excited to be a part of their lives.

Cinderella had Dana and Steven on either side of her, with her little sister curled up on her lap. They had always been told such horrible stories about Steven, but it turns out he was really just a frog in need of a little bit of work to become a prince. Now Cinderella had two families who loved her, and two younger sisters who looked up to her.

Snow White's dad still remained a mystery, but Belle saw her and Steven talking several times and she hoped Lucas would now be a father figure for her, too.

Belle glanced over at her own parents, who were so wrapped around each other, they might as well be the only two people in the world. Her dad may have been a toad back before she was born, but then he became a frog while trying to win his family back. Now he might even be the greatest prince of all. She finally understood how much he loved her and she couldn't wait to experience what she had been missing out on her entire life. What would it be like to actually have a real dad who was around all the time?

Then Belle thought about her encounter with Dave today, and how much he had changed the last year. He really was trying hard to reach prince status. Craig was already there, in her mind, but maybe someday Dave could be that prince for someone else.

Dana had explained the three types of boys last year: princes, frogs, and toads. She had made them all seem clear cut, like they were different species who were unable to cross over. But from what Belle had observed, it seemed like boys were just boys, each trying in their own way to live up to the princesses around them. And maybe, just maybe, they were surrounded by more princes than she realized, princes who just need to be given an opportunity to prove they are much more than frogs and toads.

Sneak Peek of "Forever After"

"Snow, come on! We're gonna be late!"

"Just a second!" she yelled back down the stairs to her cousins. They were impatiently waiting for Snow White to be ready so they could get to the movie before any previews started.

"Where is that shoe?" Snow White asked aloud as she continued to frantically search her room. All the contents of her closet were strewn about the floor. Her bedroom resembled the aftermath of a tornado, yet she remained shoeless. With one sneaker on, she hobbled across the carpet to look under her bed for the hundredth time. She groaned in frustration when it didn't magically appear.

Snow White got back to her feet and put her hands on her hips as she looked around. Her eyes stopped on the tall, six-drawer dresser. Then she charged forward. She yanked each drawer free and dumped the clothes in a big pile at her feet. Still no shoe. Then she dropped to her stomach and scanned underneath. She was about to give up when her eye caught sight of what looked like a blue shoelace hanging down from behind the dresser.

Jumping to her feet again, Snow White smashed her face against the wall. Sure enough, her other sneaker was wedged between the dresser and the wall. She grabbed the edge of the white, painted wood and slid the dresser out about a foot. The now empty dresser moved with relative ease.

"How did you get back here?" she asked, extending her arm as far as she could to grab it. Her fingers closed around the object of triumph and she pulled it to freedom.

With the shoe gone, Snow White noticed a little white card lying on her floor behind the dresser. One last time, she extended her arm as far as she could and raked her fingers along the carpet. Her middle finger finally touched paper and she slid it out slowly. She picked up the card and examined it carefully. She couldn't believe she had forgotten about this!

Snow White could hear a loud BEEP BEEP from Belle's car down in the parking lot. Then Cinderella's voice came up the stairs. "Do you need help? Belle, Aurora, and Ariel are in the car waiting."

"No thanks, I found it."

"Well let's go then!"

"Actually," Snow White frowned down at the little card, "go ahead and go without me."

"Are you sure?"

"Yeah, I need to take care of something instead."

Snow White listened for the front door to close, then she waited a minute longer until she heard Belle's car drive away. She held up the card and stared at it again:

Noah Wilkins

District Attorney

She remembered when he handed her the business card about four months ago and told her to call with any questions. Well she had plenty of questions! And her mom wouldn't tell her anything about why the lawyer had come in the first place. Snow White decided it was time to take matters into her own hands.

With a racing heart and trembling fingers, Snow White pulled out her cell phone and began to dial.

Don't miss out on the final book in The Princess Sisters trilogy — Coming October 2014!

About the Author

Stacy Lynn Carroll has always loved telling stories. She started out at Utah State University where she pursued a degree in English, learned how to western swing, and watched as many of her fellow students became 'True Aggies'. She then finished her BA at the University of Utah where she got an emphasis in creative writing. After college she worked as an administrative assistant, where she continued to write stories for the amusement of her co-workers. When her first daughter was born, and with the encouragement of a fortune cookie, she quit her job and became a full-time mommy and writer. She and her husband have three children, two Corgis, and a fish named Don.

If you enjoyed this book, Stacy would love and appreciate your reviews on Amazon and Goodreads! She also loves to make new friends! Follow her on Facebook:
https://www.facebook.com/authorstacylynncarroll
Twitter: @StacyLCarroll
Or visit her website: www.stacylynncarroll.com

Made in the USA
Monee, IL
03 April 2022

94071994R00164